'Flicking between the present and stories and extracts from the past, the pace never lets up in an excellent addition to this unique genre of literature'
Your Family Tree

'At times amusing and shocking, this is a fast-moving modern crime mystery with genealogical twists. The blend of well fleshed-out characters, complete with flaws and foibles, will keep you guessing until the end'
Family Tree

'Once I started reading *Hiding the Past* I had great difficulty putting it down - not only did I want to know what happened next, I actually cared'
Lost Cousins

'This is a must read for all genealogy buffs and anyone who loves a good mystery with a jaw dropping ending!'
Baytown Genealogy Society

'This is a good read and will appeal to anyone interested in family history. I can thoroughly recommend it'
Cheshire Ancestor

'*Hiding the Past* is a suspenseful, fast-paced mystery novel, in which the hero is drawn into an intrigue that spans from World War II to the present, with twists and turns along the way. The writing is smooth and the story keeps moving along so that I found it difficult to put down'
The Archivist

About the Author

Nathan Dylan Goodwin was born and raised in Hastings, East Sussex. Schooled in the town, he then completed a Bachelor of Arts degree in Radio, Film and Television Studies, followed by a Master of Arts degree in Creative Writing at Canterbury Christ Church University. A member of the Society of Authors, he has completed a number of successful local history books about Hastings, as well as several works of fiction, including the acclaimed Forensic Genealogist series. His other interests include theatre, reading, photography, running, skiing, travelling and, of course, genealogy. He is a qualified teacher, member of the Guild of One-Name Studies and the Society of Genealogists, as well as being a member of the Sussex Family History Group, the Norfolk Family History Society, the Kent Family History Society and the Hastings and Rother Family History Society. He lives in Kent with his husband, son and dog.

By the same author

Hiding the Past
by
Nathan Dylan Goodwin

I would like to dedicate this book to my son,
Harrison River

Prologue

6th June 1944

When Emily woke, everything was dark and everything was still. The angry, vicious weather from the previous day had subsided and yet something outside wasn't quite as it should have been. It couldn't have been an air-raid — they had stopped three months ago. Quietly rolling back her woollen blanket, Emily sat up in bed and listened. She was thirty-one and effortlessly beautiful, even now, after a bad night's sleep. She gently switched on her bedside lamp, not wanting to disturb her precious baby boy, who slept silently beside her in his cot. The lamp cast a low, amber glow over his face. Whatever it was that had disturbed her, had not stirred her son.

Emily padded over to the window and lifted the heavy blackout curtains. It took a moment for her to process the sensations she suddenly experienced: a charcoal-grey curtain of thick smoke, reeking of a chemical she couldn't quite place, enveloped the beloved orchard which surrounded her home, as enraged orange flames fought their way towards the house. Emily snapped back to reality, let the curtains fall into place and quickly scooped up her child, still blissfully sleeping. She turned and picked up the small brown suitcase beside her bed, which she had hastily packed last night.

Carrying the boy close to her chest with one hand and the suitcase in the other, she hurried into the kitchen, wearing her white, silk nightie. There was no time to change or search for her shoes. She paused at the front door, momentarily unwilling to loosen the bolts that kept her safe inside. Placing her hand on the first metal bolt, she suddenly placed the chemical stench outside, which was now seeping through the cracks and crevices of the kitchen — petrol: she was being driven out.

Emily pointlessly looked around the room for another means of escape, another plan, but she knew it was hopeless. Insidious tendrils of smoke began to creep from the bedroom ceiling, licking their way towards her.

The baby began to cry, a soft, mournful sound that broke Emily's heart. It reminded her that nothing was real. This life that she had made was not real. Her home was not real. Even her name was not real.

With a final glance around the room, Emily unbolted the brass fastenings. *Maybe there is time to run, to get away from here,* she thought. She pulled open the solid oak door and could see only blackness tinged with the muted light from the raging fire at the rear of the house. Despite the darkness, she knew that someone was there; waiting in the shadows for her.

Emily held the baby tightly and ran from the house. She navigated the orchard easily - nobody knew it better than she - and made it to the periphery of the woods. As the baby began to scream and pain spiked her bare feet as she ran, she knew she could never escape, yet she kept running – pushing further and further into the darkness, her nightie catching and snagging on branches. Behind her, the crunching of heavy boots was gaining ground, easily homing in on the sound of the screaming child. She pulled him tightly into her bosom, hoping to stifle his cries. From the blackness behind her, an unseen hand reached out and grabbed Emily's shoulder. It was over.

Chapter One

2013

Wednesday

Morton Farrier was perplexed. He was sitting at home running an online birth search and, according to the indexes, the man for whom he searched hadn't ever been born. It was a rare occurrence for a birth not to have been registered, he had to admit, but it wasn't *that* extraordinary. Nothing to get over excited about. In his twelve years of working as a forensic genealogist he had come across it maybe once or twice before. Although, now that he actually thought about it, he could only bring one specific case to mind, a job he had worked on two years ago. It certainly didn't warrant the unnecessary histrionics that his new client, Peter Coldrick, had displayed when he had visited him for the first time yesterday afternoon.

Morton had found Peter living an austere life in a run-down council estate on the outskirts of Tenterden, a charming Kentish Weald town not far from his own home in Rye. Peter's house was crammed with an abundance of genealogical books and guides. Years of personal research and three redundant genealogists later, Peter Coldrick had come to the conclusion that any antecedents prior to his father had been wholly obliterated. It was for the birth of Peter's father, James Coldrick, that Morton had searched in vain. He ran one final check at Ancestry, his favoured website for birth, marriage and death searches, but came to the same answer: there was no James Coldrick. He was pondering the implications of this when his mobile rang. It was Juliette, his girlfriend.

'What was the name of the guy that you went to see yesterday?' she asked. *Typical Juliette, storming straight in with a random question*, Morton thought.

'What?'

'The man you're working for, what's his name?' she asked in an impatient whisper.

'Coldrick, Peter Coldrick. Why?'

'I'm guarding his house while SOCO are inside; he's dead, Morton.'

Her words struck him like a rock to the head. 'What happened?'

'Well,' Juliette began, lowering her voice so that Morton struggled to hear her, 'we'll know more when the Scene of Crime Officers are done but it looks like suicide.'

'Suicide?'

'Uh-huh. Look, I can't talk long, just thought I'd let you know.'

'Thanks,' Morton said absentmindedly.

Juliette paused. 'Listen, Morton, I'm going to have to tell the sarge that you visited him yesterday and that he phoned our house last night,' she warned.

'That's fine,' Morton answered.

'Got to go. See you later.'

'Bye.'

He pocketed his mobile and thought back to Peter's garbled voice message, which he'd left within two hours of Morton having left his house. The message asked Morton to phone back as he'd found something important. Morton never returned the call, figuring that it could wait. A frenetic surge of thoughts and questions bounced around his brain. The idea of Coldrick topping himself seemed ridiculous. Then he remembered the money. Coldrick had paid Morton *way* over and above his usual fee. *Who pays someone all that money in the morning then kills themselves that same night?* It didn't make any sense.

The sun was shrouded behind voluminous, concrete-grey clouds when Morton set out, rendering the drive an uncomfortable fusion of stickiness and claustrophobia, which only worsened as the ten-mile journey progressed. By the time he reached Peter's house on Westminster Rise, his skin was clammy and his pulse racing. He didn't know what he was expecting to find when he got there – one police car and a few nosey neighbours maybe – but the reality was very different: an angled police car dramatically blocked the road, its blue warning lights flashing rhythmically, matching the beat of two further police cars and an ambulance parked behind it. A strip of yellow tape proclaiming in thick black letters: POLICE LINE DO NOT CROSS, cats-cradled its way between lamp-posts and gateposts across the street. Behind the cordon were what appeared to Morton to be half of Kent's emergency personnel, idly chatting and drinking hot drinks. And behind it all quietly stood the mournful little council house containing Coldrick's dead body, penned in like a quarantined animal. He felt slightly sick as he parked up and climbed from his car. Morton, handsome with a boyish face that belied his being in the final few weeks of his thirties, was dressed casually in a loose-fitting, white t-shirt and faded jeans. He ran his fingers through his short, dark hair, as his chestnut-brown eyes surveyed the scene before him; he blended well with the crowds of spectators who had gathered on the pavement.

In his peripheral vision, a uniformed figure broke from the *mêlée*, heading towards him. It took a double-take to realise that it was Juliette, thunder etched onto her face, ducking under the cordon tape. Although she'd been a PCSO for more than six months now, he still hadn't got used to seeing her in uniform. His presence here wasn't going to go down too well.

'What're you doing here?' she demanded. Morton shrugged. He didn't know.

'I just wanted to see... Is there any news?'

'SOCO are still in there. Nothing else to report. There's no need for you to be here, Morton.'

'I'm sure he wouldn't have killed himself, you know, Juliette,' Morton ventured.

'Not what it looks like in there. Besides which, you knew him for what, six hours?'

'It just doesn't feel right. Have you actually been inside?'

Juliette nodded.

'And?'

'I'll talk to you later. The sarge is sending someone over to talk to you at home.'

'Coldrick wanted to show me something, Juliette. Can you get me in?' Morton said, knowing it to be a futile question, but hoping that she could flash her badge or whatever she did and wave him through.

Juliette laughed, glancing over her shoulder. 'You think going out with me is going to get you past that lot? No chance. Go home.' And with that she turned, stooped under the yellow tape and was reabsorbed into the sea of fluorescent yellow jackets.

Morton returned to his car and started the engine. All he needed to do was stick it in reverse and leave this unpleasant place behind. But he was mesmerised by the spectacle playing out through the windscreen, his own television set with no off button. He supposed that was why cop shows always did so well on TV; there was something strangely appealing about life going so terribly wrong for someone else. He wasn't a great fan of emergency services dramas. Juliette loved and loathed them in equal measure, usually lapping up the crime then decrying the police work with angry snorts of 'It's obvious who the murderer is' or 'That wouldn't happen in real life'. Not like this, *this* was real life and he knew that if he waited long enough, he would see it – that one defining image that he'd seen a hundred times on telly and, sure enough, it came. Half an hour later Peter Coldrick's lifeless corpse, enveloped in a black body-bag, was rolled out onto the pavement by two sombre paramedics, his head and feet cutting revealing shapes into the shiny, dark material. Seconds later, in front of the mesmerised audience, he was loaded into the yawning rear of the ambulance and slowly driven away. No sirens. No blue flashing lights.

He started the car and headed home.

Morton looked out from the lounge window of his home, a converted police station that fell in the long shadow of Rye parish church. Whilst some deemed it disturbing that Morton's nearest neighbours were the long-deceased, he found it strangely comforting to live there. As far as he was concerned, the dead were so much more predictable than the living.

He stared at a weathered sandstone grave, attempting to recall his journey home from Coldrick's house, but there was nothing for him to latch onto. After the ambulance had pulled away his mind went blank, as if somebody had recorded over his memories with white noise. No matter how Morton allowed his mind to wander, it immediately boomeranged right back to the conundrum of Coldrick's apparent suicide. *Did a few hours spent in his company really afford Morton the absolute certainty in his belief that Coldrick hadn't killed himself?*

He realised that his strong feelings might well stem from the harrowing circumstances surrounding Coldrick's death, rather than the death itself. It somehow had managed to crank open the lid of an area of his brain that he only accessed when absolutely necessary. He imagined that place to be like a small wooden chest with a tight-fitting lid that only *he* could open when *he* chose. It was the same place that he kept memories of his childhood, his mother and questions surrounding his own identity and hidden past.

Morton's addled brain leapt from Coldrick's death to his brother, Jeremy, who was on the verge of being posted to Afghanistan. *Was this how it would feel to be told that he'd been hit by a Taleban sniper?* He chastised himself for his morbid pessimism about Jeremy's ability to survive in a war-zone. As he glanced out at the erect needle commemorating the town's war dead, the thought occurred to Morton that maybe he was projecting his own inadequacies onto his brother. He often thought

6

that he would have been a conscientious objector if he had been alive in either of the World Wars, although he was never quite sure if this was from cowardice, or with the benefit of hindsight.

His disjointed thoughts were interrupted when a Volvo V70 police car, with luminous blue and yellow bodywork, parked outside his house and two officers climbed out and knocked officiously on the front door. Morton showed them into the lounge where they peeled off their hats and introduced themselves as PC Glen Jones, who gave Morton the stark impression of being on day-release from the SAS, and WPC Alison Hawk, a feline-like creature with cold grey eyes.

'Had you known Peter Coldrick long?' Jones asked, the very moment that they were seated.

'No, I first met him yesterday morning,' Morton answered.

'And he phoned you last night?' Hawk asked, scrunching up her face. Morton met her stare, fixed on him, unblinking, ardently scanning for inconsistencies. He nodded, went over to the answer-phone and duly pressed play. *You have one new message. Message left yesterday at six twenty p.m. Morton, it's Peter Coldrick. Can you come over as soon as you get this? I've got into my dad's copper box and found something.*

'Having seen you yesterday morning, why do you think he was so desperate to see you again in the afternoon, Mr Farrier? What do you think he had found?' she asked, pen poised over a notepad in anticipation of his answer.

Morton shrugged. 'I've no idea. I wish I'd gone over there now – maybe he'd still be alive if I had.'

'And what was the nature of your relationship with Peter Coldrick?' Jones asked.

'I was working for him,' he answered.

'Doing what?' Jones asked.

'He paid me to research his family tree, that's all. I'm a forensic genealogist.'

'Can I ask how much he paid you?' Hawk asked.

Morton paused, knowing that the figure would sound preposterous to them. It sounded preposterous to *him*. He also knew that there was no way of withholding the information: they would undoubtedly be able to produce a breakdown of his bank account faster than he could. 'Fifty thousand.'

'Fifty thousand pounds?' Hawk repeated. 'Peter Coldrick paid you *fifty thousand pounds* so that you could tell him who his family was?' She cast an ominous look to her colleague, and Morton felt sure that he was about to be read his rights.

'Yes, that's right,' Morton answered, finally regaining his confidence and realising that he hadn't actually committed a crime. Thank God he had a PCSO as an alibi for last night. 'He paid me a lot more than I have ever been paid before or ever will be again, I'm sure. You're right, it does sound strange. But if you are listening to me, you'll also realise that I received that money in good faith.'

Jones produced, seemingly from nowhere, a small white envelope bearing Morton's name. 'Open it,' he directed.

Morton took the proffered envelope and tentatively withdrew a short, typed letter. He felt strangely obliged to read it aloud, despite a rather large obstruction unhelpfully lodged in his larynx. 'Morton, please stop the research. I've realised that it's all irrelevant now my parents are gone. Please keep the money and enjoy it. Peter.'

'Of course,' Hawk said with a caustic smile and a knowing glance to her esteemed partner, 'we don't yet know if the letter is genuine. We *will* be having it analysed. Is there any reason you can think of as to why Mr Coldrick would take his own life the very day he paid you such a significant sum of money?'

'No.'

'And how did he seem to you?'

Morton shrugged, having nothing to compare it to. 'Not suicidal.'

There was a pause as Morton watched a whole conversation passing unspoken between the two police officers.

WPC Alison Hawk suddenly stood up and Morton felt sure that she was going to arrest him. Would they handcuff him even though he wasn't resisting? *How ironic*, Morton thought, *living in a former police station*. Maybe they should just convert the cellar back into a cell. It wouldn't take long: the four-inch-thick metal door was still intact, as were the bars on the window. A life sentence with boxes of Christmas decorations, old school reports, congealed tins of paint and thirty-nine years' worth of general detritus.

'We'll be in touch, Mr Farrier,' Jones said. 'We'll see ourselves out.'

Morton said goodbye and watched from the lounge window to make sure that they actually left. The Volvo left the square with gratuitous speed, leaving in its fume-ridden wake a welcome silence.

He emitted a long and protracted sigh when he realised that it was all over. Everything was finished now that Coldrick was - whether by his own hand or another's - deceased. Whatever mystery might have lurked in his family had died with him. And that was that. Job done, thank you very much.

'Tell me everything,' Morton said, the very moment that Juliette had stepped across the lounge threshold.

'Let me get in first, Morton. Jesus. *Hello?*'

'Sorry. Hello,' he said, kissing her on the lips.

Juliette sighed and made a meal of removing her steel-toe-capped boots before she answered. 'It's suicide, Morton. No sign of forced entry, no suspicious prints. Ballistics, forensics; everything points towards him killing himself. Not to mention that there were suicide notes, including the one to *you:* imagine how that looked. "Morton Farrier, isn't he your bloke, Juliette?" Christ.'

Morton resented the implication that he was somehow to blame for Coldrick's suicide note, but knew better than to change the tracks along which their discussion was running if he wanted further information. He wondered if he could really have it so wrong in his mind when all the weight of the evidence was stacked against him. Then he considered what Juliette had just said. 'Ballistics?'

She nodded. 'Uh-huh.'

Calm, passive Peter Coldrick had shot himself? Morton couldn't imagine a less likely method of suicide. Riding an elephant into an electricity pylon seemed only slightly less of a plausible way to die. It was so absurd as to be laughable. 'It can't be right, Juliette.'

'Well, we'll find out soon enough - there'll be an investigation and inquest after the post-mortem in the next few days. It's going to be a thorough one, the Chief Constable of Kent has decided to descend upon us for a few days. Some procedural, quality assurance monitoring thing or other, which is just what we need. With her breathing down our necks, you're pretty much guaranteed a meticulous job,' she said, heading to the bedroom.

'That's something I suppose,' Morton mumbled, keeping close to her heels.

'I might be able to find out more tomorrow. I'm on at five in the morning standing outside the damned house,' she complained, pulling on a pair of tracksuit bottoms and loose-fitting t-shirt that had been purchased with the unfulfilled idea of a regular jogging routine.

'Does that sound normal to you?' Morton asked. 'Have you ever guarded the house of a *suicide* before? Murder maybe, but not suicide.'

9

Juliette paused then shook her head. 'But that doesn't mean anything. Like I said, the big boss is in so we've got to go OTT on everything.'

Morton didn't get it. What were they worried about, that Coldrick's dead body might return? He thought about it for a moment and the idea came to him that maybe he could use this abnormality in police procedure to his advantage.

'Will it just be you there?' he asked tentatively.

'I expect so now that SOCO have done their bit; might be two of us. Why?'

'You need to let me get inside,' Morton said.

Juliette laughed as she left the bedroom and dumped herself down into the sofa. Morton trailed in behind her.

'I'm serious, Juliette. Turn your back, do whatever you have to do. I really need to see if I can find what Coldrick wanted to show me.'

Juliette rolled her eyes. 'Why do you care, anyway? Surely the job's finished now he's dead? Does it really matter what he wanted to show you?'

'Yes,' Morton answered. Granted, it was the shortest-lived case of his career, but one that had piqued his curiosity – what if Coldrick's suspicions held even a nugget of truth? Kent Police might not find Coldrick's death suspicious, but he sure did. Maybe it was simply that he had nothing better to do. Whichever way, he wanted to get inside that house. 'Please, Juliette. I just need five minutes in there.'

'No, Morton. Anyway, I might get to the station tomorrow and be doing something completely different.'

Morton sighed and sloped off into the kitchen to make dinner, hoping that by making his disappointment evident, she might take pity on her dejected boyfriend and change her mind. She didn't. She did what Juliette did best, and changed the subject. 'Did you get the email from Jeremy today?' she called.

'No, what was that?'

'Invite to a leaving party Saturday night. It's all a bit rushed as his regiment's being posted out on Monday.'

Morton had known that the day of Jeremy's posting overseas was looming ever closer, but he'd put it to the back of his mind, hoping that the day would never arrive.

'We've got to be at your dad's house at seven.'

Morton groaned. 'I suppose that means he'll be there, then.'

'Of course he'll be there. Did you think Jeremy wouldn't invite his own dad or something?' Juliette asked, appearing at the kitchen doorway. 'It's been ages since you've been to see him or spoken to him. It won't hurt you.'

'I spoke to him on his birthday,' Morton countered.

'That was two minutes on the phone five months ago, Morton.'

She was right: it was time to make an effort. It just didn't come naturally to him and even saying the word *dad* felt like he was speaking in tongues.

'Are we supposed to get him a going away present?'

'Don't be so cynical, Morton,' Juliette said, circling her arms around his midriff as he began to prepare the dinner. 'It's okay to be worried about him.'

Morton exhaled, allowing his tense muscles to relax in her embrace. As he considered his brother out in Afghanistan, he became aware, possibly for the first time since he was eighteen, of a bond between him and Jeremy. Was it a genuine fraternal bond? Or just the type of bond that forms when two people live in the same house for several years? A lone tear ran down his cheek and plopped unceremoniously onto the chopping board.

'Bloody onions,' he muttered.

Chapter Two

Thursday

Morton woke with a start and sat bolt upright, his breathing out of control and his heart feeling like it was about to burst from his chest cavity, just like that scene in *Alien* that had scared the hell out of him when he had stupidly first watched it at the age of nine. He had been dreaming of Peter Coldrick without the benefit of the roof of his mouth. Peter had looked right at him, shouting, '*Come over; I've found something. Come over; I've found something.*' Morton strained his eyes to see the clock: five forty-nine a.m. He needed to get up and clear his head. His tired mind was whirring as he stumbled from the bedroom towards his study. What was he doing, continuing to research the family history of a dead man with no known family? With Coldrick dead, he could just take the money and run. What was the point in continuing? He searched inside for the answers. First of all, he had no other work on at the moment, having cleared a good two weeks in his diary for researching Coldrick's family. Secondly, he felt that his obligation to find Peter Coldrick's family still stood, since payment had changed hands. Lastly, and perhaps most significantly, no prior job had ever held such intrigue before. He needed to give it more time. Morton sat at his cluttered desk and pulled open the cardboard wallet containing the research notes taken at Coldrick's house on Tuesday, as he reflected on the visit. He'd spent six hours in Peter's company trying to build a picture of the Coldrick family, asking probing questions which ultimately led nowhere. Despite the severe lack of leads emanating from the meeting, Morton felt a strong affinity with the pitiful man before him. A man, like himself, struggling to connect with his identity. The only difference between them was that Peter was labouring under the weight of his past, while Morton did his best to ignore his. He decided that he really liked this man.

Slowly, he read aloud what he'd written, trying to absorb the information as he spoke. 'Peter Coldrick, born 1971. Only child of James and Mary Coldrick, née Balfour, married 1970. Mary died in a house fire 1987, James of cancer 2012. Peter, no siblings. James Coldrick, no known siblings. Parents unknown. Born 6th June 1944 in Sussex village of Sedlescombe. Taken to St George's Children's Home and spent childhood there until fifteen. Worked as a general labourer on various farms.'

Morton studied the piece of paper. It was very little to go on – much less, basic information than he was used to gathering on an initial visit to a client's home. What was it that Peter had said on Tuesday? *It's as if my family are all enclosed in a walled garden which has no door. If you're going to get anywhere with it you need to find another way in.* And another way in he would most certainly find.

Also in the wallet was a faded, sepia photograph that Peter had found amongst his father's papers last week. Finding the picture was the catalyst for Peter to hire him. Morton scanned the photo at a high resolution and within seconds the image was in front of him. The photo was of an attractive, young woman – he guessed early thirties - holding a small baby. Centering into the woman's dark eyes, Morton saw pride and joy at the child she held in her arms. He estimated that the baby was around a month old. Despite the age and quality of the photo, the woman looked to Morton as someone who cared what she looked like - her eyes, hair, lips and skin appearing flawless. The woman's clothing and waved, side-rolled hair, coupled with the *Box Brownie* style of photo, suggested to Morton that it was taken shortly after James' birth in 1944. Behind her was a light-coloured building of some kind, surrounded by trees. To the west was a tall herringbone-brick chimney.

The next step was to undertake what three years studying history at University College London had taught him – a forensic examination of the photograph. The photo analysis was actually pretty simple: it took Morton under an hour to deduce the exact date on which the photograph had been taken. Not bad going, he had to admit. He even knew the time of day that it was taken. Photo analysis was one of Morton's specialties, having achieved full marks in the Photo Forensics module at university. His maverick lecturer, Dr Baumgartner, on a three-year secondment from the Forensic Science Service, was a man who encouraged his students to think outside the box and to 'become more knowledgeable of the minutiae in a photograph than of your own body.' He had taught them how to interpret everything from architecture to historic weather patterns, clothing fashions to the breeding habits of bluebottles and pretty much everything in between.

First, Morton measured the angles of the shadows in the photograph, cross-referencing these against online solar patterns, which gave only two possible possibilities in 1944: at 3.58pm on 7 May

13

and 15 September. Since James Coldrick was born in June, Morton's initial assessment was that the photo was taken on 15 September. But that didn't add up with what he found next. The trees in the picture, which he'd identified as being Victoria plum, were covered in a nascent blossom, which by September would have been replaced by fruit. Either James Coldrick's birth didn't occur in June or, for the first time in his career, he'd made a mistake with a photo analysis. He was inclined towards the former option and tentatively noted '7th May 1944?' on a scrap of paper, which he attached to the photo. Morton took the precautionary step he always took when dealing with other people's photographs, and backed up the image.

Why was James Coldrick's childhood so shrouded in mystery? He needed somewhere to start. The records for St George's Children's Home seemed like a good place.

Google helpfully informed Morton that the children's home had long since closed down, the local authority instead preferring to farm out their abandoned youth to the more personal care of fostering. The building now served as St George's Nursing Home, for which Google provided contact details and a pin-point location.

Morton dialled the number and explained the reason for his call.

'I started here in nineteen eighty-three, when it became a nursing home,' the duty manager, Linda said, in a thick Yorkshire accent. 'The records of the home *were* here for a while, until they were eventually transferred to the local archives at Lewes. I think because us and the children's home were both Local Authority, there was no big hurry to shift the files over. After that point we didn't keep anything, I'm afraid, love.' Morton wasn't overly surprised by her answer. They were hardly likely to keep such potentially sensitive records stashed in the corner on the off-chance someone might require access years later.

'Is it likely they would have had personal information in them?' he asked.

'Oh, I'm sure. I mean, I didn't like to be nosey, but there were filing cabinets full of the case histories of the poor kids that were held...' she stopped herself, '...living here.' Linda lowered her voice. 'Some of those poor kids, I tell you. What I read was just awful. Good job it were closed down, to be frank with you. Wouldn't be surprised if it were another one of them homes as ended up in the news, if you know what I mean.'

'Yes,' Morton agreed absentmindedly. He thanked Linda, hung up and got himself ready for a trip to Lewes.

Morton took the last space in the pot-holed, makeshift car park adjacent to East Sussex County Archives. Some bright county official had once felt that housing the entire archives for East Sussex in the most unwelcoming, unreachable and inadequate building in Lewes was a good idea. Well, it certainly stopped casual passers-by. You *really* had to want to go there. He longed for the imminent opening of *The Keep*, a modern, purpose-built facility on the outskirts of Brighton.

Once inside, his jovial mood promptly dissipated. The lobby was guarded by Miss Latimer, a pit-bull of a woman who delighted in throwing out amateurs who had 'popped in on the off-chance' without the requisite raft of identification. In all the years that Morton had been visiting the archives, she had never once smiled or passed a single pleasantry. She was all rules and regulations. *Fill in that form. No pens allowed. You can't take your laptop bag into the archives.* He sometimes wondered if she had a condition that meant she couldn't actually physically smile.

'Good morning,' Morton said brightly.

Miss Latimer scowled. 'Kindly fill in that form, so we know why you're here.'

'Of course, Miss Latimer,' he said, smiling, as he signed the declaration of adherence to the rules that he had never actually read.

'Does that say *Moron?*' she asked flatly.

Very amusing of the ancient spinster, he was forced to admit. 'Morton,' he corrected, pushing all of his prohibited items into a locker. He made his way upstairs to the search room, where the conspiracy to marginalise the public continued with the air conditioning being set permanently to freezing. All in the name of archive preservation, Miss Latimer had told him when he had complained on a previous visit.

He handed his reader's ticket to Max Fairbrother, the softly spoken, bald-as-a-mushroom stalwart, who had been the senior archivist there for more than thirty years. He passed a moment of small talk with Max before setting down his laptop on one of the large tables in the centre of the room. He headed over to the burgeoning shelves and selected a thick file pertaining to Sedlescombe. The folder housed an index to all archives relating to the village. If what he was looking for existed, it would be catalogued here. He located St George's Children's Home and thumbed through an index to a range of records

15

- pages of indexes to governors' meetings, accounts, special fund-raising events, building developments, photographs and newspaper cuttings. He reached the admission registers, which were neatly marked with an official red stamp in the bottom right corner: 'Closed for 75 years.' This was common practice for such sensitive documents but it didn't faze him in the slightest; being on first-name terms with Max usually meant that such rules were negotiable. The negotiation being that Miss Latimer didn't find out.

Morton carefully examined the index. Something was wrong. Next to the register for 1944 were three small, typed words which sent a bundle of pins down his spinal cord: 'Missing on Transfer'. He considered the possibility that it was a coincidence that the records were missing and flicked through the rest of the documents: the admission registers for 1944 were the only files listed as missing.

He hurried to the front desk and, in hushed tones, briefly informed Max what he was searching for.

Max reached across the cluttered desk and took the ledger from Morton. He flicked back and forth through several pages, his lower lip curling as he searched. Morton knew that Max had no idea why the register might be missing. 'It doesn't give a reason,' he answered finally. 'Sometimes it will say that the document wasn't supplied by the donor. I don't know, sorry.'

Morton nodded like a suspicious interrogator. That volume must have been crammed with names, yet Morton felt sure that the reason it was missing was down to just one name: James Coldrick.

'Can I order up 1943 and 1945?' Morton asked.

Max scanned around the office. No sign of Miss Latimer. 'Sure,' he answered. 'Fill in the slips and bring them back to me.'

Morton returned to his desk and completed a small pink slip for each document with the reference code, his name and table number. In addition to the admissions registers, he also requested a bundle of governors' meeting minutes and a staff list that he thought he would take a chance with, plus the baptism records for the local parish church.

Twenty minutes later, in accordance with the rules, Max placed only the first three documents on Morton's desk. 'Good luck,' Max said with a smile. 'I've got a feeling you're going to need it.'

'Thanks,' Morton said. He didn't need luck. He was a forensic genealogist: he was born for this kind of work.

He dived straight into the baptism register, thumbing his way carefully to the correct decade. Baptisms in the 1940s generally gave the name of the child, parents' full names and address, plus the father's occupation. Sedlescombe's being a small, rural parish meant that Morton could search from 1930 through to 1950 in just a few minutes. No sign of James Coldrick. He extended the search into the 1960s, just in case James had chosen an adult baptism when he left St George's but there was nothing even close.

He closed the ledger and opened the 1945 admissions register for St George's, hoping that the apparently unborn James Coldrick was deposited at the home in the year following his birth. He flicked through the pages and ran his finger meticulously down the list of names. Predictably, there was no mention of James Coldrick. Had the name appeared there, then it would have told Morton everything that he needed to know: birth date, parents' names, occupations and address. Ordinarily, he would have felt largely disappointed at the setback, but he felt nothing but exhilaration at this latest twist. Someone had worked hard to remove all traces of James Coldrick's birth. He knew at that moment that he wouldn't find any reference to him in the files, but still he painstakingly trawled both registers, cover to cover, hoping to spot an anomaly.

After several hours of diligent searching, all Morton had discovered was the barbaric nature of the home, at which Linda, the manager of St George's had hinted. Almost every child had faced ritualised corporal punishment for the most minor of misdemeanours. *G placed in solitary confinement for insolence. R given ten taps of the cane for rudeness.* Taps of the cane: there was a euphemism if ever Morton read one. Poor kids. Morton thought that it was of little surprise that James Coldrick had maintained a veil of silence over his childhood.

The large tome of governors' meetings revealed little more than the passing of a minor array of insignificant decisions. The staffing list of the time only served to provide some fresh stock for Morton's collection of bizarre names: *Ada Drinkwater, Elsie Flowerdew, June Berrycloth, Betty Beebee, Bill Goozee, Kathleen Menghini.*

Max's announcement that the office was about to close broke Morton from his reveries, where he was envisioning the character of Betty Beebee. Old, short, ration-starved, hair in a tidy bun. Her name didn't suggest she was a cruel abuser of neglected children. She sounded jolly, the kind of person always ready with a smile and a warm hug.

Morton typed up the document dates, references and findings, adding them to the growing file on the Coldrick family.

'Excuse me, Mr Farrier?' Morton looked into the glare of Miss Latimer, who hurriedly scooped up the ledgers from Morton's table, as if she had caught him about to secrete them down his trousers. Miss Latimer indicated the clock at the back of the room. 'The office is now closed,' she said dourly.

Morton wanted to smile and issue an acerbic retort, but instead he answered, 'That's fine. I'd finished anyway.'

Morton nodded a goodbye to Max and headed out of the office, depositing a stack of his business cards on the foyer stand, which stated in bold type that he was a 'Forensic Genealogist'. He knew full well, however, that Miss Latimer would likely throw them all in the recycling as soon as he was out of the door.

After a throaty and heavy-sounding few seconds, his car finally turned over and he began his journey home. On a whim, Morton pulled into a petrol station and grabbed a bottle of white wine and the ingredients for Juliette's favourite meal of wild mushroom and goat's cheese risotto.

Tired and drained, Juliette had arrived home and changed into a pair of white jeans and a loose-fitting t-shirt. She had removed the numerous grips which held her hair neatly under her PCSO hat, allowing the dark waves to fall freely over her shoulders. She leant casually on the doorframe to the kitchen, watching as Morton dished up the risotto onto two waiting plates. When she was off-duty, Juliette took a lot of time and care over her appearance, spending an inordinate amount of time in front of the mirror applying a range of creams and make-up, the function of which Morton could never hope to understand. It was how she appeared now, relaxed and natural, that Morton found the most attractive.

'Did any more come to light today about Peter Coldrick?' Morton asked, carrying the two plates of steaming dinner over to the dining room table, where he'd set two glasses of white wine. Juliette followed and sat opposite him.

'Well,' she began taking her first mouthful of dinner, 'I logged onto the PNC and-'

'PNC?' Morton queried, not being *au fait* with the overwhelming abundance of police acronyms.

'Police National Computer. I thought I'd take a look at Peter for you. Nothing came up – no previous convictions, no arrests, no cautions – he's a model citizen. Not even a parking or speeding ticket.'

Morton was unsurprised. Coldrick had hardly seemed the type to have been up for murder or running a drug cartel somehow. 'Anything else?'

'I spoke to Malcolm Burrows in CID about Peter and they're definitely going down the suicide line. It's going to the coroner and ultimately it'll be her decision.'

'Did nobody question why a man like Coldrick would *shoot* himself? Where does Malcolm Burrows think he got the gun from?'

'I don't know, but I guess that'll be investigated.'

'Do you know what type of gun he used?' Morton asked, guns being another specialism of his.

'Just a regular shotgun, I think. He could have got it from anywhere. His ex-girlfriend didn't seem to think he owned a gun.'

Morton took a sip of wine and shot an interested look at Juliette. 'Ex-girlfriend? Did you happen to get her name? She might be worth a visit.'

Juliette took a moment to finish her mouthful, her analytical face showing that she was searching for the name. 'Soraya Benton,' she said finally.

'Soraya Benton,' Morton repeated, making a mental note to look her up after dinner.

'What about your day?' Juliette asked.

Morton spent the rest of the mealtime relaying his trip and its findings to Juliette. She always professed interest in his work, even when Morton was conveying dry, historical facts about a family she knew nothing about.

Ordinarily, Morton would have helped Juliette to clear away the dinner; on this occasion, he left Juliette to load the dishwasher by herself, whilst he quickly logged onto his laptop to run an electoral register search for Soraya Benton. He punched in her name on an online electoral register website. Four results. Only one in the whole of the south-east and she was living in Tenterden, just a few miles from Peter Coldrick's house. Bingo. He scribbled down the address and phone number then shut the lid on his laptop. Morton stared at the paper with Soraya's name on it and wondered if she could shed any light on the mysterious Coldrick family. Maybe being Peter's ex-girlfriend meant that she knew something of how a man living in a council house could afford to pay such a huge fee for his services. From the way Peter had spoken at their one and only meeting, he was unemployed and had been for some time. The thought of how Peter could find such a vast sum to pay him hadn't really crossed his mind at the time but now he weighed the possible options of where the money had come from. Lottery win? *Unlikely - what were the odds? Fourteen million to one?* Redundancy? *Possible - but no mention was made of any previous job.* Savings? *Possible but unlikely.* Inheritance? *Possible - his father had died last year, about the right time for his estate to pass through the hurdles of probate.* His searches at the beginning of James Coldrick's life were proving fruitless, so perhaps it was time to start looking at the end of his life for answers.

'You're day-off tomorrow, aren't you?' Morton called into the kitchen.

'Uh-huh.'

'Fancy a trip to Brighton?'

Juliette appeared at the lounge door. 'Why?' she asked suspiciously.

'Just thought it would be nice to have a shop, meal out and walk along the beach,' he answered.

Juliette laughed. 'When have you ever suggested going out shopping? What's the real reason?'

Morton smiled. 'Brighton District Probate Registry.'

Juliette's eyes narrowed and Morton was sure that he could see the workings of her brain behind her hazel eyes, processing the information. 'And what goes on there?'

'It's a government building where wills and administrations are housed.'

'Right,' Juliette said, the tone of her voice encouraging him to continue.

'The public can go in and search the indexes to wills. I want to find out how much money James Coldrick had when he died last year. Something doesn't add up with the amount Peter paid me compared with his house and his life.'

Juliette groaned, slumped into the sofa and switched on the television. 'Yes, fine. Can we stop talking about this job now?'

'Yep,' he said, casting a quick glance at Soraya Benton's scribbled contact details. They could wait until tomorrow. Morton sat beside Juliette, coiled his arm around her back and pulled her in close. He was

20

starting to realise that this was not going to be an ordinary research job. His previous employment had simply been *jobs*. *The Carder job. The Dungate job. The Ashdown job.* This one needed a more appropriate title. *The Coldrick Case.*

Chapter Three

Friday

On this occasion Morton was happy to confer the driving seat over to Juliette. Not that she minded. She hated his driving. She said that he overtook far too much. Her only concession to recklessness was the additional ten percent of speed she knew that she might get away with if she were ever pulled over by the likes of WPC Alison Hawk or PC Glen Jones. Not that she would get pulled by them, it would much more likely be Traffic Police, Juliette had explained to him in great detail one day after they'd driven past a car accident. *They're not Road Traffic Accidents anymore, they're Road Traffic Collisions. Car crashes are rarely accidents.*

Juliette pulled into the Churchill Square car park in the city centre and found an empty parking bay close to the exit to the shops.

'Right, I'm going to go and look at some clothes,' she said, climbing from the car. 'You do whatever you've got to do and we'll meet in Starbucks. An hour enough?'

'Perfect,' Morton said, as they made their way from the car. He knew that Juliette would be fine once the magnetism of the shops had worked its magic and pulled her in. Once she set foot over Karen Millen's threshold it was like she'd passed into a time-warp and time meant nothing. She kissed him and then they parted. He strode quickly through the busy shopping arcades, out the other side and along a quiet side street until he reached the Probate Office on William Street, a plain, brick building fronted by a wide run of steps upon which was assembled a collection of smokers.

Morton headed through a small lobby area which fed a staircase and several key-padded doors to which the public were not permitted. He approached a tiny serving hatch, behind which were half-a-dozen suited workers floundering around an open-plan office. Nobody seemed in any particular hurry to do whatever jobs they had been charged with undertaking. Morton waited impatiently for someone to acknowledge him, as tiny molehills of sweat pushed to the surface of his forehead. He wiped his face and emitted a polite cough. Several sets of eyes glanced in his direction but only a woman who looked slightly crazed approached the hatch. She had a mop of tightly-permed, bleached-white hair and dark, squinty eyes framed by a bizarre pair of horn-rimmed glasses.

'Hi, I'd like to have a quick look at the probate indexes, please,' Morton said with a courteous smile.

'Hang on.' She disappeared momentarily and then a door opened to Morton's right.

'Thank you,' he said, heading into the tiny room with a slight odour of must, where each wall was crammed with large leather-bound ledgers. It was at least ten degrees hotter in the stifling room than in the lobby area and Morton could feel the perspiration making a break for freedom down his back.

'Have you been here before?' the lady asked, leading him over to a solitary microfiche reader.

'Yes, I have.' He had been several times - it was a quick and free way of finding out if someone had left a will and, importantly, how much they'd bequeathed. It would only provide him with basic information – if he wanted more he would need to order the full document.

'Okay, so you know that wills 1858 to 1980 are on the shelves and 1981 onwards on microfiche?' she asked, somewhat suspiciously, as if he were being tested. She pronounced *fiche* as *fish*.

'Yes.'

'Right then,' she said, 'I'll leave you to it.' Except she didn't. Instead, she stood with her arms folded in the corner of the room, watching as Morton started up his laptop.

When she saw that Morton was more than capable of switching on the reader all by himself, she sighed and returned to the office, sending a momentary welcome burst of cool air into the room. He picked up the thick folder of microfiches and selected the first of two, covering wills administered in 2012.

He slid the fiche under the glass slider and the minuscule white lettering on a dark blue background became instantly magnified. Shifting the plate around until he came to the letter C, Morton quickly located *Coldrick*. Rather unsurprisingly, James Coldrick was the sole entry for that surname.

Coldrick, James of 15 Westminster Rise, Tenterden, Kent, died 3 January 2012, probate Brighton 18 March Not exceeding £780,000, 9851305366G

Morton was stunned. He didn't know what figure he was expecting to see but to discover that Peter Coldrick, living an austere wartime existence in his dreary council house had been sitting on more than three-quarters of a million pounds' inheritance when he died shocked him. *Where had his father got that kind of money from?* The general labourers that he'd ever encountered in his genealogical work usually had a pittance at the end of their lives; James Coldrick conversely had a small fortune.

The white-haired lady suddenly pulled open the door. 'Found what you were looking for?' she asked. Morton didn't want the woman to see what he was looking at and hurried to type up the entry.

'Yes, thanks,' he answered. She moved into the room and stood behind him, her hot breath heavy on his nape.

'Blimey, he did alright for himself, didn't he?' she muttered. 'Did you want that printed?'

'No,' he snapped, hoping that his abruptness might make his feelings perfectly clear but no, she remained uncomfortably close as he saved the file, closed the lid of his laptop and switched off the microfiche reader.

'All done?' she said, sounding rather disappointed.

'All done.' Morton thanked her and hurried from the claustrophobic building.

Once outside, the sweat on his forehead instantly abated. He breathed deeply, grateful to be out of the stuffy office, and made his way down the steps. One of the smokers standing in front of him, a man in his forties, wiry and grubby-looking with crew-cut blond hair, dragged a heavy black boot over a half-smoked cigarette, then took the steps two at a time. As he levelled with Morton, a box of matches fell from his jacket pocket. Morton picked them up. 'Excuse me, you've dropped these.'

The man stopped in his tracks and turned, allowing Morton a full view of his face; not the most aesthetically pleasing chap he'd ever clapped eyes on. A giant pink fleshy scar ran from his right eye almost to the corner of his mouth.

'Thanks,' he said tersely, taking the box.

'That's okay,' Morton said, mesmerised by the man's magnificent scar. He wondered what kind of accident, operation or fight could have caused his face to open from eye to mouth.

He looked at his watch – he had more than half an hour before he had to meet Juliette. He pictured her trying on a veritable mountain of

24

clothing but not actually buying as much as a pair of knickers. Wrong size. Wrong colour. Wrong style. Wrong label. He never could work that out.

Taking a leisurely saunter through the crowded North Lanes, Morton stopped occasionally to look at passing window displays of the tiny shops which adorned the rabbit warren of thin passageways. He paused at an antique shop specialising in war memorabilia and studied the items in the window. You never know what you might find in such places. The highlight of an extensive ten-week research job into one lady's family history was his serendipitous locating of her grandfather's First World War medals in a junk shop. No such trinkets sprang out at him today.

Morton passed into a quieter part of the city where the shops gave way to café bars and restaurants, outside of which sat half-dressed youths on metal chairs.

As he turned into a side street, Morton heard the heavy thud of footsteps behind him, quickly becoming louder. He turned at the last second, just as his bag was brutally ripped from his shoulder, spinning him round from the force of the theft.

He stood dumbstruck, his brain frozen.

A flash of grey and denim disappeared out of sight, carrying his bag.

'Damn it! Stop! He's got my bag!' Morton yelled, as soon as he was able to assimilate his thoughts into the understanding that he'd been robbed. By then the thief was long gone.

A small group of middle-aged men were sitting outside the nearest café, just metres away from where Morton stood. They must have seen the perpetrator. 'Excuse me, I've just had my bag stolen,' Morton said shakily. 'Did anyone see the bloke who did it?'

Most looked away. One or two shook their heads.

'I think he was about five-ten, grey hoody,' Morton persevered. 'Did anyone see him?'

'No. We didn't see him,' one of them finally answered.

'Thanks,' Morton muttered, walking away. He headed in the general direction taken by the mugger in the vain hope that he might find the bag discarded in a shop doorway. Not that it mattered: the important, valuable things like his laptop and wallet were bound to be long gone.

Just as Morton was taking a long breath in, trying to stop himself shaking, a hand fell onto his shoulders. He whirled around, ready to hit whomever was touching him. Juliette. His body went limp.

'What's the matter?' she asked.

'I've just been mugged. Had my laptop bag stolen.'

'What? When? What happened?' Juliette probed, taking his hand and staring him in the eyes.

'Just some bloke came out of nowhere and wrenched it from my shoulder. Five-ten with a grey hoody – that's about the only description.'

Juliette pulled her phone from her pocket. 'Right.'

'What're you doing?'

'Finding out where the nearest police station is.'

Morton put his hand over hers. 'No. I don't want to report it,' he said.

Juliette looked incredulous. 'Why on earth not? At the very least you can report it, get a crime number and claim for it on the insurance.'

'I'm just not feeling much confidence in the police at the moment. Come on, let's go home. I've had enough of this place.'

With a disbelieving shake of her head, Juliette pocketed her mobile and the pair walked silently back to the car park.

The drive out of Brighton was a welcome one for Morton. A whole ugly, shadowy underworld faded into the hills behind him like a bad dream. A *den of iniquity*, his father had once called the city. Maybe he was right. Juliette had been uncharacteristically quiet for some time, which he guessed was the after-effects of his refusal to report the mugging. He knew that when he told her that, she'd never be able to detach herself from her job and see it from his perspective. All she would see was that a crime had been committed which needed reporting. It was as simple as that in her world. That might have been what was bugging Juliette initially but there was something else wrong now. She was gripping the steering wheel so tightly that the sinews rose defiantly on the backs of her hands. Morton's suspicions were confirmed when the speedometer crept over seventy. On a sixty road. Very un-Juliette.

'Are you okay?' he asked.

'Yeah,' she answered half-heartedly. 'Just a car behaving strangely behind us.'

'Behaving strangely how?' Morton began to crane his head.

'Don't look round! Jesus, Morton!' Juliette snapped. 'It's been following us for the last six miles.'

Morton inched back into his chair, trying to catch a glimpse of the car in the wing mirror. He couldn't see any car behaving strangely. 'Which one?'

'He's just dropped back. A black BMW X6. He's speeding up a bit now, see him?'

Morton angled his head and caught sight of a black car – was that a BMW? He had no idea, but the car was gaining ground. 'How do you know he's following us, though? We've pretty much stayed on the same road since leaving Brighton.'

'He's trying not to be seen, speeding up, slowing down, taking odd decisions.'

'Are you sure you're not just being paranoid?' Morton asked.

'Hold tight,' Juliette said, 'and get the plates.'

Morton was about to ask what she meant when she yanked up the handbrake and hard-locked the steering wheel. The tyres squealed like dying pigs as the car spun round one hundred and eighty degrees. A split-second later and the black BMW sailed past at top-speed. Morton forgot the plates as soon as he saw the driver and recognised him; the question he had posed to Juliette about her paranoia had been answered.

There could be no mistake, the man who had followed them out of Brighton in the BMW was the same man who had dropped his matches on the steps of the Brighton District Probate Registry. As Morton sat at the desk in his study with his research notes spread out in front of him, it crystallised in his mind that Peter's death, the mugging and the car-trailing were anything but coincidences. Even Juliette was beginning to understand his reticence in reporting the robbery. The first thing that Morton did when they returned home was to jot down all that he could recall typing into the notes about the case so far. When he finished, he sifted through the folder until he came to Soraya Benton's address and phone number. *Should he call her or visit?* He would usually phone first and explain who he was and why he was making contact, but he didn't want to take a chance that she wouldn't be willing to meet in person. He decided to pay her a visit.

When Morton parked outside the address that the electoral register search had provided, he was relieved not to have his fears confirmed that he would arrive to find Soraya's bludgeoned corpse being stretchered out by paramedics. The quiet tree-lined road was close to

Peter Coldrick's house, but on the more affluent side of town. The house was a chunky Victorian semi with a carefully trained yellow-flowered honeysuckle enveloping much of the façade.

He double-checked the rear-view mirror and was as certain as he could be that he hadn't been followed. With a final glance in the mirror, Morton approached the house and pressed the doorbell.

A moment later a woman in her early forties appeared at the door in jeans and an over-sized cream jumper, with tousled brown hair tied back in a loose ponytail. Could *she* be Soraya Benton? If so, then Morton was both impressed and astonished that Coldrick had managed to attract someone so... well, someone so *way* out of his league. She was not at all the frump he'd conjured up in his imagination on the journey over here.

'Hi there,' Morton began, 'are you Soraya Benton?'

She looked baffled, her eyes narrowing as if she were struggling to recognise an old school friend. 'Yes,' she said warily.

'My name's Morton Farrier, I hope you don't mind me dropping by like this-'

'-Ah, I wondered when you might make an appearance,' Soraya interjected with a shy grin. 'Come in.' She stepped aside, showing Morton into a bright hallway. He was puzzled by her cryptic greeting. He'd anticipated a long and protracted doorstep discussion, especially if Soraya and Coldrick had separated acrimoniously. This was quite baffling to him. Soraya moved past him and he followed her into a large and comfortable lounge.

'What did you mean, *you wondered when I might make an appearance?*' Morton asked. Soraya smiled and invited him to sit down.

'I was expecting you – I knew that if you were as good a forensic genealogist as your website claimed that you'd find me somehow. You see, I was the one who suggested Peter employed you.' Morton was still perplexed – *he* might never have found her, were it not for Juliette mentioning her very existence, but he wasn't about to reveal *that* snippet of news; he was enjoying the view from the pedestal she had placed him on. She spoke so calmly and confidently that it unnerved him slightly.

'Well, here I am,' Morton said, adding after a pause, 'I'm very sorry about Peter's death.'

'Me too,' Soraya said, her expression suggesting that such simple words couldn't even begin to express what she was feeling. He could see entrenched sadness and sorrow implicit in her eyes and couldn't

28

imagine what she must be going through. 'I've just opened a bottle of red – can I persuade you to help me out with it?'

Morton nodded. 'That would be lovely, thanks.'

Soraya left the room then returned with a glass. 'Can I ask what you think about Peter's death,' she asked.

'Well, he only hired me on Tuesday, but…' Morton's voice trailed off. He didn't know how much he wanted to say, how much he could say.

'But?'

'But he didn't seem the suicide type,' Morton answered, hoping that his answer was diplomatic and pointed enough without cutting a fresh wound in her grief.

Soraya set her glass down on the table between them. 'No, he wasn't the suicide type at all. Even if he had wanted to kill himself, he never in a million years would have used a gun. I mean, he didn't even *own* a gun. Why go to all that bother when there was enough paracetamol in his bathroom cabinet to fell a large horse? Or a kitchen full of knives?'

'It doesn't really add up,' he agreed.

'Well, I *know* for certain he didn't do it.' The way that she emphasised the word *know* suggested to Morton that she must be sitting on some kind of irrefutable evidence, which surely she had shared with the police?

'How can you know? The police seem fairly convinced it was suicide.'

'I know they are, but they've got it wrong. Very wrong.'

'Hmmm.'

'No, *really* wrong. Follow me.'

Morton put down his glass and followed Soraya down the hallway where she gently pushed open a door and stood back, allowing Morton to stick his head inside. The tightly drawn Incredible Hulk curtains should have been sufficient enough clue for him, but it wasn't until his eyes fell upon a sleeping child, right leg dangling precariously from a messy cabin bed that it registered in his brain: Peter had a son. An heir.

'Finlay Coldrick,' Soraya said in a whisper, confirming his assumption. Morton was stunned. He hadn't seen *that* one coming. He still couldn't imagine Soraya and Coldrick sharing the same house, much less a child. Soraya pulled the door shut and they returned to the lounge.

'Peter would have gone to the ends of the earth for that boy,' Soraya said quietly, tucking her legs up under herself. 'They had such a close relationship – there's no way he would have done anything like this. Fin spent the day with him on Tuesday. He wasn't feeling well and Peter looked after him while I was at work. He's supposed to have shot himself around seven thirty – half an hour after I left to bring Fin home. The police were like a dog with a bone about our separation – like he was some Fathers for Justice martyr or something,' she said, a mild undertone of anger in her voice. 'But that couldn't be any further from the truth. We never saw the need to sort out custody arrangements or make anything official, we've always been perfectly amicable and put Fin first.'

'I guess it's just the police looking for a motive,' he said, surprising himself by sounding like Juliette.

'Well, they're wrong: he didn't commit suicide. It's got something to do with his family, I know it,' she said resolutely, as if that was her final word on the subject, regardless of any investigation.

'It'll be the coroner's decision, I guess.'

Soraya scoffed. There was a slight pause before she said tentatively, 'Do you think you can find out what's going on, Morton? For Finlay's sake?'

'That's what I'm here for.' The new knowledge of Peter's son only reaffirmed Morton's commitment to finding out the truth about the Coldrick's family history.

'So, what do we do now?' she asked.

'I'm going to need to know *everything* about James and Peter – their hobbies, friends, political views, jobs - the lot.'

Soraya took a mouthful of wine. 'Okay,' she said with an uncertain laugh. 'Where to begin?'

'The beginning.'

Morton had been taking scribbled notes for more than three hours. His hand ached from the writing and his brain ached from the sheer monotony of the father and son's lives. He felt like he knew their frankly dull existences inside out, including James' preponderance for *The Shipping News* and *The Archers* and his fear of flying but love of caravan holidays in Wales. 'James sounds…' Morton racked his brain for the correct word. A polite word. 'Well, *ordinary*.'

'I suppose he was. He was certainly a very reserved man. He'd sit quietly in the corner of the room – always on the periphery of what was going on — just observing with a gentle smile on his face. I never once heard him raise his voice or become embroiled in an argument or complain about his cancer. Just a very, very kind and placid man who liked the simple things in life.' Morton nodded. James Coldrick *sounded* like a plain and simple man; but for one thing. It was time to bring up the bank balance.

'Something's bothering me,' he ventured.

'Go on.'

'James lived in a run-down council house for most of his adult life, having worked as an agricultural labourer, yet he was sitting on a sizeable amount of money when he died last year,' Morton said.

Soraya laughed. 'You have been digging, haven't you? Well, neither of us could fathom it when he died and the solicitor told Peter about it. It came as quite a shock, I can tell you. As far as Peter was concerned, there was no inheritance for him. As it turned out, he left it all to Finlay for when he reaches twenty-one.' She paused momentarily for breath. Morton thought that he detected an undercurrent of resentment in her voice. She continued, 'James didn't have a car, didn't have any expensive habits or luxuries and he only upgraded to a colour telly about ten years ago and that was going halves with Peter. He was forever scratching around for loose change to walk up the shop with.' Soraya paused again. 'He even bought a lottery ticket every week! Can you imagine! What would he have done with the winnings, for God's sake?'

'That's bizarre. Where did Peter think the money came from?'

Soraya shrugged. 'He hadn't got a single clue. At first he thought that maybe his dad was unaware he had the money until Peter asked at the bank. They wouldn't say much, data protection and all that rubbish, but they did say that he'd had the money in a high-interest account for a long time and received regular statements, so he certainly knew he had it. I think Peter suspected that his dad had inherited the money or that it was somehow connected with his family. Again, it all comes down to genealogy and *you.*'

'If only it were that simple,' Morton muttered.

'I've got every faith in you.' Soraya smiled.

'Thanks.'

'Is there anything else you want to know?'

'I think that'll do for the time being,' Morton said. 'I'll leave you my mobile number. If you think of anything else, give me a call.' He handed over one of his business cards and Soraya scribbled her own mobile number on a scrap of paper. Above it she scrawled what looked like her name, though the letter *a* bore more resemblance to the number nine.

'I'll be in touch when I've got something to report.'

Morton drove into the blood-orange sunset, the overwhelming heat finally abating. It was a curious and unforeseen end to the day. He had in no way anticipated leaving Soraya's house under the employ of a young child that he had not known existed four hours ago. *How old was Finlay Coldrick?* From the restricted view he had, he estimated him to have been about six, but then what did he know? His only experience of children was when he was a child himself and that didn't really count. And yet he felt an odd affinity with Finlay Coldrick, both of them having a similar rupture in their parentage. Although he had to admit that being told your father's head was blown off at close range won the title of potentially most messed up childhood. Whoever had killed Coldrick must have been waiting, watching the house until Soraya had collected Finlay at seven o'clock, before persuading him to open the door. It had to have been meticulously planned, not some arbitrary burglary that had gone horribly wrong.

Morton was moments away from home when it hit him – if Soraya had only collected Finlay at seven o'clock then he had been with Peter when he'd made the phone call at six twenty, practically begging Morton to see him. *What if Finlay had seen what was in the copper box?*

He slammed on the brakes, being half-tempted to mimic Juliette's impressive handbrake turn but he just knew that it would all go wrong and he'd end up upside down in the hedge, so he settled for the more acceptable three-point turn and sped back the way he'd come.

He banged his fist on Soraya's front door. Four hard thumps later he realised that Finlay was asleep, but by then it was too late. The damage was done. Soraya opened the door with a deep-set frown, about to lay into the idiot hammering on her door late on a Friday night, when she realised who it was.

'That was quick.'

'Sorry for the racket. I just got all the way home and realised that Finlay would have been with Peter when he phoned me Tuesday night and I think he might know what Peter wanted to show me. I know it's not ideal but can you wake him up so I can talk to him?' Soraya looked uncomfortable and Morton knew he'd made a mistake in coming back.

32

'I don't think so, Morton, not tonight. He's not sleeping for long as it is. The poor kid's devastated. The last thing he needs is an interrogation. I'll speak to him in the morning and see what I can glean. Sorry.'

'Fair enough. Sorry, I wasn't thinking.'

'That's okay,' Soraya said, about to close the front door when a small face appeared at her side.

'Who's that, Mum?' Finlay said shyly, folding an arm around Soraya's waist. He was a small, thin boy with dark hair, dark eyes and a neat pillow-scar that ran down his left cheek. Yet there was more to him than that: those mournful eyes that told of a dark past belonged to Peter Coldrick. Morton was sure that he could have identified those sombre eyes in a line-up of thousands.

'This is Morton, he's a nice man who's come to help us. Say hello.'

'Hello,' Finlay mumbled, his face meshed into Soraya's jumper.

'Come on, why don't I make you a hot chocolate and you can have a quick chat with him.' Finlay didn't seem convinced in spite of Morton's inane smile.

The three of them went into the lounge and Morton returned to the chair he had previously occupied that evening, while Finlay and Soraya took the large white leather sofa. Finlay snuggled up to his mum.

'Fin, there's something that Morton needs to know from you, if you can possibly remember. When you were at Daddy's house on Tuesday,' Soraya began, knowing full well that she was heading blindly into a minefield, 'did you see him open a box kind of thing?' Morton wanted the ground to open up and swallow him whole; it was horrific. The poor kid's bottom lip began to quiver, he tightened his grip around Soraya's arm as tears began to flood down his face and he lost control and began to wail. Morton could only meet the child's despairing look, those dark eyes punishing Morton. Soraya pulled him in closer, telling him it was alright. She shook her head at Morton – it was more of a *'this isn't happening tonight'* look she gave rather than *'thanks very much.'*

'Come on, let's get you back to bed,' Soraya said soothingly. He nodded and the wailing became more subdued as she led him by the hand out of the room.

Morton felt nauseous. *Now what was he supposed to do? Just walk out of the front door, or wait?* She could be hours settling him back off to sleep. He shouldn't have come back. *What was he thinking?*

Outside, the car was dead. Completely dead. Rigor mortis had even set in since nothing happened at all when he turned the key. A marvellous end to a marvellous evening. If he'd just kept on driving home things would have been a lot happier for everyone. It really was time to scrap the damned car. Then he remembered the money. It would be cleared any day now and he could walk into any car dealership and just pluck a car from the forecourt – no need for finance options or drawn-out bank loans, just grab the keys and drive away with the wind in his hair.

He turned the key again, but it might as well have been for a different car for all the good it did inside the ignition. There was no point in him lifting up the bonnet, it was like a different planet under there and he was very unmanly when it came to cars. He just had no interest in them apart from whether or not they drove. And this car didn't, so he'd lost all interest. Hammering on Soraya's door for a second time that evening wasn't an option. He had no choice but to phone Juliette and ask her to collect him.

Juliette's trusty Ka swooped in, her headlights momentarily dazzling him through the windscreen. He was ready to get into her car and head home but then she instructed him to open the bonnet. In fact, she probably already had jump leads stashed in her boot along with the red triangle, a more comprehensive first-aid kit than is carried by most paramedics, tools, spare wheel and all manner of other emergency equipment. *She really must have been a scout leader in a previous existence,* Morton thought.

Morton opened the bonnet and watched silently from the pavement as Juliette, torch wedged firmly in her mouth, carefully hooked a bundle of wires between the two vehicles like an heroic doctor performing an emergency transfusion.

'I'm going to get a new car tomorrow, I can't put up with this pile of junk anymore,' Morton moaned from the confines of the pavement. He secretly hoped that she wouldn't be able to fix it. Not *just* because he felt rather emasculated but because she would more likely agree that he needed a new car if even *she* couldn't get it to start. But he knew she would be able to fix it. She always could.

Juliette ignored his comment and instructed him to try the key and keep his foot on the accelerator. Predictably, the car sprang to life. After a moment of delving into the engine, she shut the bonnet and told Morton she would see him at home.

He had followed her back, matching her religious obedience to the speed limit all the way. Now, sitting in front of the telly, Morton was wondering how to broach the subject of a new car, since she'd taken his previous comment so flippantly. He decided to just come out and say it. After all, he was earning the money. 'I'm telling you, I'm getting a new car,' he said as empathically as he could muster, 'The money will be cleared any day now, so I'll go and get one.'

'It's fine, Morton. You say it like I'm going to stand in your way. It's your money, do what you like with it. Maybe you can put some of it towards *something* for your wonderful girlfriend of thirteen months who rescued you tonight?' Juliette said with a wry smile.

'We'll see.' Morton knew that she was alluding to her desire to flash a large rock on her left ring finger, although, actually he knew that she would have settled for *anything* on her left ring finger. Even one of those ring-shaped jelly sweets would have got her down the aisle. She was always complaining that she was the last of her group of school friends without a husband – some were selfishly already onto their second – or with a brigade of children around their ankles.

Juliette examined her left hand. 'Gold suits me best,' she muttered.

Maybe he would buy Juliette a nice piece of jewellery. He was thinking of a necklace. A nice one, something classy. Maybe with an inscription. Just not *that* particular piece of jewellery. Not yet.

Morton's thoughts drifted towards a happier time when his mother was still alive and his ignorant view of his family was still intact. Just days after his mother's funeral his father had sat him down and told him that he was adopted. He had blurted out the words, as if he was telling him that dinner was ready or that Morton had known all along but it had somehow slipped his mind. *Well, I really didn't think you'd react like this, Morton. You're sixteen now, man, come along. It's all a load of biology, chemistry and whatnot. You're my son today just like you always have been and always will be.* But he was no longer his parents' child; his real parents had apparently surrendered him forty-eight hours after he had first drawn breath. The only comfort that Morton had taken at the time from this bombshell was the revelation that he didn't share a single shred of DNA with Jeremy, the natural son of his parents. He was one of those miracle babies that infertile couples who adopt seem able to produce all of a sudden.

As the years had passed since the adoption revelation, Morton had gradually become increasingly dislocated from his surname and now no longer felt any connection to it. It would be ridiculous for Juliette to take his name upon marriage when it really didn't belong to him in the first place. She might as well dip her finger into the phonebook and take her pick. Or she could have one of the names Morton had harvested from parish registers over the years, for no other reason than that they sounded amusing. *Proudfoot. Ruggles. Arblaster. Stinchcombe. Catchpole. Winkworth. Peabody. Onions.* Yes, that suited her, Juliette Onions. It would make her stand out in the world of crime prevention. Nobody would forget PCSO Juliette Onions.

Chapter Four

5th June 1944

Emily pulled a hand-made shawl over her shoulders, staring fixedly through the kitchen window into the orchard. Alarmingly high winds – stronger than she thought she had ever known – thundered furiously through the trees, callously ripping the tiny Victoria plums from their branches and scattering them heartlessly onto the sodden ground. She looked, almost without blinking, through the torrential rain to the tall, brick chimney in the distance, standing defiantly against the squally weather. She wondered what was being discussed in the house about the current war situation. *Did they know what was coming?* She had been strictly forbidden to leave the confines of the house in the orchard – it was part of the deal – but two nights ago, shortly after midnight, curiosity had driven her to determine the source of the constant, deep rumblings emanating from the village. What she saw took her breath away. Dozens and dozens of lorries, jeeps and tanks, over-spilling with Allied troops, clattered down the main road. Silent villagers peered through their black-out curtains at the spectacle before them. Emily guessed where they were heading – towards the coast ready for an imminent invasion of France. *What did this mean? Was the war finally coming to an end? What about Hitler's secret weapon that she had heard murmurings of? This wasn't supposed to be how it all went. This wasn't the plan…*

Emily shuddered as a sudden gust of wind violently shook the window. She turned to the baby to see if it had disturbed him: he was still sound asleep in his cot. She wondered what would happen to him with the war's latest twist, but couldn't bear to follow her train of thought to its obvious conclusion. Moving away from the window, Emily quietly sat at the large oak table and picked up the only photograph she had of her and the baby boy. Apart from only one other photograph of her, she had destroyed all other images of her family, burning them in a memory-erasing pyre in May 1940. She set the photograph down, took a pen and a pad of notepaper and began to write the letter that she had hoped she would never have to write.

With painful tears cascading down her cheeks, Emily signed the letter and tucked it inside an envelope. There was little sense in sealing it. If what she sensed was going to happen actually did, then they would tear this place apart pretty soon.

Emily carefully placed the letter and the photograph of her and the baby inside the beautiful copper box, which had been created for the wedding that would now never take place. Drying her eyes, she put the copper box inside a small brown suitcase and then set about packing essential clothes for the both of them.

Chapter Five

Saturday

Morton was woken by the sound of his mobile ringing from somewhere in the house. He would usually have switched it off at night, preferring not to hear whatever bad news someone wanted to share, but in light of recent events he thought it better to leave it switched on. He followed the trail of noise into the lounge, like a child following the Pied-Piper playing the iPhone ring tone, where he found his mobile. Jeremy's name appeared onscreen and Morton's heart sank.

'Morning. Not too early is it?' Jeremy asked.

'Nope,' Morton answered, a little too sharply and then regretted it when Jeremy said, 'I just wanted to check you were coming tonight; you didn't reply to my email.'

'Sorry, I've had a lot on my mind,' Morton said.

'So, are you coming then? It'd be really good to see you before I go. It's been ages.'

'I'll do my best. Like I said, I've had a lot on my mind.' He was being too harsh, he knew that, yet he couldn't stop himself. He needed at least to *try* to be more upbeat. 'Are you all set for your adventure then?'

'Think so, ready as I can be,' Jeremy said. There was a long pause, Morton not knowing what else to say. He wanted to tell Jeremy to take care and be careful and keep his eyes open and not to treat it as a big game. Not to go at all, in fact. *What would their father do if he had his head blown off by the Taleban? Or what if he ended up in a wheelchair? Then what? Who'd look after him?* He wanted to say all of this but instead said, 'Okay, we'll hopefully see you tonight, then.'

Jeremy said goodbye and hung up.

'Damn,' Morton chastised himself.

Now that he was awake, and with Juliette already at work, he might as well get on with something constructive. He poured himself a strong coffee and headed to the confines of his study. He switched on the radio and immersed himself into the *Coldrick Case*. Enclosed by sheets of scribbled notes, Morton weighed his possible next options. Given James Coldrick's confinement in St George's Children's Home in 1944, it seemed logical that he was born in the vicinity of Sedlescombe. When he had arrived there and under what circumstances, Morton did not know, but the home and the village had played a significant part in the formative years of his life. Morton fired up Juliette's laptop and started with a simple Google search of Sedlescombe, following a myriad of links of varying usefulness and quality about the history of the village. The parish council had done an excellent PR job on the village website. A history section provided a potted narrative from the Stone Age until more recent times. According to the website, St George's Children's Home was built in 1922 by the firm, Dengates, when the local workhouse was demolished. Past research had taught him that life for anyone in a workhouse, especially children, was gruelling, severe and bleak. However, given his findings at East Sussex Archives, Morton wondered if conditions were any better for the poor children at St George's.

After an hour's research, the heat was getting unbearable. Morton stripped down to what had once been his best boxer shorts, but which were now stretched and faded beyond all recognition. He remembered the way that his mother used to carefully iron the household's clothing every Monday night without fail, including the underwear. She even ironed tea-towels and pillow cases. It was her generation. 'A woman's work is never done,' he remembered her saying on a daily basis. He wondered what she'd make of his relationship with Juliette, who shared none of his mother's domesticity: you'd never catch Juliette ironing anything that wasn't absolutely compulsory. Doubtless his mother's religious background would have caused her to frown on their living together but he was certain that she would have thawed eventually. Maybe things wouldn't now be so strained between him and his father if she were still alive. It was incredible that his mother had missed out on more of his life than she'd been there for. He was sixteen when she died, still navigating his way through puberty, flailing around discovering his own identity. To all intents and purposes, she never really knew Morton at all. He didn't like to think of her too often because no matter how happy the memory he was recalling, the story always ended the same: in her death.

Morton tried to ignore the latest news bulletin on the radio: more British soldiers had been killed in Afghanistan. He held his finger to the off-switch, wanting to avoid the intimate biographical details of the deceased men but he couldn't quite bring himself to do it. *Two British soldiers serving with the First Battalion Grenadier Guards have been killed after the vehicle in which they were travelling came under fire, the Ministry of Defence has*

40

confirmed. Corporal Brian Scott and Corporal Lance Adams, both nineteen, died after the vehicle they were travelling in... He switched it off. Jeremy was going to be deployed there any day now. *Deployed*, it all sounded so organised and meticulously planned - not quite the reality that Morton had witnessed in the media.

The idea of Jeremy out there in the desert, with a real gun and real people to kill, was so incomprehensible as to be almost laughable. Morton was sure that he wouldn't last ten minutes. Despite their strained relationship, whenever Morton heard the word Afghanistan, it was like someone had hooked him up to a dialysis machine and replaced his blood with a thick freezing sludge.

Morton had had enough and was feeling claustrophobic in the airless room. He loved living in the former police house, right in the epicentre of Rye's historic past, but at times the house reached uncomfortable, stifling temperatures. He decided it was time to get out of the house and pay a visit to Sedlescombe.

Morton found a parking space beside the Post Office and stepped out onto a tidy, triangular village green, wearing dark shorts, white t-shirt and sunglasses. He drew in a deep breath, laced with the scent of freshly cut grass, and took in the picture postcard surroundings that he had viewed online: white, weather-boarded and Sussex peg-tiled houses surrounded an award-winning village green, upon which was housed a handsome, now redundant pump. At the top of the gradually sloping main road was a pub, *The Queen's Head* and a three-star hotel, *The Brickwall,* outside of which sat a gaggle of lazy geese. The quintessential, quaint and sleepy English village. *Was it this perfect during James Coldrick's childhood,* he wondered? *Or was it all just a wafer-thin veneer?*

One building stood out from the rest – St George's Nursing Home, formerly the children's home. The parish website, with its carefully chosen images of the building, conflicted with the horrific piece of architecture in front of him. Morton crossed the deserted main street to get a better look at the monstrous edifice. It was a huge, gothic-style building with fairytale turrets and crenellated parapet walls. A simple wooden name-plaque raised high on two stakes proclaimed the name 'St George's Nursing Home'. Below, in smaller letters were the words 'Formerly St George's Children's Home, erected with the generosity of Sir Frederick and Lady Windsor-Sackville of Charingsby'.

It took Morton a few moments of staring at the name Windsor-Sackville to recall its familiarity to him: it was the name of the current, widely ridiculed Secretary of State for Defence. With a surname like that, he had to be related to the founders of St George's.

Morton's eyes moved from the plaque back to the building. This was the place where James Coldrick had spent many of his younger years. He wondered what had gone on behind the huge oak door that needed to remain secret all these years. Did it *really* warrant Peter Coldrick's death, covered up as a suicide, the removal of the 1944 admissions register for St George's Children's Home and the theft of his laptop?

A thought struck him. What if St George's had kept a record of the archives transferred to Lewes? It was a long shot. A very long shot but worth a try.

Morton headed up the stone path and felt a cold shudder pass over him. He wasn't a believer in auras, ghosts or ghouls but the building had some intrinsic negativity hanging over it. Some unseen darkness. Maybe he was just being paranoid.

He pulled open the heavy door and entered an immaculately clean, white-washed lobby, filled with a copious quantity of pungent white lilies, their stench trapped in the arid lobby. Not really the kind of flowers that Morton felt were appropriate for the entrance hall of a nursing home. A bit too funereal for his liking.

He opened another door that led into an air-conditioned reception area adorned with yet more perfumed flowers. It occurred to him then that maybe these *were* funeral flowers. He was pleased to see a mauve-rinsed lady single-finger-typing at a computer like a timid hen, pecking for grain. She raised a hand with ridged veins and liver spots to her temple. Morton guessed her to be the wrong side of seventy. He might have mistaken her for a resident but for her white coat.

'Be with you in one second, love.'

Morton nodded and looked around the high-ceilinged room. He could just catch a glimpse of a large open room where a group of idle residents sat chatting, sleeping and reading. It was difficult to picture how the building would have looked in James Coldrick's time here.

'Right, how can I help you, love?' she asked, her Yorkshire accent revealing her to be Linda, with whom he had spoken yesterday.

'Hi, I spoke to you yesterday about the records dating back to when this place was a children's home,' Morton said, offering his best smile.

'Oh yes, did you try the archives?'

'Yes, I did but unfortunately the file I wanted has gone adrift.'

'Oh dear,' she said, a large frown set on her forehead. 'Not sure what else you can do then, love. As I said to you on the phone, we've not got anything here at all.'

'You said you were here when the records were transferred?'

'That's right.'

'I was just wondering if the archives gave you any kind of receipt or anything which said exactly what they took?' Morton asked, hopefully.

Linda screwed her wrinkly face. 'It's possible but I can't remember back that far, love. I wouldn't even know where to lay my hands on something like that if we did keep it. Have you got a fax?'

Morton nodded.

'I tell you what I'll do, give me your fax number and I'll have a dig around and see what I can find. How's that sound?' she asked. 'We've got folders and filing cabinets full of old junk upstairs.'

'Perfect,' Morton answered, scribbling down his fax number on a proffered piece of scrap paper, which he was sure Linda would lose within half an hour. 'Thanks very much, I appreciate it,' he added, hoping that a bit of sincerity might encourage her to go rummaging. Morton thanked her again and left St George's.

With so much of Morton's work involving being shut in confined spaces with little or no natural light, he took a great deal of pleasure in being outdoors and greatly appreciated the hot sun warming the nape of his neck. He trundled through the archaic village, nodding respectfully to a gaggle of old ladies on their way to the post office, consciously absorbing the detail of the village. He scanned the village, dismissing houses or street furniture erected since the forties. He began to feel and understand the place in which James Coldrick was raised.

With sweat beginning to bead on his forehead, Morton walked from the village centre up a long, straight road with a gradual incline towards the parish church. The road, unimaginatively named *The Street*, was dotted with expensive, substantial homes with high fences and security gates. Of some luxurious houses Morton could only catch a glimpse through gaps in the dense shrubbery and carefully maintained trees.

The pavement rose and eventually veered to the right, terminating at St John's Church, a typical sandstone-coloured building with a chancel, nave and tower. Without any serious attempt at studying the architecture, he guessed the earliest parts dated back to the fourteenth-century with other additions being added in the latter centuries. He cast his eyes across the churchyard at the range of memorials in front of

43

him. Very recent, polished marble graves stood adjacent to ancient, lichen-covered headstones, the names of the deceased occupants having been weathered into obscurity.

Three pristine white graves stood side by side in commemoration of the village's fallen war heroes. Three brothers taken within weeks of each other in 1943. He thought of his own brother fighting in a war-zone and a feeling of dread dragged inside him as he remembered that tonight was his leaving party. He turned his head from the graves and tried to shake his despondency.

Morton refocused his attention to the task in hand: he needed to find James and Mary Coldrick's grave. When told by Peter where his parents were buried, Morton found it very curious that a man with such unsettled beginnings in the village should want to be forever entombed within its parish boundaries. Given all that he had discovered since Tuesday, he now thought it absolutely inexplicable that they were here.

Ordinarily, he would have conducted a meticulous, thorough search of the churchyard, using a range of techniques to decipher even the most worn inscriptions. Today, however, he knew exactly where he was headed. Peter had told him that his parents' grave was to be found in the shadow of a yew tree in the south-west corner of the churchyard. Morton spotted the ancient yew, with its gnarled and contorted trunk pushing into a thick green canopy above, and made his way towards it. The Coldrick headstone - polished black granite with gold, engraved lettering - stood innocuously among other modern graves under the protective shade of the yew. *In Loving Memory of Mary Coldrick 1946-1987. A much loved mother and wife. Also, James Coldrick 1944-2012. A much loved father.*

'Forever trapped in the place of your unhappy childhood,' Morton remarked to himself, as he took a couple of shots of the grave on his mobile.

'Pardon?' a sprightly voice piped up, startling him. Morton was jarred from his daydream and turned to see an old-timer with a grey handle-bar moustache, expensive olive-green suit and maroon neckerchief limping towards him.

'Sorry, just talking to myself,' Morton replied.

'Lovely day.'

'It is rather,' Morton said.

'I'm just going to open the church if you wanted to have a peek around.'

'That would be lovely, thank you.'

Morton followed the old man inside the church. The temperature suddenly plunged to the same arctic conditions as at East Sussex Archives. In the vestibule he noticed a burial plan of the churchyard. It was a crude, hand-drawn piece of paper that someone had helpfully laminated. Morton quickly verified that there were no other Coldricks buried in the church then wandered along the nave, stepping on worn marble tombstones dedicated to ancient clergy.

'I haven't seen you around here before, are you on holiday?' the man asked, tidying a stack of dishevelled hymn books.

'Well, I'm actually researching a family tree—Coldrick—do you know the name at all?' Morton asked.

The old man frowned, his preposterously lengthy eyebrows eclipsing his vision, as if he were trying to recall a private members' club in Islington. 'Doesn't ring any bells. How do you spell it?'

Morton took care to enunciate each letter carefully.

'No, I don't think so, old boy,' he replied eventually. 'Queer sort of name, wouldn't you say? Doesn't sound very Sussex to me.'

'No, I don't suppose it does,' Morton replied, not really sure what a 'Sussex' name was.

'When did they live in the village?'

'Around 1944 – possibly earlier.'

'Sorry, I can't help you there – I was on active service in Egypt at the time. There aren't many of us left who can recall much from that period with any clarity. It certainly isn't a name I've seen in the parish records in my time as church warden.'

'Not to worry – thank you anyway,' Morton said. He took one last look around the church and made his way out into the stark heat, where he was convinced that the temperature had risen by at least five degrees. Morton slowly walked back to his car, allowing his mind to mull over the case. As he fired up the car, Morton took one last look at the quiet, unassuming village. It looked so normal, so harmless. But that indefinable gut reaction, upon which he so heavily relied, told him that for James Coldrick, this village hadn't always been as normal and harmless as it now seemed.

Morton was lying prone on the bed, telling Juliette about his day whilst she transformed herself from Police Community Support Officer 8084 to Miss Juliette Meade, social butterfly. He was happy with either incarnation but, as she stood straightening her hair in a curvaceous, low-cut black dress, subtle make-up and killer heels, he was forced to admit that she looked more stunningly beautiful than the drab black, monochromatic uniform of the police force would ever allow. He'd not bothered getting dressed up for the occasion and was content in jeans and t-shirt.

'It's certainly an intriguing one, isn't it,' Juliette said in response to his discoveries with the *Coldrick Case*.

'That's an understatement.'

'Doesn't it make you wonder about your own family?'

Morton's insides tightly recoiled at the prospect of having a conversation about his own veiled past, a subject which he categorically avoided at the best of times. He sauntered over to the bedroom window and caught her reflection. Her eyes were narrowed and one hand rested defiantly on her hip. She wasn't about to let this one go.

'It must make you wonder, though,' she persisted. 'Your real parents could be walking past our house right now for all we know.' Morton glanced out of the window at the passers-by. He felt sure that he would recognise someone in whom he had once lived. 'Why don't you just go for the counselling, then see how you feel? You don't even have to find out who they are if you don't want to.'

'I don't see why I should,' Morton answered indignantly. It was the seemingly random quirk of law that anyone born before 12 November 1975 must seek counselling before discovering their birth parents that most irked Morton.

Counselling. It all sounded so unnecessary.

Juliette sighed, checked herself in the full-length mirror and waltzed from the bedroom, the transformation complete, leaving Morton with an unpleasant burning inside. Just how he needed to feel moments before seeing his father and brother again.

Morton and Juliette arrived at his father's smart 1930s semi in Hastings; the same respectable house and neighbourhood in which Morton had spent his first eighteen years of life, apart from those first few memory-less hours as a new-born baby in the arms of his real mother (presuming, of course, that she had even held him at birth). Seeing the house again filled his heart with the familiar yet uncomfortable fusion of emotions he had always felt coming back: nostalgia, disappointment and hopelessness. It was the same on each and every occasion that he returned home, the feelings only swelling

46

and deepening with time. His hopes of a last-minute cancellation were quashed by the din spilling out from the open windows.

Juliette sensed his apprehension and grasped his hand in hers as they neared the front door, giving it a tender, reassuring squeeze.

Morton pressed the doorbell and waited. He had his own key in his pocket but the last time he'd used it – more than two years ago now - his father had reacted with such shock that he had just tottered in off the streets without prior warning that Morton had never dared to use it ever since.

A figure moved behind the obscure glass.

Morton returned Juliette's squeeze as the door opened, revealing Jeremy with a large grin on his face. In full military uniform. He looked like Action Man's child, Action Boy; all dressed up and ready to play. Morton wondered if Jeremy really knew the difference between a weekend in the New Forest paint-balling with his mates and live warfare.

'Hi, Jeremy,' Juliette said, leaning in to kiss him on the cheek.

'Hi, guys, so glad you could make it,' Jeremy said cheerfully.

Morton extended his hand to his brother but Jeremy pulled him into a bear hug, squashing Morton's right hand between them. As far as Morton could recall, it was the first time he had ever embraced his brother. He wondered if that was normal for two thirty-something-year-old brothers. Finally Jeremy pulled away and stepped back to allow them into the busy house.

'All set then, Jeremy?' Morton asked.

'Think so, yeah,' Jeremy answered, leading them through the crowded hallway. Morton hardly recognised the place. The house was teeming with men throwing Stellas down their thick tattooed necks and laughing raucously. Morton couldn't imagine for a single second what his dad thought about his house being turned into an army barracks' outpost. He'd probably gone next door to David and Sandra's for wine, cheese and a few games of Scrabble.

Apparently not.

His father appeared from the crowd clutching a cup of tea. 'Morton, Juliette,' he said, as if he was taking a register and simply confirming their presence, rather than welcoming them into his home. He looked so much older to Morton than the last time he'd seen him. He noticed that the last flecks of his naturally coal-black hair had been completely drowned by a solid sea of dove-grey. He greeted Juliette with a smile when she leant in to peck him on the cheek. Morton shook his hand.

'So, how's work these days?' his father asked him. Morton felt that he had to physically prevent his eyes from rolling and his lungs from exhaling dramatically. His father always opened conversation with questions about his work, seeming to never believe Morton could actually make money from researching people's family trees.

Juliette stepped in. 'Oh my goodness, the work's been flooding in for him,' she said. 'It took a lot to drag him away from it tonight, I can tell you.' She laughed. She was a good liar. It must have been the rigorous police training. If Morton hadn't known the truth, he might have believed it himself. 'Just this week he landed a really good deal, didn't you?'

'Yeah, a real killer, this one,' he said sardonically.

'Good show, that's what I like to hear. Doesn't do a chap good to be out of work these days.'

'Indeed,' Morton agreed.

'Here you go,' Jeremy said, thrusting a bottle of beer into Morton's hand. Morton took a large gulp. He was going to need something strong to help him get through this evening. 'What did you want to drink, Juliette?'

'Just water'll be great, thanks,' she said, before qualifying, '...driving.'

'You've decorated, I see,' Morton said, vaguely directing his statement towards his father.

He frowned. 'You must have been here since then. Must have been a good eighteen months ago.'

'It looks nice. Very modern,' Morton said, ignoring the oblique undertones to his father's statement.

'Jeremy and I decided it was about time we gave it a lick of paint.'

'Fantastic,' Morton said, making no effort at all to sound genuine. He just couldn't be bothered. And nor, it seemed, could his father who had spotted someone more interesting to converse with across the room and silently wandered off.

Jeremy returned with Juliette's drink. 'Here you go.'

'Cheers,' Juliette said, as her glass met with Morton's and Jeremy's bottles.

'You two really should come over more often you know, we miss you up here,' Jeremy said.

'Yeah,' Morton said half-heartedly.

'Could you do something for me, Morton?' Jeremy asked.

'Uh-huh,' Morton answered, warily.

'Will you call in on Dad more often while I'm away? He's getting on a bit now and he'd love to see more of you.'

Morton took a deep breath, resenting the implication and doubting the statement. 'Yeah, sure.'

'Great, thanks. It'll be a big weight off my mind.'

'Do you know when you're likely to be back?' Juliette asked.

'Hopefully six months, but you never know,' Jeremy answered. 'Anything could happen.'

'We could declare war on *any* unsuspecting part of the Middle East if there's enough oil there,' Morton said, taking a large mouthful of beer and receiving an admonishing hand squeeze from Juliette. He really needed to tone down the sarcasm.

'How's your work going, Juliette?' Jeremy asked. 'Enjoying rounding up criminals?'

'I love it. Well, apart from the late nights and dodgy shift patterns.'

'What sort of things do you have to do? Is it like the regular police?'

Juliette laughed. 'Well, the regulars call us CHIMPS – Can't Help in Most Police Situations. That about sums it up. Mostly we confiscate alcohol from fourteen-year-old boys, liaise with the community and direct traffic,' Juliette said with a laugh.

The doorbell sounded and Jeremy excused himself to answer it.

'Morton, stop being such an idiot,' Juliette whispered as soon as Jeremy was out of earshot.

'Just listen to them,' Morton said, quaffing his beer and indicating a large group of soldiers in the doorway, 'All this macho bear-hugging and back slapping.'

Juliette took a deep breath and moved across the room towards a table of buffet food. Morton headed into the kitchen, pushing past more army clones. The place was like a wartime working men's club, he thought. *Keep up the good work, chaps. Don't let old Blighty down.* He cracked open another beer and took a swig. Busy washing up at the sink was a smartly-dressed lady with white hair in a neat perm. She turned and smiled. 'Hello,' she said brightly. 'Are you Morton?'

Morton nodded, having no previous recollection of the woman. He realised that he was projecting his resentment at being there onto the poor lady. 'Yes, that's me,' he said with a smile.

The lady pulled off her yellow Marigolds and offered her hand. 'Madge,' she said. 'I'm a friend of your father's.'

'Nice to meet you,' he said tentatively, shaking her hand.

'I've heard a lot about you. You're a genealogist, aren't you?'

'That's right,' Morton answered, surprised to find that his father had discussed him at all, much less his career. He took another mouthful of beer and listened as Madge spoke, her eyes suddenly lighting up.

'That must be a wonderfully interesting job. All those stories and personal histories you're uncovering - how exciting! I dabbled with my family history a few years ago before everything went online and you had to haul out huge ledgers for each quarter of each year just to locate a person's birth, marriage or death. Just finding my grandfather's birth entry took me nigh on a whole day once! Now it's all there at the click of a button.'

Morton remembered the hours and hours he had spent in the early years of his career at the Family Records Centre in Islington, a building always bustling with amateur and professional genealogists alike, all vying for precious desk space in which to place the voluminous tomes containing thousands of names. 'I must have spent half my life trawling through records there,' Morton recalled. 'And the censuses were just as bad, with only the 1881 census having been indexed.'

'Oh yes, they were all microfilmed weren't they? Amazing to think how quickly things have changed. What is it that you're working on at the moment?'

Morton took a deep breath and explained the highlights of the job to her, enjoying the fact that he had a genuinely interested audience. Madge asked questions along the way but had little to offer in the way of suggestions or avenues he had not yet considered pursuing.

After a while, Morton excused himself and, feeling the need for some quietness, went upstairs to his old bedroom. He had occupied this room for eighteen years. It was filled with more memories than any other place in which he'd lived; illicit teenage drinking sessions and clumsy gropes all took place here. He had his first kiss on that very bed. It had all gone horribly wrong when his puckered lips met with Clare Smith's gaping mouth, her fleshy pink tongue trying to probe apart his clenched teeth. She said it hadn't mattered and that she wouldn't tell anyone, but by first lesson the next day he was dumped and by second lesson the vast majority of the school were puckering up as they passed him in the corridors. *Such wonderful memories*, he thought.

He sat down on the bed and finished his beer, welcoming the furring and blurring of his mind. He glanced around the room; there was no trace of his ever having resided here. Within days of his leaving for university his father had redecorated the entire room, as if that were the last time that Morton would ever go home. No thought for the long holidays or life after university. The curtains, the pictures, the carpet, the ceiling light – everything replaced. They'd even changed the door. Something about drawing-pin holes from his Madonna posters.

Morton sighed. A long time ago. A very different world. He left the room and his melancholic nostalgia behind and headed down to the kitchen. Madge was engaged in a conversation with a tall stout man in army uniform. Morton opened another beer then scoffed down two prawn vol-au-vents and a tuna sandwich. He was about to grab a handful of crisps when he heard his father call for the assembled crowd to quieten. He was going to do a speech. *Great, this party just gets better and better*, he thought.

'Ladies, gentlemen and members of Her Majesty's armed forces, could I please have your attention for one moment.' The lounge was packed solid and, standing on tip-toe, Morton could just catch a glimpse of his father, standing on a leather pouffe in the bay window with an arm tightly around Jeremy's shoulder.

The room fell silent.

'Thank you. I won't keep you long, I know you've all got plenty of food to eat and beer to drink. I just wanted to say how proud I am of Jeremy; a sentiment that I'm sure would be shared by his late mother, Maureen. It takes a lot of courage to join the army in these unpredictable and unstable times that we're in today. I know there are others in the room who will also be joining my son, so I just wanted to wish you all the best of luck and may God's good grace keep you all safe out in Cyprus.'

The assembled crowd murmured their agreement, with glasses being raised and hands being clapped.

Morton was confused. 'Cyprus?' he said loudly, to no-one in particular.

A beefy man in front of him turned. 'Yeah, we're off to Cyprus for a tour of duty.'

'I didn't know we were at war with Cyprus.'

The large man frowned and said something but Morton wasn't listening. For no apparent reason, an image of Peter Coldrick being blasted in the head at close range appeared in full clarity in his mind

51

and at that moment his stomach decided to show the world what semi-digested vol-au-vents, tuna sandwich and beer look like. All over the hallway carpet.

Chapter Six

Sunday

The memory of the previous evening made Morton's eyes ping open involuntarily. Though his brain was suspended in what felt like a thick, mucous-like sludge, he could still remember his vociferous protestations that the beers he'd consumed *weren't* the reason that he'd thrown up all over his father's fancy cream carpet. He had tried to explain (particularly to the beefy man whose shoes had been caught in the blast) that he was working for a dead man who had shot himself in the head. That was the moment that Juliette had shot through the crowd like a raging bull and bundled him straight out the front door. No questions. No goodbyes. No explanations. Just dragged unceremoniously from the house and shoved into the back of the car.

Morton touched his left bicep – the arm that Juliette had used to lever him out of the house – it was bruised and aching: a reasonable punishment, he supposed. Probably best not to complain about it.

'Morning,' Juliette said from beside him, her voice flat and emotionless. She was sitting upright in bed reading and Morton wondered what she was thinking. He rolled over and placed his arm across the top of her thighs. 'Don't even *think* about it,' she warned.

'What?'

'Trying to sidle up to me,' she said, without taking her eyes from the page. 'You've got a lot of grovelling to do today, Morton Farrier.'

Ah, those precious, wonderful words: Morton Farrier. She only used his name like that when she was faking displeasure. She wasn't *really* annoyed. Maybe just a tiny bit. It wouldn't take him too long to get back on her good side.

'I know. Sorry,' he said, hauling himself up and hoping that his brain wouldn't fall out. 'Breakfast in bed?' he asked. It was the single last thing on earth that he wanted to do and he hoped desperately that she would say no, or that she'd had her breakfast hours ago. *What was the time?* He looked at the clock: ten twenty.

'Yes, please, that would be a good start,' she answered. 'The full works.'

Morton had to work hard to restrain the whimpering cry in his larynx as he twisted his body and placed his feet on the floor. He hadn't collapsed or died yet. That was achievement enough. With a

53

deep breath and a concerted effort, Morton hauled himself up and waited for the room to stop merry-go-rounding in front of him before trudging to the kitchen like a decrepit old man in need of a hip replacement. He was grateful to have made it all the way to the kitchen without succumbing to death, and poured himself a welcome glass of orange juice. Someone had once told him that drinking orange juice after alcohol lessens the severity of a hangover. Well, it was better late than never, he guessed, as he sunk the glass much too quickly and then promptly regretted it.

A while later Morton carried a tray of scrambled eggs on toast, glass of orange juice and mug of filter coffee through to Juliette. She set down her trashy romance novel and smiled.

'Perfect,' she said, fiercely attacking the breakfast. 'Are you not having any?'

'I had a bit of dry toast, it was all my poor stomach could cope with,' Morton said, lying down at her feet with a groan, hoping for a little sympathy.

'It's your own stupid fault.'

Morton made a strange whining noise in agreement.

Two hours later, Juliette was sporting a thick fluffy white dressing gown that they each owned after 'stealing' them during a long weekend in Gleneagles last summer, a treat after Juliette had been accepted to become a PCSO. They liked to tell people they'd stolen the dressing gowns but actually the hotel had added the cost of them, sixty quid each, onto their credit card bill, which Morton only discovered the following month. In hindsight it wasn't the best start to a career in law enforcement.

'So what have you got planned for today?' Juliette asked.

'First things first is to make sure that money cleared,' Morton said, fully dressed, showered, breakfasted and ready to go. The hangover had at last lifted, like a thick fog leaving his brain.

'Well, I'm going to spend the day in my dressing gown watching my backlog of soaps,' she announced, curling up prone on the sofa and switching on the television.

'Enjoy,' Morton said, making his way upstairs to the study. He dialled the bank and waited unitl a sullen voice confirmed that his balance now stood at fifty thousand, two hundred and twenty-two pounds. Morton took the news surprisingly morosely. He'd never had such a huge amount in his life, but the money came in tandem with

Peter Coldrick's death. His thoughts were interrupted by a loud beep from the fax machine, heralding that the seldom-used machine was about to spring to life.

Morton waited patiently then tore off the disgorged piece of paper. It was sent from St George's Nursing Home. On the top sheet was written, 'Found it! Regards, Linda.' Unexpectedly, she had managed to locate the inventory of the records taken to East Sussex Archives. His narrowed eyes passed quickly down the typed list of records until he reached the admission registers: 1944 was removed along with every other record on the page. According to the inventory, the register had left St George's on 1 December 1987.

Yet it had never arrived at East Sussex Archives.

Morton turned to the last page to see the name of the person who had transferred the documents – maybe they still worked at the archives and could be held to account. Squiggled neatly at the bottom of the page he found the unambiguous signature of Max Fairbrother.

Morton's pupils dilated and his heart kicked into a new, heavier rhythm as he studied the signature. There was no question about it; Max's name was right there in front of him. Morton remembered Max's baffled face when he had enquired as to the whereabouts of the document. That was the opportunity Max had to say, 'Oh, *that* register, yes I lost it. Just one of those things. I do apologise.'

'I can't believe it,' Morton said, entering the lounge.

'Can't believe what?' Juliette asked.

'Max Fairbrother. He's only the one who took the file admissions file from St George's that I wanted to see.'

'Max who?'

'Max Fairbrother,' Morton ranted, 'he works at the archives.' Juliette looked perplexed. 'Max,' Morton repeated, as if that would help. It didn't, but his thoughts had run too far away to bother with explanations so he just said, 'It doesn't matter,' instead.

The car miraculously started first time, as if aware that its life hung in the balance and it should start to make an effort. But Morton had made up his mind and drove directly to the car showroom.

He pulled into the customer parking bay tucked behind the shiny glass building, which Morton presumed was a deliberate way to separate the vehicular wheat from the chaff. He stepped out into the relentless heat and headed towards a racing-green Mini Cooper SD that had caught his eye when he had previously driven past. He cupped his hands over the driver's window and gazed longingly inside. Long no longer, Mr Farrier.

'She's a beautiful car, this one,' said a keen youth, fresh out of salesman school, who had appeared from the heavens and startled Morton. He was sporting an ill-fitting suit and an eager eye. 'Hundred and forty miles per hour top speed, hundred and seventy-five HP nominal power, nought to sixty-two in five point six seconds, automatic aircon, sports seats, chrome interior, navigation system, hi-fi loud speakers, rain sensor, bi-xenon lights, the list goes on: beautiful!'

Morton didn't know what bi-xenon lights were or whether one hundred and seventy-five HP nominal power was a good thing or not. It sounded impressive, though, he had to admit.

'Would you like to take her for a test drive, sir?'

'No. Thank you, though,' Morton said, watching the salesman's smile turn upside down as he realised he'd made another wasted journey from the confines of the air-conditioned showroom.

'I'll take it. What will you give me for my old Mondeo over there?' Morton asked, quickly regretting the use of such a depreciative adjective.

The man introduced himself as Paul and extended a hot hand towards him. He rubbed his hands together. 'If you'd like to follow me, sir, I'll see what I can do.'

Morton followed him into the glass-walled office and was quickly handed a polystyrene cup of tea by a lugubrious secretary while Paul went out to make an assessment of the Mondeo. He returned ten minutes later with the news that it was worth no more than seven hundred and fifty pounds, but that he would give an extra five hundred quid as a 'good-will gesture', leaving Morton with a mere seventeen thousand-pound balance to pay. A drop in the ocean for a rich forensic genealogist like him. Morton knew that he was being fleeced, but continued regardless. He stripped the Mondeo of the scratched case-less CDs, handful of loose change and outdated road map; an hour and a half later he was sitting in the plush virgin leather interior, speeding from the garage without so much as a cursory glance back at his old car, festering in the shadows of the showroom.

Morton grinned as he tore along the country lanes, zipping in and out of traffic like he was a Formula One driver. He swung into a parking space in the car park adjoining East Sussex Archives and marched confidently into the ice-cold office, riding on the fresh burst of energy supplied by the thousands of pounds sitting in his bank account.

Quiet Brian, the slim taciturn man who appeared sporadically and without routine at the archives was on duty in the lobby. He was either exceptionally shy or, more likely, Morton thought, had had his personality frozen out of him by Miss Latimer.

Quiet Brian handed Morton the adherence to the rules form, which he duly signed and handed back. Morton glanced over to the shelf on which he had placed his business cards and, sure enough, they had all gone. It was a bit of a stretch of the imagination to think that they had been snapped up enthusiastically by the general public in three days. Miss Latimer had to have discarded them.

Morton bounded up the stairs clutching the fax from Linda, his heart beginning to race as he pulled open the search room door and ventured inside the wintry room. He had no idea exactly how he was going to broach the subject with Max. Maybe he should just come right out with it in a loud, bold voice, as if he were in court. *I put it to you, Max Fairbrother that on the first of December 1987 you wilfully removed the 1944 admissions register from St George's Nursing Home and kept it for your own personal gain…*

Miss Latimer was sitting at the research desk, holding her glasses millimetres above the bridge of her nose as she studied a document on the desk in front of her. Morton knew that he had entered her peripheral vision and that she was deliberately ignoring him. He shuffled lightly on his heels to try and attract her attention and he wondered if he should cough politely.

'It's downstairs, first door on the right,' Miss Latimer said loudly, without moving as much as an eyelash.

'Sorry?' Morton said, before he realised to what she was referring, but it was too late to stop her.

'The *toilet*,' she enunciated, 'it's downstairs, first door on the right.'

'I don't need the toilet –'

'Then would you kindly stop wiggling about in front of me,' she said, finally condescending to look up at him. She placed her glasses down and stared at Morton. He guessed that was his cue to talk.

'Is Max here?'

'Mr Fairbrother is not available at the moment. What is the nature of your enquiry?' she asked.

'Confidential,' Morton said with a caustic smile, 'could you call him, please? It's important.'

Miss Latimer sat rigid, contemplating his request. Finally, she picked up the phone. 'Sorry to disturb you, Mr Fairbrother. I've got somebody here to see you. He says it's important.' She covered the mouthpiece. 'Who are you?' Morton knew she was feigning ignorance but played along regardless.

'The forensic genealogist, Morton Farrier,' he said dryly. Miss Latimer scowled.

'Mr Farrier. Right.' She set down the phone and began tapping at the computer. Moments later in strolled Max Fairbrother wearing a brown leather bomber jacket and light blue jeans. He was either going for the young and trendy look or the Biggles look. Either way, he looked ridiculous.

'Morning, Morton. Back so soon?' he said cheerily.

Morton smiled, unsure of how to tackle him. He rummaged in his bag and pulled out the fax from St George's and approached the front desk, where Max stood behind Miss Latimer.

'Max, do you remember I was looking for the 1944 admissions register for St George's last week?'

Max's brow furrowed for a moment. 'Oh yes, I do. It was missing on transfer, wasn't it? Or something?' *Or something* was about right. Morton nodded and thought that Max was acting the part very well. If he hadn't seen the signature for himself he might have believed him. Maybe he should have been an actor rather than an archivist.

'Well, a funny thing happened. I contacted St George's and luckily they had an inventory of what was removed on the…' Morton looked down at the faxed account, Max's name just out of sight. '…first of December 1987.'

Miss Latimer set down her glasses, intrigued by the exchange taking place between the two men. Max's cheeks had flushed crimson.

'Apparently,' Morton continued, his eyes boring into Max, '*everything* was removed, including the 1944 admission register.'

'Pass that to me,' Miss Latimer instructed, thrusting out her hand.

Max dived across and snatched the paper. 'It's okay, Deidre, I'll deal with it.'

Morton looked at Miss Latimer's disgruntled face. *Deidre*. He never had her down as a *Deidre*. She was an Agatha or an Eileen or a Camilla. Deidre Latimer, the spinster archivist.

'Do you fancy going out for a coffee, Morton?' Max asked, his face continuing to burn. 'Nero's okay for you? I find coffee places are all much of a muchness these days,' Max quipped cheerfully.

58

'Sure,' Morton answered tersely, riled by Max's blasé attitude. He was desperate for a caffeine injection, and to get away from Deidre was probably the best solution for everyone. Particularly for Biggles and a confession that could cost him his job.

Morton took a table in the back corner of the coffee shop, which he was grateful to find largely deserted. He didn't trust anybody at the moment, least of all the man heading towards him with a tray of coffees and two muffins. *Max had actually bought him a muffin?* Morton found it vaguely disturbing, as if they were old chums on an annual get-together.

'I got a blueberry and a double-chocolate – take your pick,' Max said brightly. Morton reluctantly took the blueberry muffin – well, he was hungry after all. Max sat back in the leather armchair, crossed his legs at the ankles and took a bite from his muffin. His nonchalance irritated the hell out of Morton.

'Who told you to remove all the old records from St George's to the archives, Max?' Morton said, barely able to contain his fury.

Max cleared his throat and blew out his cheeks, his lips vibrating together. 'County. They'd been asking us to archive all sorts of records for a long time, from schools, the local authority, hospitals, parish councils but we simply didn't have the resources to achieve it all quickly enough. St George's was just one of many.'

Morton was perplexed. 'But then? Why 1987? What was the urgency? Those records had sat there untouched for years.'

'I haven't the foggiest,' Max said, shaking his head and steepling his fingers. 'Let's just say that I was *persuaded* by someone to make St George's a priority.'

'So it was someone in County who told you to pull the admissions register?'

'No, at least not that I'm aware of.'

'Who was it then?'

Max shrugged. 'Not the nicest acquaintance I've ever met.'

'Do you know his name?' Morton pushed.

Max's brow furrowed. 'If memory serves me correctly, it was a man called William Dunk.'

'Why did he want the records?'

'I don't know, Morton.'

'Did he want any others?'

Max shook his head. 'That was it.'

59

'Do you know what happened to the records once he'd taken them?'

'I imagine that whatever they contained needed destroying – why else go to such extreme lengths? Lots of people would love to get their hands on original documents which show their family – sometimes touching and holding something one's great, great grandfather once held or signed is the closest one can ever get to them – but nobody would do what Dunk did for that reason.'

Morton's instincts agreed with what Max had said about the records likely having been destroyed. He glared across at Max, wondering what had made someone with such a passion for preserving the past want to blatantly sabotage it. 'Why did you do it? Money?'

Max shifted uncomfortably in his seat. 'Well, I didn't get a choice in the matter,' he answered, his voice trailing off, as if encouraging Morton to jump in with a moral condemnation. Morton preferred to stay quiet and give Max all the rope he needed to hang himself. Max continued, 'First of all he showed up at the archives and I told him to bugger off, to put it mildly, then the next day he showed up at my house brandishing a weapon. So, I handed the file over. After that I never saw him again.'

'Why would someone be so desperate to remove an admissions register?' Morton said rhetorically. 'Seems a bit extreme.'

Max met Morton's hard stare. 'I've asked myself the same questions over the years, but I still have no idea.'

Morton considered the scenario carefully. As an historian, if he had been put in Max's position the first thing that he would have done would be to pick over every word of that admissions register with a fine-tooth comb to discover its hidden secret. 'You must have taken a look inside,' he said finally.

'Yes, I did. I took it home and read it cover to cover. Then I re-read it and re-read it again. Nothing out of the ordinary. Nothing. Just the names of children being admitted to a children's home. I didn't get it. In a funny way, that kind of made it easier to hand over. It wasn't like I was giving away the Domesday Book.'

'I don't suppose you recall seeing the name Coldrick in there?'

Max shook his head. 'As I said, nothing stood out. I couldn't now tell you a single word that was written in there.'

Morton didn't trust Max but he felt that he was being honest with him. 'Who did this William Dunk work for?'

'I don't know, he never said and I never asked.'

'How could I find him?' Morton demanded.

'He's probably six feet under by now, I shouldn't wonder. He was at least in his seventies back then.'

'In his seventies? And he threatened *you*?' Morton said, slightly incredulous that a beefy man like Max could be intimidated by a pensioner. He had visions of this Dunk character propped up outside Max's house on his Zimmer frame.

'When I say that he came to the house, I meant that he was *inside* my house. With a crowbar held over my wife's head.'

That revelation slightly dampened the damning fires of Morton's moral condemnation. Still, he couldn't quite let Max off the hook; he could have reported it to the police or something. 'Oh,' Morton said.

'Exactly.' Max paused. 'Look, Morton, I know it goes against everything that I've ever worked for and I do feel guilty about it, but I'd like to meet the man who offered a polite 'no' to William Dunk and his crowbar. The question is, what are you going to do now that you know I took it?'

'Hadn't thought about it,' Morton said, dismissively.

'Can I ask what *your* desperation is to locate this one register?' Max asked.

Morton took a leisurely sip of his drink before answering. He didn't want to divulge a thing to Max. 'Just a case that I'm working on, that's all.'

Max smiled. 'You think I'm still working for them, don't you?' he said. When Morton wasn't forthcoming with an answer he added, 'I'm not, you know.'

'Whatever you say, Max,' Morton said glibly. He downed the last of his coffee, burning the roof of his mouth, and marched indignantly back to his car.

Morton left Lewes with a fresh piece of jigsaw to add to his case notes: William Dunk. If Max was correct, and Dunk was now dead, then the implication was that a lot of people had been working for decades to cover up the past – a task which was continuing to this day. He had no doubt at all that the removal of the admissions register was because of James Coldrick. As he zipped through along the High Street in Rye towards his house, he contemplated his next step. To connect this new piece of jigsaw to the bigger picture, Morton needed to know more about William Dunk.

As he turned into Church Square, he noticed an aged war veteran, standing proudly by the church entrance wearing a blue beret and a full selection of medals, collecting money for charity. His mind flashed to the future – *would Jeremy survive an army career in these unstable times and be standing outside a church in his seventies?* He felt happier that he was now, at least, headed somewhere that the Foreign Office hadn't blacklisted as a travel destination. He needed to stop being so damned morose and think about something more positive. Like Juliette. She'd be home watching television, waiting for him. Maybe they could do something nice together.

'Hiya,' he called into the lounge when he got home. The television was off and there was no sign of her. Her car was still on the drive but he couldn't see a note or any clue as to where she might have gone. Ordinarily he wouldn't have paid it any heed, but after all that had occurred, visions of her being bundled into the back of a blacked-out van sprang into his mind. He chided himself for being so melodramatic. He picked up his mobile and called her. She answered. Thank God.

'Are you alright?' he asked, trying to conceal his concern. She sounded breathless.

'Fine, I'm just out for a jog. What's up?'

'Nothing, I'm home and just wondered where you were,' Morton replied. *Jogging? In this heat? Was she mad?*

'You sound weird,' Juliette puffed.

'No, I'm fine; I'll see you in a bit.'

'Okay. Bye.'

Morton hung up, relieved. Since she was out frying herself in the heat, he had a moment to switch on her laptop and run a search in the online death indexes for a William Dunk, born *circa* 1917, give or take ten years. The results flashed up on screen.

William Dunk, 1 May 1913 – May 1993, Havering, Essex
William Dunk, 7 Mar 1902 – Mar 1999, North Somerset, Somerset
William Charles Dunk, 1 Apr 1913 – Jul 2002, Hastings and Rother, East Sussex
William Edwin Dunk, 21 Dec 1911 – Nov 1986, Hackney, London
William George Dunk, 6 Aug 1910 – Sep 1993, Shrewsbury, Shropshire
William Isaac Dunk, 12 Mar 1911 – Jan 1998, Leeds, Yorkshire
William Joseph Dunk, 1 Jun 1912 – Mar 1997, Poole, Dorset

William Roy Dunk, 11 Oct 1934 – Nov 1989, Grimsby, Lincolnshire
William Thomas C. Dunk, 21 Jan 1915 – Jul 1985, Chorley, Lancashire

He looked at the list in front of him. Several of the men's ages ruled them out. One would have been way too old and one too young to pass for a man in his seventies in 1987 and two of the men were dead by that time. That left five men to choose from. Dorset, Yorkshire and Shropshire as places of death were possible, yet seemed unlikely, somehow. That left William Charles Dunk, who died in East Sussex in 2002 as the most probable candidate.

Morton jotted down the details and went to order the certificate. He decided that it was worth spending the extra money to receive the certificate on the priority, twenty-four-hour service. A few simple clicks later and the certificate was ordered.

He opened the *Coldrick Case* file. It was now starting to bulge under the weight of paperwork that he had generated. Never before had he produced so much documentation with so few answers. The first page contained the scribbled notes made at Coldrick's house five days ago. *Five days – was that really all it had been?* He re-read the notes and was suddenly struck by Mary Coldrick's date of death: 1987. He had never been a great believer in coincidences before but if this case had taught him anything, then it was that a coincidence was simply a connection waiting to be made. Peter had told him that his mother had started looking into the Coldrick family tree just before she died which just *happened* to be the same year that the 1944 admissions register disappeared. *Coincidence?* He didn't think so.

Morton dialled Soraya Benton's mobile. She picked up straight away.

'Hi, it's Morton Farrier here. I've got some questions about Peter's family.'

'Sure, fire away,' she answered.

'I was just wondering if you knew anything about Peter's mum's death.'

There was a short pause. 'Well, it was way before my time. Peter said it was a house fire, I think. He was at school when it happened and his dad was out somewhere. That's about all I know.'

'Do you remember what the cause was?'

'I think it was an electrical fault or gas maybe. Why do you ask?'

'I was just wondering, that's all. Trying to tie up loose ends. Explore all avenues, that sort of thing.'

'You don't suspect foul play, do you?' she asked.

'No,' Morton replied, unconvinced by his own answer.

The front door slammed shut and Juliette called out his name. She sounded worried. He covered the receiver and called down to her. 'I'm on the phone. One second.' Then back to Soraya. 'I'm just looking under every rock. I've got to go, thanks for your help. I'll get back to you.' He ended the call just as Juliette bounded into the room, red-faced and slightly out of breath. Her damp hair was pulled up in a ponytail over a translucent-grey tide-line of sweat on her t-shirt. She *was* worried.

'What's the matter?'

She inhaled sharply. 'We're being watched.'

'What?'

'We're being watched. There's a guy at the top of St Mary's Church with a pair of binoculars,' she said, moving towards the lounge window. Morton followed and stared up through the nets to a dark blurred outline on top of the church tower. 'I'm going to call it in, get him picked up.' Juliette pressed some buttons on her mobile.

'Wait,' Morton said. 'I don't think that's a good idea.'

'Why not? He might be a lead.'

'Well he's gone, for one thing,' Morton said. 'For another thing, what would you have him charged with exactly? Carrying a pair of binoculars?'

Juliette looked up to the empty church tower and folded away her phone. 'I don't like this, Morton.' She had regained her breath and placed her hands on her hips the way she did when she wanted to exert her PCSO authority. 'You need to start trusting the police. This is getting out of hand.'

'How do you know he's not just another tourist?' Morton asked. There were always people up there with cameras and binoculars taking advantage of the sweeping vista out to the coast. Maybe she was just being paranoid.

'How many tourists with secret service style ear-pieces and top-of-the-range binoculars trained on our house have you encountered before?' It wasn't a rhetorical question. 'Hmm?'

None, he was forced to admit.

Chapter Seven

Monday

The skies were ominously dark as Morton walked the short distance from his car to Ashford Library on Church Road. After discovering that he was being watched yesterday, Morton was on high alert. He had checked his rear-view mirrors like he hadn't done since he had taken his driving test aged seventeen. On his way to the library he'd taken random and sudden turnings in an attempt to throw off any potential chasers, though what good it would do him if someone really wanted to stalk him he wasn't sure. He was as confident as he could be that he hadn't brought any nefarious followers with him as he entered the library. If he had been followed, then his pursuers would just have to take a book down to the bean-bag-thronged 'Chillax Zone' and wait for him, evidently a place favoured by the bizarre combination of foreign students and tramps. The new-look library even boasted a Costa Coffee concession with the caveat that food and drink could only be consumed within the Chillax Zone, so Morton resisted the urge to grab a large latte and instead took a vacant table in the Reading Room. He looked around the quiet tables: he was safe; his neighbours were a group of old men too tight to buy their own newspapers, grunting and making comment on the day's headlines.

In the name of reserving his seat in this surprising hive of activity, he placed his bag containing a notepad and pen down on the table and approached the customer service desk. Behind the counter, a rotund teenaged girl was taking an inordinate amount of pleasure spinning a skinny purple-haired youth with tight black jeans on a swivel chair. Neither were in any hurry to serve him.

'Can I help you?' the girl said acerbically, bringing the chair to an abrupt halt.

'I'd like to see any newspapers which cover the Tenterden area for 1987.'

'*Kentish Express*, *Kent Gazette*, *Sussex Express* or *Tenterden Times*?' the girl said.

'*Tenterden Times*,' Morton answered, plumping for what seemed the most likely. The other papers sounded too general.

'You want the whole year?' she asked incredulously.

'I'm not sure,' Morton said, 'I'm looking for a particular story. Can I start with December and work my way backwards?'

'Whatever,' she said with a shrug. She waddled through a door behind the desk, leaving the skinny lad staring at Morton like a wide-eyed baby. Moments later she returned, struggling to squeeze herself and two string-bound parcels of newspapers through the door.

'Give us a hand,' she asked, and he went to her rescue, taking one of the bundles and dumping it on the counter in front of Morton. The two packages were labelled 'November' and 'December'.

Morton muttered his thanks and carried the stacks over to his desk. He sat down, carefully removed the string wrapping and plucked the final *Tenterden Times* of 1987 from the pile and began to skip through the paper. He wondered how much of a feature the fire story would be in a paper whose headline story shouted 'Outrage over plans to close allotments!' He meticulously searched each and every page until the paper was finished, then set it to one side and began the previous week, slowly building up a picture of the highs and lows of the small Kentish town. *Crash Biker was High on Cocaine. Why can't Tenterden have more Doctors? Guest House Owner's Dog Bit Neighbour. Town under threat from Europe!*

It occurred to him then that Peter Coldrick's death would have featured in this week's paper and might make for interesting reading. If the collection of headlines he'd just sifted through were anything to go by, then Peter's apparent shotgun suicide would have dominated at least the first twenty pages.

An hour later, Morton was re-threading a string loop around the December newspapers when his mobile rang: the ultimate sin in such a hallowed place. The walls were adorned with laminated pictures of mobiles with bold red lines struck through them, so it was of no surprise to him when the grumpy old men at the adjoining tables tutted and threw disgusted scowls at him, followed by disbelieving looks to one another.

A withheld number.

The glares worsened when Morton dared to press the green button and take the call. 'Hello?' he whispered.

'Hi, Morton,' an upset voice said. Whoever it was had been crying. 'Can you come round at all? I've just had the coroner's report on Peter's death.' It was Soraya.

Morton headed into the Chillax Zone where 'Quiet Talking is Permitted' and mouthed the words 'large latte' to the woman behind the Costa Coffee counter. 'What does it say?' he asked Soraya. He heard her draw in a lengthy breath.

'I'd rather just show it you,' she sniffled. 'Can you pop round?'

'Yeah, sure. I'm busy for the moment, but I'll be round as soon as I can.'

'Thanks, Morton. See you in a bit.'

He said goodbye, ended the call and paid for his coffee. He sagged down onto a bean bag and sipped his drink, as he stared up vacuously through a large skylight just as fat, swollen droplets of rain began to explode above him, gradually more and more until the skylight came alive with dancing water. He was fleetingly mesmerised until his thoughts turned back to Soraya. He took the fact that she was upset to mean that the coroner had taken the police view that Peter had topped himself. It still seemed like the most unlikely thing in the world to Morton.

He finished his drink, switched his mobile to silent and returned to his desk, where he unstitched the November pile of papers and began skim-reading more stories that were blown out of all proportion by the local newspaper. He had reached page six of the Friday 27th November 1987 edition of the *Tenterden Times* when he located the single-paragraph story.

Neville Road Fire

Police have confirmed that a woman's death in a fire at her Neville Road home last week is not being treated as suspicious. Mrs Mary Coldrick, 41 is believed to have been asleep in an upstairs bedroom when a cigarette started a severe fire which engulfed her home last Thursday. Mrs Coldrick's husband and son, who were not home at the time of the accident, are being comforted by friends. Fire fighters removed Mrs Coldrick's body from the burnt-out building after a man described by police officers as 'a local hero' failed to battle the flames to save her.

Morton read the story three times. Just twelve days after Mary Coldrick's death, the admission register at St George's was removed. Definitely not a coincidence. *But why?* Something happened before Mary's death that prompted William Dunk to remove the very file which would reveal the identity of James Coldrick's parents. Yet it was *still* only circumstantial evidence. He imagined PC Glen Jones and WPC Alison Hawk's reaction if he barged into the police station to report the crime. *He'd* probably end up being arrested for wasting police time.

He pushed the newspaper to one side and turned to the newspaper for the previous week, which had as its headline story, 'Woman Missing in Fire' and a large, full page photograph of the burning building. Morton stared at the picture. It seemed somehow barbaric and cruel to show what was essentially Mary Coldrick being cremated. She was in there, burning alive as the firemen hosed on gallons of water and the *Tenterden Times* photographer eagerly snapped away, knowing his pictures would make the front page. The sheer size of the photo pushed the actual report of the blaze to page two.

Fire

A severe fire swept through a house in Neville Road yesterday, leaving a local woman unaccounted for. More than forty firefighters were called to tackle the blaze shortly before 14.00 BST. Mrs Mary Coldrick remains unaccounted for. It is not yet known if she was in the house at the time. A neighbour, who was evacuated from her home due to the intensity of the blaze, described how a passer-by responded to her pleas for help, "I was shouting out that there was a fire and this man tried to get into the back of the house but it was too fierce and he came back out with his cheek all cut up and bleeding." Police are waiting for the house to be declared safe so that they can conduct an investigation. Anyone with any information should contact Detective Olivia Walker.

Morton imagined the local hero staggering from the flames, his face cut and bleeding, devastated at not being able to save Mary Coldrick. He wondered why the man hadn't stepped forward to accept the hero's praise and possible front page of the *Tenterden Times*.

Then an image smashed into his mind. The Brighton Scar Face. *Another coincidence?* If the feeling in his gut was anything to go by, then this 'local hero' had actually gone inside the house to make sure that Mary Coldrick would not escape the blaze. Had she given him the facial injury, as she struggled to flee the inferno? He felt nauseous as he looked back at the photo of the burning building. Perhaps it was a good thing that Peter Coldrick was dead. How on earth would he have told him *that? By the way, Peter, your mum didn't painlessly lapse into unconsciousness from smoke inhalation, she was probably thrown into a wall of flames by a psychopathic madman who inexplicably wants your whole family dead.*

Morton took the two newspapers over to a self-service photocopier, pumped in a handful of twenty pence pieces and received black and white copies of the stories. He tucked the photocopies into his bag, re-bound the stack of newspapers and left them on the vacant Customer Service Desk.

The automatic front doors to the library parted, encouraging him to leave the warm and dry confines and step out into the torrential downpour. It was hard, vertical rain that had been waiting patiently to be unleashed for several days. He pulled his coat in tightly and made a run for the car, as a dramatic flash of lightening illuminated the sky and zig-zagged through the black clouds.

Morton was eternally grateful to get a parking spot directly outside Soraya's house. He was fairly confident that nobody had followed him, although the thick curtain of rain had prevented him from seeing much beyond a car's length behind him. He waited in the Mini for a few minutes, hoping that the rain would ease up a little, but it only seemed to worsen. He decided to use the opportunity to flick through this week's edition of the *Tenterden Times*, which he'd picked up at a newsagents on his way here. Just by looking at the headline Morton knew that this was going to be a pointless exercise. *Hunt on for Mystery Lotto Winner.* And, sure enough, Peter Coldrick's death didn't raise as much as a paragraph in the paper.

Morton dialled the main office of the *Tenterden Times*. A chirpy female receptionist answered, 'Good afternoon, Weald Newspaper Group, Melanie speaking, how can I help you?'

'Good afternoon, I'm ringing to enquire about a story in the *Tenterden Times.*'

'Oh yes,' Melanie answered pleasantly, encouraging him to continue.

'Well, I say a story in the *Tenterden Times* but it's actually a lack of a story. I wondered why you failed to report on the suicide of Peter Coldrick last week? He shot himself –'

'One moment, I'll just put you through to our news team,' Melanie interrupted.

The opening bars of *Endless Love* were cut short by a growling male voice that didn't bother with all the company niceties. 'Yes?'

'Good afternoon,' Morton said, attempting to tame the lion aurally, 'I'm wondering why the inscrutable death of Peter Coldrick last week wasn't reported in the *Tenterden Times?*'

The line went quiet. Was the lion tamed, or dead?

'We didn't think it warranted space in what was a news-heavy week. People commit suicide all the time; it's hardly a scoop,' he answered gruffly.

Morton couldn't help himself. 'I'm sorry – *news heavy* - you say? Do I need to read the headline about the search for someone who might have purchased a lottery ticket from the newsagents on the High Street and who, by your own admission, might not even be a local! This man, Peter Coldrick is supposed to have shot himself, but I'm telling you that-'

'I'm sorry – who is this?'

'Investigate it,' Morton implored, before ending the call. He reached across to the passenger seat and picked up the photocopies that he had just made at Ashford Library. He wondered if he should share the information with Soraya but decided against it. He wanted more evidence first. He filed the papers away in his bag and decided to make a run for it. The rain was never going to ease up. Morton grabbed the bag and ran towards the house, hammering histrionically on the front door.

Soraya appeared with the artificial smile of a bereaved woman. 'Come in.' Morton stepped inside and she took his drenched coat from him. 'Thanks for coming.'

'That's okay,' he said, following her into the lounge. She looked as though she needed a hug but he wasn't the type to just embrace a relative stranger. He blamed his conservative upbringing for such arrant unsentimentality; he couldn't recall a single childhood embrace from either parent.

'Take a seat,' Soraya said quietly, raising a finger to her bloodshot eyes.

'Thanks,' he said, eying an A4 white envelope that she was clutching tightly.

'Here,' Soraya said, passing it to him.

Morton opened the envelope and withdrew two sheets of paper. The first, headed with the Kent County coat-of-arms was a short and succinct letter from the coroner, offering his condolences with the accompanying post-mortem results. He turned the page, passing over Peter Coldrick's personal details.

External Examination...the body was that of an underweight male of approximately the age stated. Height 5 ft. 8 inches, Weight 56 kg. Rigor mortis was present in the limbs and there was hypostatic staining of the posterior body surfaces. There were no external marks of violence. Natural teeth were present in the mouth.

70

No scars were identified. Trace soot and propellant staining to both hands…concentric seared circular wound of 5.4cm to left temple.

With an increasing sense of nausea, Morton scanned his eyes down the page, unable to take in the gruesome level of detail. Internal Examination, brain 1637g …Cardio-Vascular System…Respiratory System…Gastro-Intestinal System…Genito-Urinary System…Endocrine System…Conclusion…The necropsy appearances indicate that death is the result of a self-inflicted single gunshot wound to the head….Cause of Death: Suicide.

'Suicide,' Soraya said flatly when Morton met her gaze. She sat herself down beside him. 'Not even an open verdict or the *possibility* of murder. I mean, not even a mention of the suicide note being typed with no signature. I phoned the coroner as soon as it arrived but she just regurgitated everything she said there.' A lone tear ran down over her right cheek. 'At least the body's been released for a funeral now.' She said 'the body' carelessly, as if referring to a dead gerbil or stick insect. Morton reminded himself that death affected everyone in different ways. After his mother died it was his father's way to repeatedly deep-clean the oven; it was Jeremy's way to entirely stop talking for the best part of three months.

Morton abandoned his fear and put his arm around Soraya's shoulder. For a brief moment she froze and he thought that he had overstepped the mark, lecherously taking advantage of a grieving woman, but she buried her head in his chest and burst into tears. The words forming in his mouth all sounded trite or clichéd, so he said nothing and just held her closely.

Soraya released herself and semi-circled her thumb under each eye before taking a deep breath. 'They've finished at his house, too,' she said. 'Will you come with me while I look through his personal effects? I've no idea at all of his…*wishes*. It's just not the sort of thing you ask someone in their thirties.'

'Yeah, of course I will,' Morton said.

'I was thinking about going over there today if you're free?'

'Yeah, sure,' Morton answered. Maybe he would find whatever it was that Peter was so desperate to show him the night he died. 'We can go now if you like?'

Soraya nodded, wiped her face and stood. 'It would be good to get it out of the way.'

71

They travelled in near silence for the duration of the ten-minute journey to the other side of Tenterden. Soraya had asked him for a progress update and he responded vaguely, never liking to reveal too much to clients mid-way through a job. Normal family histories were littered with unpredictable twists and turns; this case was anything but usual, so to reveal what little he actually knew would be a futile exercise. When they arrived at the quiet estate, Morton parked as close to Peter's house as he could. All the drama from Wednesday was totally over. The house now resembled all the others in the street.

Soraya fumbled in her handbag, pulled out a large bunch of keys and opened the door, stepping wet footprints onto the worn doormat. The house was deathly silent and dark, all the curtains having been pulled to keep out prying eyes. She flicked the light switch in the hallway but nothing happened. 'Bloody hell, they've turned the power off already. Can you believe it?'

'They don't waste time, do they?' he replied, inexplicably feeling the need to whisper.

Soraya entered the lounge and opened the sun-bleached, ruby curtains. 'That's better.'

Morton followed her into the lounge, an uneasy feeling unsettling his stomach. He wanted to leave before he had even begun. 'Do you know where his personal papers would be?'

Soraya shook her head. 'Bedroom maybe? It's the front bedroom upstairs. I'll take a look in here.' The bedroom was the one place he *didn't* want to look – Juliette had informed him that it was in this room that Peter had died.

Morton entered the dim hallway, placed his foot on the bottom stair and looked up, wondering if he really wanted to see upstairs. He thought of Juliette and what she would do – bound up the stairs, two at a time, like a curious puppy – then began the ascent. With slow deliberate footsteps, Morton climbed the shadowed stairs.

At the top, he was confronted by three closed doors. He gently pushed open the first door, revealing a surprisingly clean and modern bathroom. Coldrick had seemed much more of a grimy avocado suite man, he thought. He moved across the landing to the second door and turned the handle: he found a small box room with *Dr Who* curtains and matching duvet set on a child's bed. Morton cast his eyes over an open-fronted bookshelf crammed with children's books, toys and stuffed toys; Fin's room was an unlikely location for the copper box.

He backed out onto the landing and then opened the remaining door: Peter Coldrick's bedroom. The scene of the crime. Instantly, he was struck by the smell. Six days on and a potent acrid mix of rusting iron and fresh sea salt rushed into his nostrils. He covered his mouth to stop himself from being sick. He couldn't imagine it being something that the SOCO guys could ever get used to. He guessed that was why they were always suited up like Michelin men whenever they were called to crime scenes. Like the rest of the house, the room was filled with a muted darkness. Keeping his mouth covered, Morton cautiously entered the room. As he moved to open the curtains something in his peripheral vision caught his attention. The bed. Whoever had their finger on the trigger Tuesday night, had pulled it right here. A shallow indentation in the smooth, cream duvet betrayed where Coldrick had sat; confirmed by the disgusting quantity of dark – almost black – blood which splayed out in a perfect formation across the pillows and headboard. No Bodily Fluid Removal Team had swept through, changing bed linen, vaxing the carpet or touching up the magnolia walls: everything was just as it had been the day a cold metal bullet passed through Peter Coldrick's left temple into his brain.

Morton pulled open the curtains and tentatively inhaled, filling his nostrils with the stale air that smelt like a stagnant pond. With a little stretch of his imagination he could attribute it to the house having been closed up for several days and *not* from the spilling of several pints of Peter Coldrick's blood. He supposed that everyone involved in the death industry passed their way through the various stages of desensitisation. How else could a coroner slice open Coldrick's head like it was a boiled egg to determine that his brain weighed 1637g? *It must be a fine line between coroner and psychopathic killer,* he reasoned.

He began the uncomfortable task of rooting around a stranger's belongings, tugging open doors and drawers around the room, casting his eyes over the contents for either the copper box or anything else which might help the case. He opened the cheap, flat-pack bedside cabinet and rifled through a lifetime's worth of junk. He found nothing. The only two other items of furniture were a large oak wardrobe and a chest of drawers, which he quickly discovered was filled with clothes, towels and an abundance of hot water bottle covers. He pulled open the wardrobe. Inside were rows of multi-coloured jumpers, all carefully ironed. Morton didn't think that Coldrick was the type to even own an iron, much less use one, judging by the state of his clothing the day that he had met him. A solitary black suit book-ended the run of clothing, which Morton guessed would be the final piece of clothing Coldrick would ever wear. He'd never understood the idea of dressing a dead person in a perfectly good suit and he made a mental note to tell Juliette his last wishes when he got home: cardboard coffin; woodland burial; naked; no flowers. At the base of the wardrobe were a pile of ancient blankets and three tatty suitcases. Morton pulled the cases out and, at the back of the wardrobe, noticed a small copper box the size of a paperback. Was this *the* copper box Coldrick had mentioned in the answerphone message? It had to be. He lunged at it and pulled it out of the wardrobe. The lid was emblazoned with an intricately decorated coat of arms. He carefully prised open the lid. Empty. Completely empty. Whatever Coldrick had found inside was long gone.

'Morton,' Soraya yelled from downstairs. It was an 'I've found something' kind of a call, as opposed to 'I'm about to be shot' kind of call, so he took his time replacing the cases in the wardrobe before making his way back downstairs.

'I found this on the shelf,' Soraya said, handing him a hardback book. Morton read the title and his heart rate began a new, thumping rhythm. *All About Sedlescombe*. 'Look inside.'

Morton opened the book and withdrew a fragile letter with a photograph attached by a rusty paperclip. He instantly recognised the crudely cut headshot as being the woman holding James Coldrick as a baby. Even though he guessed that Soraya had already read the letter, he felt compelled to read it aloud.

'Fifth of June 1944. My Dear Baby, I am placed in an abominable situation and one which I prayed would never occur. The war has taken many deviations and wrought much destruction but nothing to what I fear will happen to you, my precious boy, whom I have loved more than any other. There is so much to say and yet so little time; I pray that you will be spared any involvement in the injustices of this war and that you may live a quiet, protected life when justice, peace and all that makes life sweet will reign over the earth. Your ever loving mother, M.'

'So that's Fin's great grandmother writing that?' Soraya asked, leaning over to get another look at the letter.

'That's the way it looks,' Morton said. He remembered his analysis of the photograph of James as a baby. The letter added weight to his belief that James Coldrick was born sometime in April or May 1944, not June. He re-read the letter and spoke out loud those parts that most troubled him. '...what I fear will happen to you... so much to say

74

and yet so little time...' He looked across at Soraya. 'Does it sound to you like a goodbye letter?' She nodded in doleful agreement. Morton looked back at the decapitated photo. A body-less arm to her left suggested at least one other person was present at the time the picture was taken. He looked at the signature, *M.*

'History isn't my best subject; do you know what was going on in the war at that point that might mean she has to leave him?' Soraya asked.

'Well, D-Day had just started over the Channel, but there wasn't much going on locally to my knowledge. I think the air raids had all but ceased and the doodlebugs hadn't yet started...' Morton shrugged, having nothing to suggest that made any kind of sense.

'Well, I think James certainly lived a quiet and protected life but I'm not sure about justice and peace.'

'Maybe the price of peace was that he lived a quiet life and didn't ask questions – unlike Peter.'

'Maybe.'

'Where was the book?' he asked.

Soraya tapped on the top shelf of the nearest bookcase. 'Right here. Under our noses.' Morton looked at the shelf where her hand rested – right on top of *Tracing Your Family Tree* – then down at the bold title on the binding of *All About Sedlescombe*. He was as sure as he could be that the book had not been there on Tuesday when he had visited the house, as the row of books to which Soraya referred - *Ancestral Trails: The Complete Guide to British Genealogy and Family History, Tracing Your Family Tree, Explore Your Family's Past, From Family Tree to Family History* – had been a topic of discussion between him and Peter.

'I'm sure that wasn't here on Tuesday,' he said to Soraya.

'How can you be sure?' she asked.

'Peter and I were discussing all the avenues he had explored to research his family tree and the books came up. I would have noticed that book.'

Soraya shrugged dismissively. 'Maybe the police moved things around during their investigations?'

'Maybe. Anyway, look what I found upstairs,' he answered, holding up the copper box.

Soraya took the object and turned it over in her hands, not quite sure what she was supposed to be looking at.

'Peter mentioned it to me in a phone message - it belonged to his dad.'

75

'Oh, right. Does it help?'

Morton shrugged. 'Maybe. I was really hoping to find something *inside* the box but maybe it was the box itself that Peter wanted to show me. The coat of arms could be a lead. Heraldry isn't my forte so I'll have to get it checked out.'

Soraya half-heartedly pulled open another drawer. 'I can't find anything about his *wishes*,' she said, making 'wishes' sound like a demand. 'I mean, who the hell do I get to take the ceremony? He never went to church so far as I'm aware – does that make him a humanist or just a lazy Christian? I've got no idea.' Soraya looked at Morton for help, but he had no idea either. Six weeks of the *Tenterden Times* revealed an alarming trend in modern funerals – for young people at least – no black clothes, a large photo of the deceased on an easel by the coffin, *Angels* and/or *I'll be Missing You* (the Puff Daddy and Faith Evans version – *never* the Police version), a mixture of friends' tributes and the odd religious passage followed by a burial in a football shirt. Not really something Morton could suggest for Coldrick.

'Just get a Church of England minister and keep it simple,' he suggested.

'Hmmm.'

Other family members would be the obvious next step but Morton knew that was a blind alley. 'Any friends?' he suggested tentatively, knowing the answer before Soraya answered.

'Not really…' Her voice trailed off, leaving the silence to finish the sentence.

'Are you going to let Fin go to the funeral?'

Soraya looked dumbstruck, as if this was the first time she had even considered it. The blood appeared to drain from her face as she weighed the prospect of her eight-year-old son attending his father's funeral. She shrugged and turned her back to him, returning her focus to the stack of paperwork in the bureau behind her. Her rummaging became more frantic until a huge pile of papers fell to the floor. 'You know what, I can't do this. You're right, just keep the funeral simple. If he wanted a special all-singing, all-dancing service then he should bloody well have told someone.' She burst into tears and Morton now felt comfortable in pulling her into an embrace. Soraya clung to him, sobbing gently on his shoulder. 'I just want all this to be over.' She released her hold and took a deep breath. 'Sorry.'

'It's fine,' he reassured. 'Come on, let's get out of here. There's nothing more to be done here today.'

Morton carefully placed the copper box and the book containing the letter and photograph into his bag and led the way out of the macabre house into the pounding rain.

Morton pulled up outside his house, the impacting rain relentlessly hammering the car. He switched off the engine and stared out into the grey gloominess. He hoped that Soraya would be okay by herself after she had insisted she wanted to be alone when they left Peter's house. 'I've got some bits to do before I collect Fin from school,' she'd said, so he sat and watched as she ran from the car with her coat pulled up over her head. Seconds later she was gone inside and he made his way home.

Morton picked up his bag from the back seat of the car and dashed inside his house. He slammed the door on the foul weather and picked up the collection of damp post squashed against the wall. He set down his bag and flicked through the pile of dreary bills and correspondence; at the bottom was a white envelope with the familiar red stamp of the General Register Office emblazoned on the front: William Dunk's death certificate. Morton tore it open and scanned the content.

Date and place of death: Eighteenth July 2002, Conquest Hospital, Hastings
Name and surname: William Charles Dunk
Sex: Male
Date and place of birth: 1 April 1913, Stepney, London
Occupation and usual address: Handyman (retired), Smuggler's Keep, Dungeness Road, Dungeness, Kent
Name and surname of informant: Daniel Dunk
Qualification: Son
Usual address: Smuggler's Keep, Dungeness Road, Dungeness, Kent
Cause of death:
(a) Myocardial infarction
(b) Left ventricular hypertrophy and coronary atherosclerosis
(c) Diabetes mellitus

It was correct; it had to be the right William Dunk. Morton read the certificate three times and wondered what a 'handyman' - a euphemism if ever there was one - born in London and living in Dungeness, was doing coercing Max Fairbrother into stealing the 1944 admission file for St George's.

He scooped up the rest of the day's post and made his way upstairs. Juliette was on a late shift, so the house was deserted. Still feeling paranoid about the house being watched, Morton tentatively checked that each room was definitely empty, even going as far as looking in the wardrobe and under the bed. Outside, Church Square stood deserted, the inclement weather deterring tourists and nefarious visitors alike. Satisfied that he was completely alone, he made himself a coffee and a cheese sandwich and sat down at his desk with the death certificate, the copper box, the headshot photo and letter. No matter how many times he studied each item, he could find no common link that made any logical sense. He had two new leads: firstly to locate William Dunk's son, Daniel, and politely enquire as to his father's 'handyman' dealings in the late 1980s and secondly, to research the coat of arms on the box which, he realised, might well not have any connection to the *Coldrick Case* at all. James Coldrick could just as easily have picked it up from a junk shop as inherited it.

Morton opened up Juliette's laptop and ran an online electoral register search for Daniel Dunk. Two minutes later, the results unequivocally confirmed that Daniel still resided at Smuggler's Keep, Dungeness. Perfect.

Chapter Eight

7th May 1944

A vociferous skylark rose hastily from the noiseless orchard, piercing the calm skies which had, for the past four years, been filled with turbulence and anger. For almost two months now, the skies had been empty of the German *Luftwaffe* planes, which Emily had watched droning over in their hundreds, day and night for what seemed like a lifetime. The current tranquillity alarmed her.

'Emily, smile!' a voice belonging to William Dunk called fondly behind her, snapping her from her reveries. *Smile.* That's what she needed to do – it was no use fretting. It was always going to be a long game.

'Wait!' Emily said. 'I want a photo with the baby.'

William playfully rolled his eyes and waited as she passed through the white-blossomed plum trees to her home, where the baby was resting in his cot. Inside was pleasantly cool, the flagstone flooring providing a welcome barrier to the oppressive heat outside. She pushed open the door to the bedroom which she shared with the baby and found him wide awake, contentedly staring through the window at the dense woodlands in the distance. Emily smiled and watched, wondering what the darling child could be thinking about. Maybe he had some innate sense of the foreboding she felt. Maybe he knew that things were changing.

The baby turned his head and noticed Emily, the faint flicker of a smile erupting on his tiny, precious face. His first smile had appeared just four days ago, an event Emily now wanted to try and capture on camera. She picked the baby up and carried him out into the calmness of the afternoon.

'How do I look?' Emily asked her companion.

'Stunning – as always,' William replied, holding the Box Brownie camera up to his face.

'Try and get him smiling,' she said, ignoring his flirtatious comment. She carefully angled the baby towards the camera, avoiding the direct glare from the sun.

A clunk and a flash and the day was forever captured.

William set the camera down in the long orchard grass. He walked the short distance to her and leant in to kiss her on the lips but she turned at the last moment.

'No, we can't. I've told you – it's over. Now that I've got the baby...' Her voice trailed off.

'We can go from here. Disappear – it's easy in wartime. I'll pretend he's mine, I've told you.'

Emily shook her head indignantly. 'I need to feed him. Goodbye, William. You shouldn't come here again - for all our sakes.'

She pulled the baby tight to her chest and strode through the orchard into the house.

William, used to her brashness by now, watched and wondered.

Chapter Nine

Tuesday

Dungeness really was bleak when it was raining, Morton thought. It was also bleak when it wasn't raining. All those wooden and tin shacks, dilapidated buildings and all that endless shingle. They even had tumbleweed. If anything told you that a place was uninhabitable, then it was tumbleweed. A paradise for artists, though, apparently.

Morton slowed down to ten miles an hour as he drove along Dungeness Road, the monstrous nuclear power station looming large in front of him. He'd once heard that the residents of Dungeness were issued with free iodine tablets, 'just in case' of an emergency at the power station. *They'd need a bit more than that to protect them in their balsa wood homes if that thing went up,* he thought. Maybe that was why they didn't bother with bricks and mortar down here: nothing short of a concrete bunker hundreds of feet below ground would be left unaffected if the power station had so much as a minor leak.

Google Maps had helpfully stuck a bright red pin in the exact location of Daniel Dunk's house, so Morton knew to slow to a snail's crawl, as the building drew closer. The house was a ramshackle, wooden construction with a lopsided garage slumped to one side, having lost the will to live countless years ago. The garden, comprising shingle and sporadic bursts of ugly, green sea kale, merged seamlessly with that of a neighbouring garden.

Morton indicated to pull over, though he had no idea why, since there wasn't a single soul around. Not even a seagull braved the harsh Dungeness rain. Morton leant over to the back seat and pulled out his camera. He attached a telephoto lens, zoomed into the house and snapped the bungalow during the brief seconds of clarity provided by the intermittent windscreen wiper. If it weren't for the electoral register telling him that the house was actually occupied he would never have believed that anyone could have lived here. He zoomed in to rotten window frames with tightly drawn, washed-out curtains and photographed the peeling paint on the blue door. What made anyone *want* to live here? The only explanation he could come up with was isolation. Dunk might as well have been living on another planet. He considered the nefarious goings-on which could take place in such acute remoteness. All sorts of plotting and scheming.

81

Morton moved the camera to the front of the house. 'Christ!' he exclaimed, as a black BMW X6 filled the eyepiece. It was the same car that had followed him and Juliette out of Brighton and it was parked here, on Daniel Dunk's drive. This time he was able to focus on the number plates. 'RDA 220,' he said, repeatedly snapping the vehicle. The luxurious, lavish vehicle was a stark juxtaposition to the decaying, deprived surroundings.

From the corner of his eye something moved. He swept the camera back over to the house as a thin wiry man slammed the front door shut and made his way to the BMW. The man kept his head down and, for the moment, hadn't noticed the telephoto lens focused on him. Morton caught a rain-blurred profile shot and gasped. The frozen frame in the viewfinder revealed that the man sported a large scar running from his left eye down to the corner of his mouth. The Brighton Scar Face. Was *he* Daniel Dunk?

The Brighton Scar Face started the BMW and Morton was suddenly faced with the possibility of coming face-to-face with him. He had no choice but to quickly swing the Mini onto the adjoining property and make his way up the concrete drive towards a white-washed, weather-boarded house, hoping desperately that the Brighton Scar Face was unaware that Morton had upgraded his mode of transport since their last drive-by meeting. Morton reached the house, killed the engine and slumped down in his seat, just in time before the BMW sped past.

Seconds later and the BMW had disappeared into dense sheets of rain.

With a long breath out, Morton sat back up and started to relax.

His heart skipped a beat, as a shadow passed by and thumped hard on his window. He turned to see a hoary furrow-browed man wearing an oversized yellow poncho staring angrily into the car. Morton got his breath back, opened his window an inch and discreetly centrally locked the doors.

'What do you want?' the rheumy-eyed man demanded, revealing a gummy, toothless mouth.

'I'm looking for Daniel Dunk,' Morton answered politely. The old man eyed him suspiciously and Morton wondered if he was about to get an axe through his head.

'That's his place there,' the man said, pointing to Smuggler's Keep. Morton could see rage rising in the old man's eyes. 'But you knew that already, 'cause I saw you pointing that *thing* at his house.' The old man flicked an irate finger at the camera resting on the passenger's seat. 'What do you want here, I asked you?'

Morton wasn't about to hang around and have this conversation. He turned the ignition, flung the car into reverse and raced off the driveway, sending a spray of small stones firing in all directions from under his tyres.

The old man hurried down the drive, brandishing his fist in the air and shouting furiously. Morton caught the gist of the rant; he was about to phone the police.

He reached the empty road and pushed the Mini to full pelt, quickly propelling Dungeness into the rear view mirror.

Morton's study resembled the Major Incident Room of a police station, which pleased him immensely. No previous job had ever required him to pin photos of men suspected of murder, arson and stalking to his cork board, which he had gleefully stripped of inconsequential rubbish as soon as he had returned from Dungeness. Gone were the archive opening hours, interesting snippets from magazines and reviews of books he might one day purchase. Now it was adorned with photos, certificates, photocopies, factoids and scraps of paper connected by a veritable cat's cradle of string and multi-coloured pins. At the centre of the board was a freshly printed photo of Daniel Dunk. Adjacent to the photo was William Dunk's death certificate. The two men had loitered in the peripheral shadows of the Coldrick family for the past two decades. *But why?* Morton wondered.

His mobile rang: Juliette. He'd been trying to reach her the moment he had left Dungeness but her phone had been switched off.

'Is everything alright?' she asked, a tinge of worry in her voice.

'Yeah, I think so,' Morton said vaguely.

'I saw that I had twelve missed calls from you and I thought something must have happened.' Morton could hear the concern in her voice abating as he told her about his morning. 'Oh, I thought it was something serious.'

'I need a favour.'

She sighed. 'Go on?'

'I need you to look up Daniel Dunk's number plate; I don't think it's his car somehow. It might reveal who he's working for.' It didn't take a great detective to work out that someone driving a fifty grand car wouldn't live in a radioactive rundown shed in Kent's dumping ground.

'Give me the number and I'll see what I can do.' Morton read out the licence plate from the photograph in front of him. Despite it being engrained in his memory, he wanted to be completely certain. Juliette repeated it back to him and then hung up.

Having turned that line of enquiry over to Juliette, Morton switched his attention to his other lead: the copper box. He picked it up and turned it over in his hands. It was a very unremarkable box, being without pattern or decoration but for the intricate coat of arms emblazoned on the lid. Time had aged the copper to a dull rust–brown. Tinges of oxidised light green filled the deepest of the carved ravines. He doubted it held monetary value but hoped it held value in progressing the *Coldrick Case*.

Morton set the box down beside him, switched on Juliette's laptop and ran a Google search on how to identify a coat of arms. He made his way through the first pages, adding and subtracting search criteria as he went, hoping magically to identify the arms. He learnt about shields, supporters, ordinaries, helms, coronets, compartments, and mantling but nothing specific enough just to tell him to whom the box belonged. The Institute of Heraldic and Genealogical Studies in Canterbury kept appearing in his searches as an authority on the subject, so he decided to give them a call, naively hoping for an immediate over-the-phone analysis. A pleasant-sounding lady asked him where he lived and told him that the best thing to do would be to bring the item in and they would research it for him. Morton really didn't want to venture back out into the cold and rain, he much preferred the idea of sitting with a bucket of coffee, staring glibly at his new *Coldrick Case Incident Wall,* as he had named it. He'd also hoped that Juliette would have called back by now. How long did it take to tap a bunch of letters and numbers into a computer?

He took one last look at the *Coldrick Case Incident Wall* and set out for Canterbury.

He hadn't been to Canterbury for some time. The last time was to visit their archives, housed rather superiorly in a section of the Cathedral.

If it had been anything resembling a nice day, he might have taken the time to wander around the Cathedral. He had a vague recollection of a primary school visit in the dim, dark days of his childhood. All he could remember from the day trip was colouring in a picture of a stained glass window and his travel-sick friend, Clive's vomit washing up and down the aisle of the coach all the way home.

By some strange miracle, Morton found a parking spot within half a mile of the Institute and, clutching his bag in one hand and a large golfing umbrella in the other, hurried as fast as he could to the building.

The Institute, a modest, medieval building, was on Northgate, just within the city walls. Morton wasn't sure whom he had been expecting when he got there, but, as he crossed the threshold into the air-conditioned building, he was greeted by a sweaty, rotund, black-bearded man in his mid-forties whose name badge announced him as Dr Garlick, which Morton thought an appropriate name for a man who bore a strong resemblance to a garlic bulb.

Dr Garlick took Morton into a small side office with only a tiny, latticed window for light. The walls were bursting at the seams with heavy, disorganised books and files. Dr Garlick sat behind a cluttered oak desk, switched on a powerful desk lamp and placed a pair of glasses on his nose, looking expectantly at Morton's bag. Morton carefully pulled the copper box out and watched as Dr Garlick's eyes lit up.

'What a marvellous little artefact!' he said animatedly, as he took the box from Morton and turned it over in his hands.

'Is it?' Morton said, still finding it quite unremarkable.

'Oh yes. Unusual. It'll take a bit of investigation though. Can you leave it with me?' Dr Garlick asked, passing the back of his hand over his sweaty forehead.

Morton had a flash of paranoia. *What if he's working in cahoots with the Dunk family, too?* He reasoned that he couldn't distrust everyone he came into contact with or the case would never progress. 'Fine,' he said, before adding, 'just don't let that copper box leave this building with anyone other than me.'

Dr Garlick seemed slightly taken aback but nodded in agreement. 'Of course, of course.'

The rain had faded into a misty drizzle as Morton headed back towards his car, a much lesser sense of urgency in his stride. He imagined bounding into the police station and handing a great stack of paperwork to PC Glen Jones and WPC Alison Hawk. Although, actually, he would need to speak to someone in much higher authority about it. '*Entirely* circumstantial,' WPC Alison Hawk would say. 'Do you actually have *any* concrete evidence that Daniel Dunk is responsible for the death of Mary Coldrick, Mr Farrier?' Morton would become one of those joke characters in television police dramas that return week after week with increasingly bizarre claims. *Aliens abducted my cat. My grandmother has turned into a blue tit.* No, he couldn't go to the police until he had something – anything - solid.

His mobile ringing jarred him from his wandering thoughts. He hoped that it was Juliette calling with the name of the car owner, but it was Soraya's name that flashed onscreen.

'Hi, Soraya.'

'Thursday, two pm,' she said, as if he should know what that meant.

'Sorry?'

'Peter's funeral. Thursday, two pm.'

'Oh. Okay.'

'Morton, could you do me a favour?'

'Sure.'

'Would you do a reading?' she asked, in such a light-hearted way that it sounded like she was organising a wedding or asking him to grab some bread from the supermarket on his way home. A reading at Peter Coldrick's funeral? He hadn't even made up his mind about whether or not he was even *going* to the funeral. He'd only known the guy two minutes. Soraya must have sensed his reluctance. 'It's just that I'm having trouble rounding people up. He wasn't the most sociable of people and I don't need to tell you about the situation on the family front.'

'Er…well, I hardly knew him really. It was just –'

'Just a short piece will be fine,' Soraya interjected. 'It doesn't need to be anything too fancy.'

'What do you want me to read?' he answered, hoping that his lack of enthusiasm might make her change her mind.

'I'll leave that up to you. Can I count you in?'

'Yes,' he heard himself saying.

'Brilliant, thank you,' Soraya said, ending the call.

Marvellous. An unknown reading at the funeral of a murdered man he met one week ago. Life just couldn't get any better.

Morton had been adding more string pathways to his *Coldrick Case Incident Wall* when he heard Juliette's car pull up outside. He hurried down to the kitchen and poured two generous glasses of red wine and sat patiently in the lounge, anticipating her arrival with news of the

86

registration plate. He heard her kick off her boots and trudge steadily up the stairs.

'What a day,' she groaned, pecking Morton on the lips and reaching for the proffered wine. She collapsed into the sofa and sighed heavily. 'Sometimes, you know, I just hate the police. Do you know what I had to do today?'

Morton shook his head, hoping that it would be a very short story.

She took a gulp of red wine. 'I was only sent out - on foot - on a three-mile walk to see an old man who called in a suspected burglary. Fine, whatever. So, I get my notebook out and start writing it all down – he arrived home ten o'clock yesterday morning having been into town to collect his pension, pay the bills, blah blah blah and when he gets home, he finds his house smelling of excrement – his word – and since he'd only urinated the whole day, somebody must have broken in and used his toilet.'

Morton laughed, much to Juliette's consternation. 'Come on, it is pretty funny.'

'So I asked if anything was taken. No. Was anything damaged? No. Any sign of forced entry? No. Anything else that would indicate a burglary? No. Just that his house smelt of excrement.'

'And did it?'

'Uh-huh, big time.' Morton laughed again. 'Anyway, I walk the three-mile trek back to find half the station doubled over in hysterics. Apparently, Mr Pepperdene is a frequent waster of police time. So, now I know. It's *really* not that funny, Morton.'

'Oh, I beg to differ.'

'So anyway, investigating the case of the phantom crapper meant I didn't get time to look up that number plate for you, I'm afraid.'

'Really?' Morton said, suddenly losing his grin.

'I'll do it tomorrow but it isn't easy, you know; I shouldn't even be accessing those records.'

'I wouldn't ask if it wasn't important,' Morton said, deliberately not attempting to disguise his disappointment.

'What about you, how was your day?' Juliette asked, seemingly oblivious to his displeasure. She tucked herself into a foetal position beside him.

Morton rolled his eyes as the memory of the day flashed before him. 'After I got back from Dungeness I had a call from Soraya – she only wants me to do a reading at Coldrick's funeral on Thursday. Can you imagine? I don't even want to go, never mind read at it.'

'Now it's my turn to laugh,' she said with a grin. 'What have you got to read?'

'That's part of the problem: she said it was up to me and I haven't got a clue.'

'If it's up to you then just stick your finger in the Bible and plump for the nearest moral tale. Nobody listens at a funeral anyway, they're all too wrapped up in grief to care.'

'We don't even own a Bible,' Morton answered, taking a swig from his wine.

'Isn't *Yea though I walk in the valley of the shadow of death* a funeral reading?' Juliette asked. 'Or is that for the last rights? The last funeral I went to was a Buddhist's: Gregorian chanting, swinging incense and shaven-headed women in monk's robes. Very odd.'

'Well thanks for that, that's really helpful.'

'Don't get so het up about it, Morton.' Juliette sat up to face him. 'Just Google it.'

'Hmm,' Morton answered doubtfully. Two days to plan a reading. Great. He reached for the remote control, ready to switch on the television and switch off from the *Coldrick Case*.

Chapter Ten

Wednesday

Morton woke midway through a nightmare. Dr Garlick was offering him the copper box, telling him that it was a 'most unexpected and exciting story,' but, just as Morton went to take it, Dr Garlick inexplicably morphed into Daniel Dunk who cackled maniacally like The Joker from *Batman*. Then he disappeared. Just like that.

He opened his eyes and it took a good few seconds for his brain to register that he was slumped in a hard plastic chair in the waiting room of the Conquest Hospital in Hastings. Nurses, doctors and visitors were milling about, ignoring him, as if he were just another part of the complexities of the A&E department. He supposed he was really. He felt awful and craved a hefty dose of caffeine. The small waiting room comprised a dozen similar blue plastic chairs, an out-of-order pay-phone and an ancient-looking hot drinks vending machine. There was no option for an extra shot of caffeine, so Morton chose a coffee with two sugars and stared at the posters on the wall, whilst the machine proceeded to fill a plastic cup with cheap instant coffee.

He wondered how his father was getting on with the range of tests the doctors were running on him. Morton had taken the phone call at four a.m. and, like all middle-of-the-night calls, it had set his heart pounding before the person at the other end had even spoken the words 'suspected heart attack'. Juliette immediately offered to drive them both straight to the hospital but Morton, despite his estranged relationship with his father, knew that he needed to get there quickly – *not* at Juliette's law-abiding speed. He'd hurriedly pulled on whatever clothes first came to hand and dashed to the hospital, triggering enough speed cameras *en route* to lose his licence. He was sure, though, that if it ever reached court, he could cite mitigating circumstances. He'd arrived at the hospital and ignored the pay-and-display car park signs, running into A&E where he found his father's washed-out body rigged up to more machines, drips and monitors than Morton thought his clogged veins could possibly cope with.

The coffee was beginning to have an effect, beginning to bring Morton back to some semblance of life. If only it were that simple for his father.

What time was it? Morton looked around for a clock, or even a window to give some indication of the time of day, but couldn't find either. He pulled out his mobile. Almost nine thirty. Surely there would be an update on his father now. He carried the drink over to the nurses' station, where two young women were in mid-conversation about last night's television. He waited for them to notice him and when they didn't, he interrupted. 'I'm sure it was a *really* life-changing evening for you both, but could you kindly deal with the more trivial matter of my almost-dead father, *if* you don't mind.' It was too harsh and he regretted saying it straight away. The nurses gave each other an exasperated look.

'Your father is *far* from dead,' one of them said reproachfully. 'Do you honestly think we would have left you snoring away in the waiting room if there was anything that warranted disturbing you? You looked as though you could do with the rest.'

'Sorry,' Morton said flatly, not about to be drawn into the finer points of his sleeping habits. He was sure, though, that he didn't snore. 'Can I see him?'

'By all means. He's in Bay C, second bed on the right.'

'Thank you.' He moved away from the nurses' station and heard mutterings about his rudeness. He had been rude, he knew that. Another instance of mitigating circumstances.

Morton headed towards Bay C, which sounded like he would find his father in the corner of a warehouse or a busy dockyard. The sunlit room was at full occupation, being filled with a variety of sick and injured men of similar age to his father. His bed was screened off from the rest of the ward by a floral curtain. *Typically antisocial,* Morton thought. He cautiously pulled back the screen and was momentarily shocked: his father, eyes closed, pitifully thin and frail in a hospital-issue gown, showed no signs of life. Were it not for the host of machines he was wired up to confirming life, Morton would have believed him dead. He edged towards the bed and sat down beside him. A large part of him wanted to squeeze his father's bony white hand and tell him that he loved him and that everything would be okay, but he just couldn't. Thirty-nine years without physical contact prevented their hands from uniting. *Surely his father had held him as a baby, or picked him up if he fell over as a toddler?* Maybe, but there was nothing in Morton's memory store to substantiate it. Instead, he rested his hand at the edge of the bed and stared at the pathetic sight before him.

90

Moments later, as if sensing Morton's feelings, his father's hand twitched, seeming to reach and search for his.

'Jeremy?' his throaty voice asked, lifting his head dolefully from the pillow, his eyes opening to a narrow squint.

'No, it's Morton,' he replied.

His father issued a sound resembling a sigh and collapsed back into the bed. *Fantastic*, Morton thought. Even on death's door his father couldn't hide his disappointment in him. He realised that he probably should get word to Jeremy about their father. Maybe the Army would give him compassionate leave. He thought that he would wait for some of the test results first – it was still only a *suspected* heart attack – but it didn't take Einstein to figure out that a cooked breakfast each day since his wife had died, no exercise, plus a copious quantity of whiskey and a cigar each night might eventually lead to a clogging of the arteries. The funeral flowers on Morton's mother's grave were still fresh when his father made the announcement that he would be living his life how *he* wanted to live it and exercise, temperance and healthy eating were not included. To all intents and purposes, he became a reckless teenager. At the time it sounded to Morton like his father was somehow blaming his wife's death on the fact that she tried to feed them wholesome food and encouraged the odd gentle stroll in the park.

'Are you still there?' his father asked, almost inaudibly after a few minutes' silence.

'Yes, Morton's here,' he said, just to clarify that it wasn't his natural son keeping the bedside vigil. *What did that make him? The* unnatural *son?*

'Is Jeremy coming?' his father rasped.

'Yes,' Morton said. He reasoned that telling his father that Jeremy was on his way would either be a comfort in his final hours or would be a temporary reassurance. It was a lie which immediately served its purpose: his father visibly relaxed and closed his eyes.

Morton sat back in his chair and watched his father's chest rise and fall in short, shallow breaths, allowing the rhythmic sounds emanating from the machines to gently lull him into sleep.

Sometime later, Morton's mobile sounded loudly in his pocket. His father opened his eyes with alarm, huffed when he realised the sources of the noise, and slumped back into the bed. Morton withdrew the phone and flicked the switch to mute. It was the Institute for Heraldic and Genealogical Studies calling. Morton slid the screen to answer the call and quickly stepped out of the ward. It was the receptionist telling him that Dr Garlick wanted to see him. Morton made an appointment for the afternoon, ended the call and returned to his father.

Three and a half hours later, Morton sauntered along the inside of the Northgate Canterbury city wall, his thoughts harassed by his father's knife-edge condition. Before Morton had left the Conquest Hospital, the doctors had confirmed that his father had suffered a heart attack and that further tests were needed.

Morton reached the Institute for Heraldic and Genealogical Studies and entered the cool lobby area where he asked the smiley receptionist for Dr Garlick.

'Mr Farrier!' he greeted moments later, as if they were old friends, extending his hand warmly. 'Good to see you again.'

Morton shook the proffered hand and was relieved to see that he was carrying the precious copper box. With all that had occurred recently it wouldn't have surprised him to find Dr Garlick dead and the box stolen. 'Can I get you a coffee or tea?'

'A coffee would be great, thanks,' Morton answered, hoping that it would taste better than the awful stuff from the hospital vending machine.

'Julie, a coffee for Mr Farrier and a peppermint tea for me, please,' he called across to the receptionist, who suddenly lost her smile. 'Would you like to take a seat over there?' he said, indicating an area with a coconut plant and four comfy chairs. 'Very interesting one, this,' he said, holding up the box. Morton had a moment's fear that his nightmare might have been *déjà vu* and he was about to witness Dr Garlick's sudden mutation into Daniel Dunk.

'So you've identified the arms then?' Morton asked, being slightly perturbed by the fact that Dr Garlick's stomach was resting on his thighs. It seemed so odd that his thin and pasty father was lying in a hospital bed after a heart attack while a giant bulb of garlic waddled around Canterbury without a care in the world. If Morton had been closer to his father he might have thought it unfair. Instead he just thought it odd.

'Yes,' Dr Garlick said, but there was a tentative edge to his voice. 'Though there is some confusion.' *Isn't there always?* It seemed that nothing was straight-forward with the *Coldrick Case*. He struggled to remember what a normal genealogy job was like anymore. Certainly not this one. 'It belongs to the Windsor-Sackville family,' Dr Garlick said, pausing for Morton's reaction.

'Really?' was all Morton could think to say, as he processed the information. He remembered that the Windsor-Sackvilles were the patrons of St George's Children's Home, where James Coldrick had lived as a child. Was James *given* the copper box? Did he *steal* it? Did all the children receive one as some kind of leaving gift?

'It was produced circa nineteen forty-five and belongs to the current Sir David James Peregrine Windsor-Sackville,' he said, before clarifying, 'the father of our Secretary of Defence.'

'Current? He's still alive?'

'As far as I know. He must be in his nineties by now, though.'

'Is this something that could've been mass-produced?'

Dr Garlick shook his head vehemently. 'No. Perhaps two or three were made, but more than likely just this one. Worth a pretty penny, too, I shouldn't wonder. If you are thinking of selling it, though, don't just stick it on that eBay place for goodness' sake.' Dr Garlick laughed, but at what Morton wasn't sure.

The receptionist returned carrying a metal tray with Dr Garlick's peppermint tea, a black coffee, bowl of mixed sugar lumps and a small pot of milk. She set the tray down wordlessly and flounced back over to her desk.

'Help yourself,' Dr Garlick said.

'Thanks.' He stirred in two sugars and some milk and took a sip. Filtered. *Much* better than the hospital. 'You said there was some confusion?'

'Yes. Look,' Dr Garlick said, moving the box between them. 'This half of the armorial achievement, with all the expected brisures and what have you, is pure Windsor-Sackville, dating back many generations. We know that it has to belong to Sir David because it bears his mother's arms within it. What we don't know, none of us here knows, is who the *other* half belongs to. Are you up on your Windsor-Sackville history?'

'Er, no, not really.'

'Well, David Windsor-Sackville married Maria Charlotte Spencer, distant relative of Lady Diana Spencer in 1945, yet this isn't her family arms,' Dr Garlick said, handing Morton a sheet of paper. '*That* is the coat of arms of David and Maria Windsor-Sackville, registered with the College of Arms soon after their marriage.' Morton compared the two coats of arms. Only half of each shield matched the other.

'What does it mean?' Morton asked, repeating a question that had haunted him for the past week. *Nothing* made sense.

93

Dr Garlick shrugged. 'I'm afraid my colleagues and I are at a loss over it. Taking an educated guess, it's possible that it was produced for Sir David's marriage to someone else but who that is, we've no idea. He certainly did only marry the once – I've double-checked the official records.'

'And did you find anything under the Coldrick name at all?' Morton asked, hoping that his thirty pounds an hour of research fees had gone on something more than one piece of paper and yet more uncertainty.

'Nothing, I'm afraid. The name isn't registered at all. Ever.'

Morton needed his best friend and saviour, Google, and he needed it now. He downed the hot coffee, thanked Dr Garlick for his time and handed over a cheque for a hundred and eighty pounds - surely a world record for a photocopy of the Windsor-Sackville coat of arms.

Outside, all signs of the last two days' inclement weather had completely passed. Morton took off his jacket and buried the copper box inside it and made a beeline for his car.

When he reached the Mini he called the Conquest Hospital for an update on his father and a nurse on the assessment ward told him that there had been no change in his condition. Some mercy, he supposed.

Morton parked on the drive behind Juliette's car. He looked at his watch curiously. She wasn't due to finish work for another hour. Hurrying up the stairs into the lounge, he found her in uniform, frowning, contemplative and staring at the lounge floor. Something had happened. It had to be his father. The hospital must have called whilst he was driving home. Part of him didn't want to ask. But he had to know. 'What is it?' She met his gaze and he saw that she had been crying.

She shook her head.

'It's my father, isn't it?'

'What? No, I don't know anything about your dad. I was hoping you were going to tell me.'

'He's stable at the moment. They're running every test known to man and he's rigged up to drips, heart monitors and God knows what. I'm going back up later tonight with some bits from his house.'

'I'll come with you.'

'Fine. What's the matter?'

'I've been suspended.'

'What? What for?'

'Accessing prohibited information,' she said, her voice on the cusp of an angry outburst. Morton knew he needed to tread *very* carefully.

'The number plate?'

She nodded, then prolonged his agony by saying nothing more except, 'I have to go back in for an interview at some point.'

'And?'

'The BMW's registered to Olivia Walker,' she said.

'Olivia Walker?' Morton repeated. He knew the name, but couldn't place it. He'd heard it in the last few days – some connection to this case.

'Kent's Chief Constable,' she added, as if she could tell what he was thinking.

It took a moment for Morton to digest the news. Daniel Dunk's BMW was registered to the highest ranking police officer in Kent. 'I don't get it,' he said.

'Me neither. All I know is that it's not a personal car; it's one of more than half a dozen used for the security of key members of the government, like the Prime Minister, Home Secretary, Northern Ireland Secretary, et cetera.'

'Are you sure about this?'

Juliette's body sagged. 'I was suspended. How much surer do I need to be?'

'So Daniel Dunk's working for the Chief Constable of Kent?' Morton said, as much to himself as to Juliette. Although this latest development had made the picture even more abstract, he still thought with great excitement about all the new pieces of string and coloured drawing pins he needed to add to his *Coldrick Case Incident Wall*.

'Christ knows, but something dodgy is going on. Not even five minutes after I'd run the number plate search I was hauled into the inspector's office and told to explain myself. I said I saw the owner of the vehicle acting suspiciously but he wasn't having any of it, suspended me there and then. I'm starting to think fifty grand is nowhere near enough money for this job of yours.'

'Hmm,' Morton agreed, attempting to mentally place the new acquisitions to the *Coldrick Case* jigsaw. 'You said Olivia Walker is in charge of the security of key government ministers – would this happen to include the Secretary of Defence?'

'Philip Windsor-Sackville, yeah, I believe so. Why?'

'I'll make a cup of tea and bring you up to speed.'

95

Morton strolled into the kitchen, unable to shake the name Olivia Walker. He knew her name from somewhere else. *But where was it?* He boiled the kettle, searching his mind for a match.

Then it struck him.

She had been the officer in charge of the investigation into Mary Coldrick's death.

What a coincidence!

'There's something else about your Chief Constable,' Morton said, handing Juliette a mug of tea.

Morton told Juliette *everything* about the *Coldrick Case*, even the finer details that he had previously skipped over. Juliette clasped the mug of tea like a frozen vagrant and listened intently to him, only interrupting to clarify when something had taken place. 'But this was *last* week,' she had said. 'Why didn't you tell me?' He'd told her it was because he hadn't wanted to bore her.

Morton carried the copper box and the photocopy of the Windsor-Sackville arms to his study. He carefully placed the photos of James Coldrick and his mother, along with her letter inside the box and tucked it away under his desk. Opening up Juliette's laptop, he punched 'Windsor-Sackville' into Google. Only seven million two hundred and fifty thousand websites to trawl through. The top results concerned Frederick James Windsor-Sackville.

BBC – History – Windsor-Sackville (1880-1965)
Frederick James Windsor-Sackville was a Conservative politician and prominent member of government. His much lauded welfare reforms...
www.bbc.co.uk/history_figures/windsor_sackville.shtml - 25k

Time 100: Frederick James Windsor-Sackville
The illustrious statesman who served his country in WW1 before becoming Chancellor of the Exchequer.
www.time.com/time/time100/leaders/profile/windsor-sackville.html - 33k

Windsor-Sackville – Wikipedia, the free encyclopedia
Political family headed up by Frederick James Windsor-Sackville. He was born 18 May 1880...
En.wikipedia.org/wiki/Windsor-Sackville – 359k

Morton scrolled down past generic biographies of Frederick James Windsor-Sackville, wanting to find out information about his son, Sir David and his grandson, the current Secretary of Defence. Most of the websites, on which he clicked, seemed to agree that David James Peregrine Windsor-Sackville was a rising star in the Conservative party prior to World War Two. Then, having gained a place in Churchill's Coalition Government, he secured the family's fortunes at a time when other gentry were losing theirs, by landing large re-construction contracts for his fledgling company, *WS Construction*. Having helped populate half of post-war Britain with cheap prefabs, David became a key member of the government's rebuilding programme; many of Britain's most unsightly 1950s concrete monstrosities owed their creation to WS Construction and David James Peregrine Windsor-Sackville. A knighthood followed in 1964. Maintaining his place close to the centre of the British political system, it was inevitable that his son, Philip would follow in his footsteps, ascending to the role of Secretary of Defence in the current Coalition Government. As stated by Dr Garlick, David married Maria Spencer in 1945, their first child, Philip, arriving the following year in December 1946. Morton took a page of notes before clicking on the family's own website.

The Windsor-Sackville Family
Information, quotes, speeches and biographies on this distinguished British family.
www.windsor-sackville.org.uk/ - 28k

He looked around the website 'of this most eminent of English families' designed with elegant colour-schemes and an old English style font. Clicking on the Family Tree tab, he followed the ancestral line of the Windsor-Sackvilles. He studied the screen for some time then stared at the *Coldrick Case Incident Wall*. The only logical explanation that he could come up with was that James Coldrick could have been the son of Sir David James Peregrine and Lady Maria Charlotte Windsor-Sackville. It certainly made sense on *some* kind of level. Had they placed the illegitimate James - born a year *before* their marriage - just metres away at St George's Children's Home and then bought his silence when he grew up with several hundred thousand pounds? Had they killed Mary Coldrick when she began to pry into her husband's past? Had they killed Peter Coldrick when he too grew curious and began to ask the wrong questions? Did the 'M' at the end of the wartime letter written to James Coldrick stand for Maria? *Could it really be as simple as that?* Morton doubted it. It all felt a bit too crowbarred into place, the kind of surmises dreamed up by amateur genealogists determined to find that elusive link to royalty. He'd lost count now of the number of clients who had claimed to be descendants of a mistress of Henry VIII, as if that even meant anything.

Having retrieved the two photographs of James Coldrick's mother, Morton clicked on the 'Photo Gallery' tab and scrolled down to a close up of Maria Charlotte Windsor-Sackville. He held the images close to the laptop screen and compared the photos. The profile shot of Maria on the website looked to Morton like it had been taken in the sixties or seventies and bore no resemblance to the wartime photographs in his hand. But that meant nothing; she could have completely changed over those twenty or so years. There was certainly nothing in front of him that precluded them from being the same person.

Under the 'News' tab he read that on Saturday Sir David and Lady Maria Windsor-Sackville were to open Sedlescombe Village Fete. *Might be worth a visit*, he thought. He made a careful note of the date and time and pinned it to the wall.

Morton carefully drew up a neat family tree for the 'illustrious' Windsor-Sackvilles and compared it with the cul-de-sac tree for the Coldricks. He held them side by side, wondering at the connection. *There has to be something here*, Morton thought. As he cast his eyes over the short Coldrick tree, something suddenly struck him: if his suspicions were anywhere near correct, and the Dunks and Olivia Walker were helping to cover up the fact that David and Maria had given birth to an illegitimate child, then Finlay Coldrick could be in grave danger. Juliette's suspension had just sent a major warning that he was closing in on the truth.

Morton raced down the stairs, called a garbled goodbye to Juliette and dashed out to the Mini. A moment later, he screeched out of Church Square on his way to Tenterden.

He had been sitting on Soraya Benton's doorstep for over twenty minutes when she arrived home with Finlay in his school uniform, clutching a Spiderman lunchbox. She looked much prettier than the last time he'd seen her and he wondered if it was the faint trace of make-up or perhaps the smarter clothes that she was now wearing. Her eyes were less puffy, less grief-stricken somehow. She was carrying three bulging Waitrose carrier bags.

'Well, Fin, look what the postman left on the doorstep,' she said. 'Were you expecting a worn-out-looking genealogist to be delivered today?'

Fin shook his head. Morton guessed that he was recalling their previous encounter when he had made the poor child cry.

'Hmm, me neither. What do you say we do with him? Invite him in or throw him out onto the streets?'

'Throw him out,' Finlay said seriously, a meaty frown bearing down over his eyes. *Fair enough*, Morton thought.

'Please let me in,' Morton pleaded, doing his best to overact the part, but actually wanting to skip the pleasantries and get down to more serious things. Like the fact that someone might be about to kill the eight-year-old currently barring his entrance to the house. After all, everything that was going on was because of him and his ancestry.

'Nope,' Fin answered.

Morton stood. 'It's quite important,' he said to Soraya. She nodded and thrust her key into the lock, practically pushing Fin through the door.

'Go and play in your room, Fin and I'll call you for dinner.' She turned to Morton. 'Sorry, you weren't out there long, were you? Had to pop to a friend's then a quick dash around the supermarket.'

'No, it's fine.'

'So, what's all this about then? You seem agitated.'

Morton followed Soraya into the lounge and took a seat opposite her. 'I think Fin's life might be in danger,' he announced dramatically. As soon as the words were out of his mouth he wondered if he should have gone in with a more gentle approach, but after all the time-wasting on the doorstep he needed to spell things out clearly. If Fin had belonged to him, though God knows this little encounter had cemented his resignation to never have kids, he would have run to his bedroom and checked there was nobody lurking under the bed or hiding in the wardrobe.

'What do you mean?' she asked, her face turning pale.

Morton exhaled sharply and told her everything that he'd discovered about the Windsor-Sackvilles and his suspicions regarding James Coldrick's parentage. Soraya listened impassively, allowing him to deliver the full story without interruption.

'It does sound rather worrying,' she said when he had finished. Morton stared at her. *That was a bit of an understatement*, he thought. 'I think we'll go and stay at my sister's for a while, until this all blows over. She lives in St Michaels, just outside Tenterden.'

'Will you go tonight?' Morton asked.

Soraya nodded. 'Yes, as soon as I've got a bag packed for each of us. Do you really think that Peter, James and Fin are descended from the Windsor-Sackvilles?'

This was the very reason that Morton seldom gave interim reports to clients. He was a long way from drawing *that* conclusion. 'At this stage, it's just a possibility. For decades people in the shadow of the Coldrick family having been hiding the past; it's my job to reveal it - but I'm not there yet. Certainly, they – whoever *they* are – want to maintain a shroud of secrecy over James Coldrick's birth.'

Soraya seemed to have glazed over. 'That would be a turn up for the books,' she said with a smile. 'Related to a rich knight and member of parliament. It would certainly turn Fin's life around...' Her voice trailed off, but her eyes revealed to Morton that her mind was busy making alarming connections.

'Let's not jump the gun,' Morton warned.

Soraya snapped back to reality. 'Of course. Right, I'd better get packing.'

Morton had wanted to try a last ditch attempt to get out of the funeral tomorrow but the ringing of his mobile caused Soraya to finally check that her child was still in one piece playing on his Nintendo, or whatever it was that kids played these days. Certainly not the Action Man or Meccano of his youth. It was a withheld number, which usually meant a bank. Probably about to offer him a better deal for his ever-diminishing fifty grand.

'Morton Farrier,' a male voice said, more of a statement than a question.

'Speaking.'

'You've got ten minutes to leave your house.' Not the bank then.

'I'm not in my house,' Morton said haughtily, trying to work out where he recognised the voice from.

'I know you're not,' the voice said calmly, 'but Juliette is and unless you want to be identifying her charred remains anytime soon, she needs to leave your house now.'

'Who is this?' he demanded, but the line went dead.

Panic mode set in.

He leapt up and ran for the door, yelling out to Soraya that he needed to go, at the same time speed-dialling Juliette. It rang endlessly.

The journey time back home to Rye was twelve minutes. He wouldn't make it in time. Couldn't. He looked at the clock: 5:42.

The countdown had begun.

He jumped into the car and slammed his foot on the accelerator. Something inside told him that the call was genuine and not necessarily designed to scare him, although that was a definite by-product. He *knew* that man's voice, but for the life of him couldn't give the voice a face.

Juliette's phone went to voicemail. He had to leave a message. He needed to be clear and succinct. 'Juliette, listen to me. I need you to leave the house right now. I'm not joking. Someone's made a threat. Meet me by the church. Phone me when you get this.' He ended the call, taking a corner far too quickly, almost skidding off the road. *If Juliette's going to survive, you need to calm down!* he admonished himself.

Morton slammed through the sleepy village of Wittersham. He was about half way home.

5:46. Six minutes.

He dialled Juliette again but there was no signal. *Damn it!*

He tried to clear his mind, to concentrate fully on the road. Juliette's life depended on it. Besides, it might yet be a hoax, something designed to scare him, to warn him off the *Coldrick Case*. His instincts told him that the people he was up against really didn't do hoaxes.

5:48. Four minutes.

Morton entered the village of Playden at sixty-eight miles per hour. He looked down at his phone and saw a signal had miraculously appeared. He hit the *phone* icon then selected Juliette's mobile from the top of the list. Morton's eyes levelled with the road, just as a *Jempson's* supermarket delivery lorry limped out of a side road. Morton slammed on the brakes and drew to a near-stop, just meters from the back of the lorry, the de-acceleration sending his phone to the floor.

'Juliette, are you there?' Morton shouted into the footwell, as he zipped the Mini out into the oncoming lane to check traffic. Nothing. He sped past the lorry on the descent into Rye. 'Juliette, if you can hear me, get out of the house!'

5:50. Two minutes.

Morton reached down and fumbled in the footwell. He finally found the mobile and raised it to his ear. The line was dead.

He redialled and pushed the Mini even harder.

5:51. One minute. He imagined her 'quickly' grabbing her handbag. Then her laptop. Then a few clothes because she had no idea how long she would have to stay away. If it was permanent, then she'd want to go around gathering up everything of sentimental value: her grandmother's wedding dress; the old leather-bound photograph albums of people nobody in the family could identify; her external hard drive with thirteen months of their shared life in photographs on it.

5:52. Time up.

Receiving reproaching and angry looks from pedestrians, Morton sped up Rye High Street. One wrong step by a passer-by and that would be it. He turned the corner into Church Square too sharply, narrowly avoiding an elderly couple about to step off the pavement.

He stepped on the brakes outside the church entrance. No Juliette. *Where was she?* Morton leapt from the Mini and raced towards the house, a spasm of tachycardia thumping his body. He knew that if she was still inside the house then it was too late. She wouldn't survive. The clock was nearing zero. Morton neared the front of the house.

'Morton!' a voice from behind him. Juliette's voice. She was in the churchyard, sitting calmly on a bench, like a jaded tourist weary from a day's sightseeing. No handbag. No laptop. No grandmother's wedding dress. No photo albums or hard drives. Just her with an anxious, perplexed look on her face. He jogged over to her and sat down beside her on the bench, allowing himself to breathe deeply and properly.

'Do you want to tell me what's going on?' she asked.

Morton managed to say one word just as all of the windows of their house exploded outwards in a violent, projectile eruption. They both sat, dumbstruck, as angry tongues of fire licked from the spaces in the brickwork where windows had once been.

Chapter Eleven

Thursday

It was a very strange experience for Morton to wake up in his old bedroom in his parents' house. He looked up at the brown blemish above the bed that multiple coats of white emulsion had failed to conceal over the years after a pipe had burst in the loft during a family holiday in the Lake District when he was fourteen. That stain was the only thing in the room that had existed before he left for university. He thought about how happy they had been as a family on that holiday. Just eight weeks later his mother was dead. She'd found a lump in her breast but elected not to tell anyone until she realised that it wasn't going to go away of its own volition. By then it was too late.

He wondered if it was his mother's death that had prompted his father to seemingly blurt out that Morton was adopted. Would he now be living in blissful ignorance if she were still alive? Maybe if he'd never been told he would now be dutifully keeping a stoic vigil at his father's bedside rather than studying the amorphous mark on the ceiling. He wanted to wake Juliette and point out the stain, tell her the story about the holiday to Coniston, one of a mere handful of occasions when he had felt a genuine part of the Farrier family, not like some surplus limb. But he didn't wake her; he left her curled tightly in a ball beside him, like a new-born kitten. She needed the sleep after all that had happened yesterday.

They had finally climbed into bed at three o'clock in the morning after driving from the police station to his father's house. As if watching the entire contents of his house blasting out of the windows in flames hadn't been bad enough, Morton had then been subjected to 'an interview' by the wonderful police duo of WPC Alison Hawk and PC Glen Jones. For the second time in nine days the dynamic pair had made him feel like a suspect. It didn't help that Juliette was interviewed in a separate room. With typical Juliette foresight, the first thing she did after the explosion was to 'get their story straight.' Only then did she call the fire brigade. The problem was, getting his story straight made Morton feel all the more guilty. 'Trouble seems to be following you, doesn't it, Mr Farrier?' Hawk had opened his questioning with. 'Any reason why someone would want to flatten your house, Mr Farrier?' Jones had asked, without giving him time to answer the first question.

Morton shook his head and feigned shock that the explosion was thought to be a criminal act rather than electrical or gas. He had told them the agreed version of the truth – he'd been out shopping and had returned to collect Juliette to go out for a nice meal. Simple. Except then they wanted to know where the shopping was. And why Juliette was dressed in her work uniform for an evening out. Morton triumphantly held up a packet of unopened chewing gum and said, 'Shopping.' Another look passed between Hawk and Jones. 'And as for the uniform thing,' Morton added, 'we were going to get a take-out, which was lucky, all things considered.' Another look between them and he was released, grateful that Hawk and Jones hadn't managed to whittle out of him the fact that he had received a warning to leave the house ten minutes prior to the explosion. Or that he had recognised the voice of the person issuing the warning.

Morton padded downstairs in his boxer shorts to make a large cup of coffee. Everything in the kitchen was in the same place as it had always been since time immemorial. He surmised that it was probably his father's parents who had first dictated where everything should live in the kitchen and woe betide anyone who dared to question it. 'If it ain't broke, don't fix it,' had been one of his father's many quips. Morton realised that he was thinking of his father in the past tense and didn't really believe that he would pull through. He just wasn't the type to survive illness or disease. He wasn't one of those people who could 'battle illness' and fight back. He wasn't a fighter and Morton was sure that his weak body would readily give up at the first obstacle.

He sipped his coffee and wondered where Jeremy was at that moment. After being passed from pillar to post, Morton had finally been able to speak to him in the early hours of the morning. He took the news with typical Jeremy histrionics. 'Oh my God! I'm on my way,' he'd cried. Morton had told him that he was staying at their father's house for the time being, which Jeremy took as unfettered altruism. Morton refrained from adding more drama to Jeremy's life by telling him that part of the reason for the relocation was because their house had exploded.

Morton tried to make a mental inventory of what he'd lost in the house. As huge curtains of fire poured from the gaping orifices where doors and windows had once been, the fire chief had rather optimistically said, 'It might not be as bad as it looks.' Then the roof had collapsed. No, there could be nothing left at all. What hadn't been singed, smoked, soaked or burned to a crisp would have been fatally

104

crushed. He felt strangely emotionless about losing most of it. Furniture, clothes, books, DVDs – all replaceable junk. There were a few keepsakes that had belonged to his mother that he was gutted to have lost. And then there was the fact that *everything* connected to the *Coldrick Case* had gone up in smoke. His *Coldrick Case Incident Wall* that he'd spent so much time creating was now nothing more than a pile of boiling ash. But then that was probably the reason for the explosion in the first place: to destroy every last shred of evidence that he'd compiled. Fortunately, he had backed up most of the documents.

Juliette appeared in the kitchen looking dog-rough, her hair seemingly having been blow-dried in a hundred different directions and a few ounces of fat pumped below her eyes as she slept. She was wearing an over-sized 'I Love Derbyshire' t-shirt that they'd found in his father's wardrobe.

'Shoot me,' she hissed.

'Morning!' Morton answered brightly. 'Coffee?'

'Black. Biggest cup you can find. Three spoonfuls of coffee,' she said, flopping down onto the kitchen table. 'Christ. Tell me yesterday was a nightmare and there's a *really* good explanation as to why we're here?'

He looked at her bedraggled body slumped on the table, her tough exterior having been shed overnight like excess skin. There was no way on earth she would have survived the explosion if she had remained inside. Now he knew what love was all about. He placed the steaming hot drink in front of her and stroked her hair. 'I'm afraid not.'

Four large cups of coffee and a long, hot bath later - modern devices such as a shower having never been fitted in his parents' house - and Morton was feeling somewhere near human again. He had found a packet of sausages in the freezer, which he had cooked with a tin of beans and a couple of slices of toast for their breakfast.

'So, just so that I understand, some random guy just phones you and tells you your house is going to blow up in ten minutes?' Juliette said, somewhat incredulously, as she shovelled a large forkful of food into her mouth. It was the first time that they had actually talked about the moments prior to the explosion without embellishment or omission.

'Well, not really a random guy.'

'What?' she asked, lowering the fork and giving him her full attention.

'I recognised the voice, but it wasn't until about five o'clock this morning that I realised who it was.'

'And?'

'Daniel Dunk.'

'The guy who lives at Dungeness with the car registered to Olivia Walker? Why would he do that?'

'God knows. It might have been a Mafia-style attack – a final warning to keep away from the *Coldrick Case*. If he'd actually wanted me dead, then I would be. I don't think it's a coincidence that the day we make the link between Daniel Dunk, the Coldricks, the Windsor-Sackvilles and the Chief Constable of Kent Police our house turns to rubble, do you?'

'No,' she answered definitively.

'At least we've got somewhere to stay for the time being. Every cloud, and all that.'

'Morton, that's a terrible thing to say. I hardly think your dad suffering a heart attack is our silver lining.'

'I didn't mean it like that,' he said, as he carried his plate over to the sink. Eighteen years in this house had taught him that he had to wash the dishes before he did *anything*, no matter how life or death it was. His mother would turn in her grave if she knew he had taken the decision to leave the washing up for later.

This time, Morton duly paid the parking fee at the Conquest Hospital, though he very much resented having to pay at all. It was disgusting to be charged to park in a hospital, he thought, paying for the privilege of visiting a dying relative. He'd read somewhere a few weeks ago that some NHS trusts were now offering discounts for regular visitors and terminal patients were even lucky enough to be given a free parking permit. How generous.

Juliette took his hand and they made their way to the Atkinson Ward, where his father had been transferred. They found him once again cordoned off by a plastic curtain, sitting up reading *The Daily Mail*. He looked a different man to the one Morton had last seen, life seemingly returning to his fragile body.

'Hi, Dad,' Juliette said, sounding oddly comfortable labelling Morton's adoptive father 'Dad'. Certainly more comfortable than he did. His father looked up with a smile and set down the paper.

'Hello,' he said cheerfully. 'Lovely weather, isn't it?'

Morton was curious at what went on inside his father's head for him to be screened off from the world, rigged up to more machines than your average robot and the first thing he has to say is a comment about the weather. 'Shall I open the curtain, so you can enjoy the sunshine?' Morton asked.

'No, thank you,' his father answered, waving a finger vaguely towards the curtain. Morton assumed it was something to do with the other patients. He never had been a great socialiser.

'How are you?' Juliette asked.

'Been better. They tell me I have severe atheromatous in the something or other proximal artery and something in the other one. Furring of the arteries in layman's terms. They've put me on warfarin tablets,' his father said. He pronounced 'warfarin' as 'Wolverine' and Morton imagined his father as the new addition to the X-Men.

'So it's definitely your heart then?' Juliette said.

'Yes, it was a heart attack. I've got to see a specialist dietitian and I've been told by at least two dozen doctors that a 'lifestyle' change is in order. Ha! A lifestyle change, at my age. I ask you. What do they think I'm going to do, start drinking carrot juice and pumping iron at the gym? Not on your Nellie.'

Juliette smiled. 'Maybe just cut back on some of your—'

'Pleasures?' his father interjected.

'Extravagances,' Morton corrected. His father raised his eyebrows. 'I brought you in the bits you asked for from home.' He lifted the bag and placed it on the bed, then instantly fretted about the assortment of bacteria and germs he had inadvertently transferred from the floor.

'Thank you, at least now I can get out of this awful gown they've stuck me in. Would you be able to pop back home again later and get my slippers?'

'Yes, of course,' Morton said. He hadn't wanted to broach the whole explosion thing and the fact that they had, to all intents and purposes, now moved into his house. He reasoned that it would only add more stress to his ailing heart if he knew that there was a stack of washing up festering on the worktop at home.

'How's work?' his father asked.

'Usual,' Morton said, not really considering that 'usual' couldn't have been more of a contradictory way of describing his current employment status.

'Has anyone told Jeremy?' his father asked. 'About my health, I mean.'

'I phoned him last night,' Morton said. 'He's on his way home.' He couldn't gauge from his father's voice whether or not he had done the right thing in informing him. It would be just like his father to snap, *'You can't just recall a member of Her Majesty's armed forces because of a little thing like this. I'm fine.'*

'You did, oh good,' his father said, evidently pleased that he would soon return. 'You're looking very summery, Juliette,' his father said.

'Thanks, I bought it this morning,' she answered. 'It was this or the PCSO uniform.' His father laughed, not realising that she literally now owned two outfits. Morton was actually amazed that she hadn't made more of a fuss about the loss of her colossal clothing and shoe collection, but she simply shrugged and said she'd get some new ones on the insurance. Very un-Juliette. It was probably shock or something. Pretty soon it would hit her. Then she'd hit him.

After twenty minutes, the three of them had exhausted their supply of polite conversation and Morton told his father that they needed to go.

'Make sure Jeremy knows where to find me.'

'We will,' Juliette said, pecking him on the cheek. 'Take care.'

'It's not me you should worry about, it's the others!' Another of his father's great quips.

'He looks okay,' Juliette said, as they left the hospital. 'I thought from what you'd said he was going to be much worse than that.'

'I think flat-lining is medically considered *pretty* bad, as things go,' he answered, still convinced of the inevitability of his father's demise.

Morton wondered whether or not you could be fashionably late to a funeral. They were late, fashionably or otherwise. They had left in good time and with every intention of attending the final service of the man whom they barely knew (or had not known at all in Juliette's case), but Morton had suggested that they take a detour to see the destruction the explosion had wrought. Police tape sealed off their house, although it could no longer be described as a house; it was simply a pile of unidentifiable, smouldering rubble. If Morton hadn't known better, he would never have believed that an entire house and all its contents could be squashed and compacted down into the heap of nothingness in front of him. He then understood the term 'razed to the ground'. Juliette had recognised the PCSO standing guard behind the cordon, shepherding away inquisitive neighbours and nosey rubberneckers. The PCSO had been surprised to see Juliette among the curious crowds, until she had told him that the pile of wreckage used to be her home. He told her that the murmurings among the fire department were that Semtex *might* have caused the explosion.

'At least it might make them investigate it if they suspect Semtex,' Morton had said, as they hurried to the church. He had fully expected another cover-up and anticipated 'Gas Explosion Shock!' as the headline in next week's *Rye Observer*.

Morton found a parking spot on Tenterden High Street, just in front of the town hall and they hurried along past the *Woolpack Hotel* into the side of St Mildred's Church. Morton couldn't imagine a saint being named Mildred somehow. She sounded like an aged, plump, wartime housewife with too many kids on her hands rather than the patron saint of something meaningful. Maybe she *was* the patron saint of aged, plump wartime women.

The standard exterior of the church belied the vastness that Morton and Juliette found inside, as they snuck in a few rows from the back. The size of the building amplified the indisputable fact that only eight people had turned up for Peter Coldrick's funeral (and that included the vicar and Peter himself), his plain wooden coffin carefully balanced on a trestle in the centre of the aisle. Soraya was at the front with another woman who had exactly the same hair style, whom Morton presumed to be her sister. Two rows behind them was an elderly couple. Morton suddenly felt a pang of guilt for attempting to squirm out of attending. Then there would only have been five living people here. He had a sudden, unwelcome flash of his own mother's funeral, much of which was a blur to him. The lasting image that he had was of the open casket, her waxy face plastered in foundation and eye-liner by someone who had evidently never known her in life and her abhorrence of make-up. At least her funeral had been well-attended. Standing room only.

Whilst the diminutive vicar, sporting an obvious hairpiece, waffled through a generic funeral prayer, Morton speculated at how many people his funeral would attract. More than eight, he hoped. Was fifty a good number to aim for? It would depend on when he finally died, since it was natural for your circle of friends to dwindle down to your own armchair if you hung on for long enough. Still, the way things were going with the *Coldrick Case,* he might not need to worry about longevity.

As the congregation pathetically, and almost inaudibly, stood to sing *The Lord's My Shepherd* Morton made a guest list for his funeral. He started with immediate family - his father (assuming that he could cling to life himself), Jeremy, Aunty Margaret, Uncle Jim, cousins Jess and Danielle - then moved on to his friends and former work colleagues. By the end of the lamentable song he reckoned he could scrape forty attendees. Maybe a few extra with partners, husbands and wives. Juliette, on the other hand, would fill this church twice over. Her funeral would be like the ones you read about in the papers where it's necessary to erect a screen outside for the wailing mourners to observe the service. The papers never reported tragic funerals like this one which comprised only those who felt obliged to turn up.

With the song over, the vicar returned to the pulpit and read monotonously verbatim, and without once looking up from his script, a chronology of Peter Coldrick's life. There was nothing new or noteworthy in the eulogy, just a concentration on his skills and dedication as a father. Then he called on Soraya.

Morton noticed Juliette suddenly sit up and take an interest and he wondered if she'd just nodded off or if it was due to a twinge of jealousy. He was convinced that the only reason Juliette had agreed to come to the funeral was to see if Soraya posed any threat to their relationship. She didn't, of course. There was something about Soraya which meant he would never have gone for her even if he were single. She was attractive enough, maybe even slightly out of his league in that regard, but there was something about her that made him not be attracted to her at all. Something he couldn't actually put his finger on or name.

Juliette seemed satisfied that Soraya posed them no danger and resumed looking around the church, as if she were on a nice day out and happened upon an unlocked, ancient church and was glad of a moment's respite from the midday sun.

Soraya's tribute to Peter was remarkably composed, reiterating his devotion and commitment to Finlay. She ended her speech by asking the congregation to sing Peter's favourite hymn, *All things Bright and Beautiful*. Morton wondered how Soraya knew what Peter's favourite hymn was, since, by all accounts, he had no history of religion in his life. It seemed a curious thing to have been discussed in a relationship that had barely developed beyond the conception of a child. What would Juliette say his favourite hymn had been if he were suddenly to be shot in the head? *He* didn't know what his favourite hymn was. After three verses of *All Things Bright and Beautiful* all Morton could come up with was *Morning Has Broken* – was that what it was called?

110

And it was hardly a favourite; he'd last sung it when he was ten years old. He really was going to have to tell Juliette what he wanted at his funeral. Definitely no hymns. Or religion.

'What's my favourite hymn?' Morton whispered.

'What?'

'What's my favourite hymn?'

'How should I know?'

Fair enough, Morton thought. It was hardly something that he could hold against her. What was *her* favourite hymn? His mother's was *Abide With Me* and Morton could still hear the haunting organ music in his head as her body disappeared behind the red velvet curtains for cremation. He'd wished then, as he wished now, that they'd buried her. The idea of his mother on fire appalled him. At least if she'd been buried he'd have a grave to visit. Two days after her funeral he and Jeremy were parcelled off to Aunty Margaret's for a week so that their father could scatter the ashes in the New Forest, apparently as per her request, something he still questioned to this day.

The vicar approached the pulpit. 'And now I'd like to ask Peter's best friend, Norton Farrier, to say a few words.' *Norton?* His heart began to race as he made his way to the front of the church, though he couldn't fathom what actually there was to be nervous about since he would be speaking to a near-as-damn-it empty building. Had Soraya told the vicar that Morton was Peter's best friend, or had the vicar embellished the pitiable truth to create a more sociable, affable and incorrect Peter Coldrick?

Morton tugged at the flexi-arm of the microphone so that it was level with his mouth. He took a deep breath and surveyed the congregation, who looked as emotionless as if they were at a dreary matinee performance of an am-dram play. Given the congregation in front of him, he wondered if the reading he had chosen was either wholly inappropriate or had hit the nail smack on the proverbial head. He was about to speak when he noticed a stocky man with a crew cut silently sneak into the back of the church and sit in the row directly behind Juliette. Definitely not a friend of Peter Coldrick's. Morton didn't know what to do. People were starting to stare at him. He had to do the reading. He cleared his throat and began. '*If you Should Forget Me for a While by Christina Rossetti. If you should forget me for a while, and afterwards remember, do not grieve, for if the darkness and the shadows leave a vestige of the thoughts that once I had, better by far that you should forget and smile than that you should remember and be sad.*'

He stared out into the congregation but the man with the crew cut had vanished. He ignored his hastily prepared, woolly notes that he had intended to read about 'the wonderful man' that was Peter Coldrick. He was more interested in finding this menacing visitor. He searched the shadows at the back and sides of the church but couldn't see him.

'Okay,' the vicar said uncertainly, advancing towards the pulpit, 'thank you very much for that, Norton. I'm sure nobody in this room will forget our dear brother, Peter anytime soon.' Morton left the platform and returned to his seat.

'Where did that man go?' Morton whispered.

'What man?' Juliette said.

'He just crept in and sat behind you.' He wasn't sure why but she turned just to be sure there was nobody there. It wasn't like PCSO Juliette Meade 8084 to miss something like that. Morton began to wonder if he'd imagined it. After all, it was a long distance from the back of the church to the front. No, there had definitely been somebody there.

'Did you get a good look at him?'

'Average-looking with short hair.'

'That'll make a memorable e-fit,' Juliette whispered. 'Not Daniel Dunk, then?'

'No,' Morton said with certainty.

The congregation stood for the final benediction.

'Lord our God, You are the source of life. In You we live and move and have our being. Keep us in life and death in Your love, and, by Your grace, lead us to Your kingdom, through Your Son, Jesus Christ, our Lord. Amen.'

'Amen,' Morton and Juliette said, slightly out of kilter with one another.

'There now follows a private service at the crematorium,' the vicar hastily leapt up to announce. Morton wondered if it were actually possible to have a more private service than this. He hoped that since Soraya hadn't mentioned it, Peter Coldrick's best friend, Norton might be excused from the cremation. The old couple shuffled along the aisle towards them and out the back of the church.

'Come on, let's get out of here,' Juliette said, and they made their way out into the late afternoon sunshine.

'I need to talk to you about my funeral,' Morton said.

'What?'

'Morton, hang on,' a voice called from inside the church. It was Soraya. She burst out onto the steps. 'I just wanted to say thank you for doing the reading, it was lovely, really. Peter would have been very touched.' She looked at Juliette and smiled. 'You must be Juliette?'

Juliette offered her hand. 'Pleased to meet you, despite the circumstances.'

'Likewise. I took his advice,' she said, nodding her head to Morton, 'and moved in with my sister but I think he's being a *teeny* bit overdramatic. Oh, which reminds me, here's her address. It's only the other side of town.'

Morton shook his head, taking a small yellow Post-It note with a scribbled address on it. 'I wish I were being overdramatic, Soraya. They blew up our house yesterday.' He realised how theatrical that had sounded but there was no way of playing it down.

The smile dropped from Soraya's lips. 'Surely not?' She looked at Juliette for confirmation. 'My God. I mean, you're alright, aren't you?'

'Apart from being dispossessed and having nothing other than the clothes we stand in, we're fine,' Juliette said.

'Oh golly, I'm so sorry. At least you're alive, though.'

'There is always that.'

'And you think it's because of Peter?' Soraya asked.

'I can't think of any other reason why someone would plant enough Semtex under my house to destroy a small town.'

'God,' Soraya said. 'By why, for goodness' sake?'

'That's what we're trying to work out,' Juliette said.

The vicar appeared from the church and touched Morton's sleeve. 'Lovely reading, Norton, lovely reading. He must have meant a great deal to you.'

Morton smiled politely and tried not to stare at the small furry creature resting on the vicar's head.

'Will you be joining us at the crem, Morton?' Soraya asked. 'We're going to be placing Peter's ashes in his parents' grave in Sedlescombe churchyard.'

'Sorry, we'd have loved to come but what with all that happened yesterday we've got a lot to sort out,' he said, questioning in his mind whether it was right to say they would 'love' to attend a cremation.

'I understand. I'll catch up with you in a day or two. Take care, won't you.'

Morton and Juliette stood back and watched respectfully as Peter Coldrick's coffin was carried from the church by six pallbearers and loaded into the waiting hearse.

Juliette took Morton's hand. 'Come on then, Norton, let's go back to your dad's and order a pizza or something.'

'Good idea.'

Chapter Twelve

4th April 1944

Frederick James Windsor-Sackville marched purposefully through the wide, oak-panelled hallway, having just arrived from a private Whitehall meeting with several other key members of government. At sixty-four years, Frederick's severe angular features and unforgiving eyes belied his age but not in his favour. He wore his best suit with a ruby tie and handkerchief from the breast pocket. He had a fine clipped moustache, which he trimmed religiously each morning.

'Go and fetch David?' he told one of his staff, who was following slightly behind.

'Yes, sir,' he replied, scurrying off to find Frederick's son, David.

'I'll be in my study,' Frederick barked, striding along the vast hallway, under painted portraits of his distant ancestors. He paused momentarily and looked up at his father's picture, hanging grandiosely above his study door. Frederick hoped his father would approve of all the sacrifices and difficult decisions he had taken during the course of this ceaseless conflict in order to protect the good name of the Windsor-Sackvilles, a job his son and heir, David would need to continue. He had shown excellent political wit around Parliament, becoming a genuine asset to Churchill's Coalition Government. With shrewd guidance and direction, he was sure his son could aim for the very top. The Windsor-Sackvilles *had* to benefit from the war. David's only misdemeanour so far had been with *her*, something Frederick had so far kept closely under wraps.

Frederick entered the fastidiously tidy study and sat at his desk, pensively tapping his fingers. 'Come on, come on,' he muttered to himself, despising tardiness and dilly-dallying. Of course, he knew where his son would be: in the orchard.

A light tap at the door. 'Father?' David said, breathlessly.

'Come in and sit down. Shut the door.'

David obeyed his father and sat down, knowing that his father had something significant to say.

'How is she?' Frederick asked, his eyebrows furrowed.

David's eyes lit up. 'Very well. The nurse thinks the baby will be here within the hour.'

Frederick clenched his jaw. Not the news he wanted to hear. 'Look, I won't beat around the bush, David. The war is changing direction.

Plans are afoot for something big. Something which will turn the tide of war.'

David's face fell. 'What does this mean?'

'I think you know what it means. Over the next few weeks we need to sever all ties with *Emily's* family. File everything you have in the archives ready to be destroyed.'

'And the baby?' David asked, unable to look his father in the eyes any longer.

Frederick waited until his son glanced up then shook his head solemnly.

'A boy!' the nurse called, bundling the baby up and placing it on Emily's naked breast.

Emily, tired and exhausted, smiled and held the baby tightly to her. *A boy! Exactly what she wanted. What* they *wanted. Needed. A boy to continue the family name.* A gentle breeze fluttered in from the orchard outside, cooling the sweat on Emily's forehead. She looked at the boy, tenderly squirming and writhing in her arms. Just like her, he had bright blue eyes and chestnut-brown hair. He was perfection.

'Any ideas of names yet?' the nurse asked.

'His father wants him to be called James,' Emily replied.

'Lovely name!' the nurse exclaimed.

Chapter Thirteen

Friday

Morton was sitting outside The Clockhouse Tearoom in Sedlescombe in a t-shirt and jeans, with a pair of binoculars dangling from his neck, rubbing his tired eyes. He had barely slept last night, having spent much of the night mulling over the *Coldrick Case*. He had countless more questions than he had answers, yet the involvement of the Windsor-Sackvilles was becoming impossible to doubt. As a forensic genealogist, he needed firm, concrete proof – the type to be found in archives and record offices. He had spent most of the previous evening using his father's prehistoric PC to search the National Archives website - the portal used for locating government and private documents in England and Wales from the eighth century to the present day. He began by searching general key words, leaving the date, repository, place and region fields blank, then gradually began to narrow and refine his search. As the evening wore on, he had gained a better understanding of the political roles of the Windsor-Saville family, but crucially, there were no private records pertaining to the family in any repository. All the documents he found links to, even those recently released under various closure and secrecy rules, were innocuous ones relating to the business of government – nothing which would give him the evidence he needed to find a link from James Coldrick to the Windsor-Sackvilles. Whilst he was online Morton had searched the birth index for a James Windsor-Sackville born circa 1944. He wasn't surprised to read that 'No matches found' was the answer. If James Coldrick had indeed been the illegitimate son of Sir David James Peregrine and Maria Charlotte Windsor-Sackville, then he doubted that they would have been so blatant as to have registered his birth for the entire world to see.

A young, blonde waitress set a tray down in front of Morton with a flirtatious smile. He thanked her and couldn't resist a glance at her svelte figure as she tottered back inside the tearoom. Rather inexplicably, he felt quite relaxed, as if he was on a jaunt in the countryside and had happened upon a twee, genteel tearoom, replete with floral crockery and lace doilies. Maybe it was sitting on the patio on a hot, still day that was having a calming influence on him.

As he poured himself a filter coffee, Morton looked across at the pair of tall, grand, iron gates, which barred entry to Charingsby. If answers to the questions he sought existed, then they would be found behind those gates. All that could be seen of Charingsby was a gravel, beech-lined drive cutting through a billiard-table lawn. Nothing of the house could be glimpsed from outside – probably just the way the Windsor-Sackvilles liked it. Morton was here for one very simple reason: he wanted to gain entry into the estate. Last night he had spotted an anomaly and potential lead, which he needed to explore. According to the Ordinance Survey map, the sprawling estate of Charingsby incorporated a gatehouse cottage, a run of tied workers' cottages, various out-buildings and a stable complex - something which corresponded with Google Maps. However, whilst carefully examining the whole estate using the aerial satellite function on Google Maps, Morton spotted a small, pale-coloured building set in the middle of what, according to the map, should have been solid, ancient woodland. He cross-referenced the location on an online map website, where he pulled up images of the estate from 1841, 1873, 1908 and 1949. The building appeared on the first three maps, yet was absent by 1949. A missing building on a map would not usually have warranted the plan he was about to execute. However, the fact that in the background of the photograph of James Coldrick as a baby was a small, pale-coloured building rang alarm bells in Morton's head. The fact that there was a tall chimney to the west of the building was impossible to ignore.

Morton drank a mouthful of coffee. Gaining entry was going to be difficult and illegal, much to Juliette's dismay when he had told her of his plans. She had decided that she could no longer wait for the insurance money to come through, so she called her best friend, Rita and the two of them went to Tunbridge Wells to buy some clothes. 'A lot of clothes, Morton,' she had warned him. He could hardly protest. He was happy enough for the time being helping himself to Jeremy's wardrobe and all that he had asked Juliette to buy for him was a new laptop, since he'd inadvertently lost two in just over a week. Given all that had happened, he would rather be wandering aimlessly between clothes shops than hatching a plan of how best to enter the lair of the Windsor-Sackvilles. Juliette had told him it was quite possibly the single most stupid thing he could do since they were very likely the people who had tried to kill them both two days ago. He agreed with her but made the trip to Sedlescombe nonetheless.

He had considered waltzing innocently up to the high-tech video entry system mounted on the high brick wall beside the gates and simply asking to be permitted to view their archives. Owners of such stately homes he'd encountered on previous jobs had been only too willing to allow him to delve into their private papers. Somehow, he didn't think the Windsor-Sackvilles would be so accommodating.

Morton had come prepared, having rummaged around his father's house for items he thought he might need. He found a backpack, which he filled with a pair of National Trust binoculars, digital camera, an Ordinance Survey map of the area, a torch, box of matches, a bottle of water and a notepad and pen. The addition of a pair of wire-cutters and a crowbar destroyed the image that he was the archetypal country rambler.

He took a sip of coffee and pulled out the camera to check if anything was still on the memory card. He legitimized his recent carefree rummaging and plundering of his father's personal belongings by thinking of himself as some kind of executor-in-waiting. What with his mother being dead, Jeremy away in Cyprus, it would fall to him to sort out his father's affairs. He blithely skipped through countless images of his father's garden, then came to an out-of-focus image of his father, Jeremy, a young man and an old woman holding ice-creams up to the camera. The orange time-code stamp in the corner dated the photos to last summer. He skipped the camera on to a photo of his father with his arms around the old woman, whom Morton could clearly identify as Madge, the lady who had spent most of Jeremy's leaving party washing up in the kitchen. She had seemed so nice, and yet here she was, swanning around Coniston and the Lake District with his father, Jeremy and an unidentified man. The more photos Morton saw, the angrier he became. His father had taken this woman to Coniston and seemingly revisited all the places that they had gone to as a family just before his mother had died. He wasn't sure what he was most angry at, the fact that his father was apparently seeing someone else, or the fact that he hadn't been told about it. *What was his father doing with an old, grandmotherly type like her anyway?* Then he realised that he was comparing her to his mother as she was when she died. How old would his mother be now? Sixty-nine? Christ, she'd be a wrinkly old woman herself. He hovered over the 'Erase All' option but thought better of it, switched the camera off and tucked it away back in the rucksack before he did something he might regret.

He finished his cake and coffee and left a generous tip, hoping that the buxom blonde would find the money and not the scowling frump behind the till. With his sunglasses perched on his nose, Morton casually strolled across the street to the gates of Charingsby. The village, bathed in total sunshine, was entirely deserted, as if there had been some kind of an evacuation order. It sent a sinister chill down his spine when his eyes fell on the gothic, shadowy structure of St George's Nursing Home, just a stone's throw away from the Windsor-Sackvilles. He rested his head on the cold iron bars but, even with his head pressed to them, could only catch a glimpse of the house, tiny and obscure in the distance.

Morton slowly ambled along the road beside the village green, enjoying the warm sun on his neck and a brief moment to take stock of the charming village. It looked as though Charingsby, having been occupied by the Windsor-Sackvilles since the fifteenth century, had existed long before the majority of the village. Most of the houses along the main road provided a convenient hermetic seal around the edge of the estate.

He continued steadily through the village, until he came to a public footpath post, which was slowly being strangled by an insidious weave of dark-green ivy. The sign pointed perpendicular to the road, running beside a row of delightful houses, called Riverside Cottages. The map confirmed that a river, after which the cottages were presumably named, ran across two fields then entered a wood at the edge of the Charingsby estate. Morton took a swig of water and stared at the river meandering into the distance; he just needed to follow it and he'd be inside. He downed the drink, crossed into the freshly-ploughed field and began to trudge through the calf-length grass around the edge, keeping close to the river and trying to look as much like a rambler on a pleasant walk as he could.

As the safety of the road slowly disappeared behind him, Morton wondered if he should quickly give Juliette an update. He had given her a rough overview of his plans, but thought now might be a good idea to give her his exact location. Somewhere for the search party to start looking for him if he failed to return home tonight. He took his mobile out and, rather predictably, there was no signal. That was that then.

When he entered the second field, which was being used for sheep-grazing, the footpath deviated, veering sharply away from the river in front of him. He knew that once he stepped foot off the path he lost all defence that he was simply enjoying a walk in the Sussex countryside.

It was now or never.

With a deep and decisive breath, he left the designated path behind and crossed the dry, crusty brown field towards the woods, carefully following the winding river. As the distance between him and the footpath increased, Morton half wondered if a gun-mounted jeep would suddenly roar out of nowhere, just like he had seen on television when people tried to approach Area 51 in the Nevada desert. But no gun-mounted jeep appeared, just a fat hare making a break for the hedgerow.

A few minutes later, he reached the edge of the woods and realised that his plan of simply lifting a section of fencing and passing underneath wouldn't be so straightforward; at the boundary of the woods the river was forced into a narrow, concrete tube in order to pass under a heavy-duty, two-metre-high fence topped with a vicious, double-curl of barbed wire. Morton tugged at the base of the fence but it was rigid, appearing to be fixed into the ground. He had to resort to Plan B and took out the pair of wire-cutters that he had hoped he wouldn't need. First, he scanned the woodland with his father's National Trust binoculars, which were remarkably powerful given that they were probably a free gift. There was no sign of life beyond a pair of blackbirds pecking furiously at an ant-infested mound of earth, so he pulled out the cutters and took a final, fleeting glance around him. He couldn't *see* anybody, but in these high-tech days that meant nothing. He'd once heard that the military were using satellites so powerful that they could read the text on a newspaper lying on the pavement. God only knew who was watching him from outer space as he clipped through the metal.

Six minutes later, Morton had crudely cut a hole large enough to squeeze through. He knelt onto the grass and, with a deep breath and a final check around him, he curled back the section of severed fence and crawled into the lion's den, dragging his backpack behind him. He stood up and looked around. Nothing had changed in those few feet, yet being on the inside he felt strangely closer to James Coldrick. Closer to the truth somehow. Peter Coldrick's words from Tuesday sprang into his mind. *It's as if my family are all enclosed in a walled garden which has no door.*

Maybe he had just found that door.

121

Morton pulled on the backpack, sweat beginning to bead on his forehead, and began to walk cautiously under the cooling canopy provided by mature oaks, beeches and sycamores. He judged that in three or four hundred yards he would arrive at the building.

He trod carefully but quickly through a carpet of wild garlic and late-flowering bluebells, deliberately choosing where his feet fell, so as to avoid leaving an obvious path of crushed plants. Finally, the thick woodland yielded to a grassland clearing. And there, at the centre, was the building he sought: a small, dilapidated cottage. Chunks of off-white plaster had fallen away, revealing cracked, bare bricks. Windows were either broken or boarded up. The place had suffered decades of decay and neglect. Adding to the sense of eeriness and uneasiness Morton was feeling, the plum trees surrounding the house, which he had identified in the photograph were all bare, their barren branches seeming to have died with the house.

Sweat began to trickle down his back. His heart was racing from the quick pace that he had crossed the woods, but now it refused to slow down. He slowly moved closer to the building.

Morton recalled the photograph of James Coldrick as a baby. This was definitely where it had been taken.

He knew this cottage was significant.

Despite more than sixty years of woodland growth, the top of a towering, herringbone-brick chimney was still visible in the background. The chimney belonged to Charingsby.

He took out his father's digital camera and began taking photographs. Although the original image of James Coldrick as a baby had perished, along with the rest of his *Coldrick Case Incident Wall,* he had thankfully saved a digital version to his mobile. He held his phone up and stood exactly where the photographer had snapped James Coldrick as a baby in 1944, wondering what had gone so terribly wrong for that smiling, happy woman and her new-born son.

He cautiously approached the cottage, regarding it with suspicion, as if it might be booby-trapped with Semtex or some other incendiary device. It wasn't as if these people didn't have a penchant for blowing things up. The complete and total silence around him only added to his uneasiness as he neared the building.

When Morton reached the cottage he felt the need to stand still and double-check that he was still alone. He held the binoculars to his eyes and slowly turned three hundred and sixty degrees.

He was alone.

Morton set down his backpack and approached the front door. He tentatively tried the handle, but it was either locked or seized up from years of inclement weather and disuse. He was sure that the building had played a part in James Coldrick's early life and knew that he needed to get inside. He pulled the crowbar from his bag and slowly inserted it into the rotten frame. As he exerted all his energy into the tool, the door began to flex and groan under the pressure. Suddenly, it burst clean off its hinges in a cacophony of metal and wood cracking, smashing down inwards onto a flagstone floor, echoing sonorously among the surrounding trees. *Great, now the whole estate knows I'm here,* he thought. He might just as well have buzzed in at the main gate after all.

He froze to the spot and waited, half expecting a pack of dogs or gun-wielding security guards at any moment.

Minutes later, nothing had come, so he cautiously stepped one foot inside the cottage, still fearing something terrible was about to happen. There was no way anybody had been inside here for donkeys' years, he reasoned to himself. *Donkeys' years* - that was something his father would say, not a thirty-nine year old man. Christ. He heard his father's voice telling him to pull himself together and with that ethereal voice in his mind, he strode confidently inside the cottage.

Inside was freezing and dark. Morton took out the torch that he had found beside his father's bed. The beam fell first onto a huge rack of antiquated shotguns fixed to the wall. He glanced around at the room's simplicity and realised that this wasn't a cottage at all, but a simple two-room shooting box, a relatively common sight on large estates. They were designed to provide accommodation and storage during the annual hunting season, yet this place appeared like an abandoned relic from the past, untouched for countless shooting seasons. He moved the torchlight slowly around the room; the beam illuminating the life of a forgotten past: packets of food on a large oak table; a decorative sideboard stocked with plain white crockery; a small bookcase containing a selection of classic titles; two fabric armchairs beside a loaded open fire; a grimy Belfast sink stacked with unwashed plates.

He took a closer look at the food on the table. Some of the brand names were familiar to him, yet the packaging told him that he was looking at food made somewhere in the Thirties, Forties or Fifties. The torchlight fell onto a white packet with blue writing, which confirmed for him the exact decade: *Cadbury's Ration Chocolate*. The building had stood unused since the war. *But why?*

123

The torch beam began to fade, which he thought was rather typical. He shone the fading light over to the adjacent room and hesitantly moved into the doorway. It was a small room and, just before the torch battery died, he caught sight of a neat and tidy bed, all ready-made as if waiting for the owner to return. He spotted something else in the corner of the room just as the light failed. Something that set his heart racing.

Feeling acutely vulnerable in the pitch-black room, he set down the backpack and fumbled about for the box of matches. Finally, he struck a match and the room took on an eerie, shadowy glow. He held the light over the object in the corner of the room. It was a tiny cot with blankets that, unlike the bed, were all dishevelled and unkempt, dangling precariously over the wooden bars. He bent down and picked up a knitted, beige-brown teddy bear. He drew it close to his face, knowing to whom it once belonged. Morton stood clutching the bear, contemplating the sight before him, weighing the implications of discovering an isolated shooting box, unused since the war, which contained a baby's cot. *Had this been James Coldrick's place of birth? The place where his mother had written the goodbye letter to him?* He tried to recall the contents of the letter. *What was it she had said?* Something about being placed in an abominable situation and what she feared would happen to him. A wave of nausea suddenly passed over him and he needed air that wasn't almost seventy years old inside his lungs. He moved back into the main room of the shooting box when something caught his attention. He squatted down to the door, which he believed he had just burst from its hinges, and took a closer look. The hinges *had* been forced open, but not by him and not just now. One was twisted, contorted and in the process of disintegration. The other hinge was missing entirely. The door had been held shut by three large metal straps, which were themselves time-rusted and decayed.

Morton was beginning to form an idea of what had occurred here in 1944.

A tumultuous double crack of nearby gunfire made Morton jump with fright.

They'd found him.

He blew out the match and ran for the door. The last thing he wanted was to be cornered in a deserted shooting box when nobody outside knew where he was. He peered cautiously into the woodland. The only movement was a mass exodus of birds taking to the skies in raucous screams.

Morton sprinted to the nearest thicket and tucked himself into a purple rhododendron bush where he observed a group of people with dogs striding into the clearing approximately one hundred yards away. He quickly raised the binoculars to get a better look. Five people and two golden retrievers. Hunting dogs. Brilliant. At least they weren't Dobermans, he thought. The binoculars weren't powerful enough to help identify the group heading towards him, but it looked like four men and one woman. He adjusted the plastic focus ring as they neared him, their faces gradually gaining clarity. Morton couldn't yet see the detail of their faces, but their gait and mannerisms told him that they weren't searching for an intruder on the estate, but rather were out on a shooting expedition.

The group came within fifty yards and incomprehensible fragments of their conversation drifted across to him. He tweaked the binoculars again and the group came into focus. The woman, attractive with a neat brown bob and blonde highlights, whom he guessed to be in her mid-forties, seemed wholly out of place dressed in a black pin-stripe business suit, while the four men were dressed as stereotypical aristocrats with tweed jackets, flat caps, plus-fours and half-cocked shotguns. He didn't recognise the woman or two of the men, one of whom was struggling under the weight of a mountain of luminous orange clay pigeons. The other two he categorically recognised: they were undeniably his old friend Daniel Dunk and the Secretary of Defence, Philip Windsor-Sackville. The woman leaned over and pecked Philip Windsor-Sackville on the cheek.

Morton heaved a sigh of relief as the group changed direction so that they were no longer heading straight for him. He was relieved that the door to the shooting box was facing him; from their angle, as far as they could tell, nothing had changed since 1944. They stood still for a moment, laughing and joking. Morton had an opportunity to get a decent photograph of them but the camera was in the backpack, which was inside the bedroom of the shooting box. He lowered the binoculars and gauged that if he crawled quickly over to the shooting box, he could just get back with the camera in time to take a photo before they disappeared back into the woods.

Morton dived to the ground and shimmied awkwardly through the long grass until he reached the safety of the shooting box. Once inside, he pulled himself up and grabbed the digital camera from the backpack and slithered back out into the undergrowth to get a photo.

The shooting party were still stood in the same position, buying Morton a few more seconds to switch the camera on and check that the flash was off. Rather surprisingly for his father, the digital camera was decent quality with an impressive telephoto zoom and Morton quickly had the Secretary of Defence and the woman, presumably his wife, giggling like teenagers in his viewfinder. He snapped them repeatedly.

The group began to move, back in the direction that they had entered the woods.

Morton took one last photo when suddenly his mobile loudly declared to the whole world that he had just received a text message.

He ducked down and froze, hoping that by some small miracle they hadn't heard it. Parting the tall grass, his pulse quickened as he watched the group stand still in unison, all turning quizzically. One of them, Daniel Dunk, began to turn towards the shooting box.

He needed to get out.

Fast.

Quickly and gracelessly, Morton squirmed on his stomach back to the shooting box to collect the backpack. Scooping it up from beside the bed, he slung it onto his shoulder and turned to leave the room. The stream of light flooding in through the door suddenly darkened.

He turned his head abruptly towards the shadow and was met with the sharp crack from the butt of a shotgun.

It was just how he imagined heaven to be. Deep, penetrating warmth. His head in the lap of a smiling, flaxen-haired Scandinavian with a low-cut top, her breasts nudging the side of his head. Morton brought his eyes into focus. It couldn't be heaven. In heaven he wouldn't have a nettling, wet stain in his boxer shorts or a headache like he had never felt in his life, as if his brain were full of broken glass.

'Try not to move,' the Scandinavian said in a voice that was distinctly un-Scandinavian. He knew the voice from somewhere. It was the waitress from earlier. He flicked his eyes around and saw that he was not in heaven at all, but in the middle of Sedlescombe village green with urine-stained jeans and a marble-sized bump above his left ear. He ignored her advice and sat up, trying to cover his groin. 'It's okay,' she said, 'it's just a bodily function. Involuntary. I trained to be a nurse. Well, sort of.'

126

'What happened?' Morton asked, glad that he still had the power of speech, if not of his bladder. He hoped to God he hadn't leaked from any other orifices.

The woman shrugged, inadvertently rubbing her breasts against his hair. 'I don't know. We just found you here on the green, unconscious. We've phoned for an ambulance.' And, as if by magic, an ambulance with the added humiliation of blue flashing lights pulled up beside them, flagged down by the frumpy woman from behind the counter of The Clockhouse Tearoom.

'Thanks,' he said.

Evidently the sarcasm wasn't clear enough as the waitress replied, 'You're welcome. I could hardly leave a man who left a two pound tip half dead now, could I?' Two pounds, it sounded piffling now, but when he had left it on top of a five pound twenty bill, it had seemed rather generous.

'It ain't good for business neither,' the frump added, needlessly pointing Morton out to the two paramedics hurrying across the grass towards him.

'Oh dear, what have you done, sir?' one of the paramedics said to him, as if he were a child.

'Banged my head,' he answered, figuring that the truth would only serve to complicate matters and elongate this embarrassing incident even further.

'That *is* a nasty bump,' the other medic said, running a latex-gloved hand through his hair like a meticulous nit-nurse. 'I think we need to get you off to hospital.'

'No, really – I'm fine. I don't want to go to hospital.'

The first paramedic gave him a quizzical look.

'Really, I'll phone my girlfriend. She can come and collect me. I'll be fine.'

'I told you it was a stupid idea, didn't I?' were the first words out of Juliette's mouth when she collected him from The Clockhouse Tearoom. He had been released into her care on the proviso that she monitor him for twenty-four hours. Even though the Mini's boot and entire back seats were crammed with enough bags of clothing to open a small boutique, Juliette still resented having her shopping spree brusquely curtailed by a phone call from the paramedics. 'What did you think would happen?' she persisted. He didn't really have an answer for that. Then the Police Community Support Officer in her came to the fore. 'Did you get a look at who did it to you?'

'Uh-huh.'

'And?'

'The one and only Mr Daniel Dunk,' he said.

'What?' Juliette said, shooting him an angry, quizzical look.

'I know; that's twice, at least, he's had the opportunity to kill me and hasn't taken it.'

'This has gone far enough, Morton. We know who he is, where he lives and who he works for; it's time to call this one in.'

'I'm sure they'll overlook the fact that I trespassed, damaged property and have no substantial evidence whatsoever.' The evidence he did have was on his father's digital camera, which had gone the same way as his laptop and all the evidence pinned to the *Coldrick Case Incident Wall.*

She sighed heavily and he knew that that was a sign she agreed with him but hated the fact. 'What about the others, can you describe them?'

'The woman was tall, dark hair, in a bob with blonde highlights. Quite slim, mid-forties. Pin-stripe suit. Bright red lipstick. And I mean *bright* red.'

'Quite pretty?'

'Yeah, why?'

'Sounds like an e-fit for Miss Olivia Walker to me.'

'She was kissing Philip Windsor-Sackville.'

'Oh, well it can't be her then, he's married.'

'Yeah, because it would be *so* unlike a politician to be having an affair.'

'Morton, you're so cynical all the time,' she said, which he was forced to agree with.

He reached down for his phone, remembering that it was receiving a text message that had got him struck over the head in the first place. It had better have been important. He opened his messages and read the text. *SHOPPING!!!! Hope you're having a good day, Juliette xx.* As tempting as it was to say something, he decided it was best to keep his mouth shut.

'Stop!' Morton suddenly warned Juliette, as she approached the front door of his father's house. She froze in her tracks, like a Covent Garden mime artist, looking vaguely comical with her carrier-bag-filled hands raised in front of her. She looked back at him for guidance. 'Come back here, quick,' Morton called.

Something was wrong.

'Look at the curtains upstairs,' he said, once she had reached his side. 'They were definitely closed when we left this morning, now look at them.'

'Oh God, not another house. What shall we do?' she asked, backing towards the Mini. It was very unlike Juliette to defer to him like this and that worried him all the more. *Was it okay to phone the bomb squad because you* thought *that your house might be riddled with Semtex, since you distinctly recall leaving the curtains shut?* 'I think we should ring the police and ask for their guidance.'

'Good idea,' Juliette said, pulling out her mobile.

The question of what to do next was answered for them when the front door opened. And there, with a large smile on his face, stood Jeremy. 'Afternoon. Are you coming inside, or just happy to look at the house from a distance?'

'For Christ's sake,' Morton mumbled.

Juliette managed a laugh as they headed up the path to be greeted by Jeremy, like he hadn't seen them in years.

'It's so good to see you both again,' he said with a lengthy embrace. 'How funny, I've got a pair of jeans and shirt exactly like that, Morton.'

'That is funny,' Morton answered. Jeremy seemed completely oblivious to the fact that they had moved in; he invited them to sit down for a cup of tea.

'I've just got back from the hospital,' he said. 'He looks awful, doesn't he? I had to step out because I found it really upsetting.'

It was unintentional, and he knew it was an awful thing to do, but Morton couldn't quite manage to stifle a snigger that suddenly crept up on him.

Juliette booted him hard in the shin and made his laugh turn into a yelp.

'What's the matter?' Jeremy asked.

'He's got concussion,' Juliette said, glaring at Morton.

'Have you? What happened?' He seemed genuinely concerned.

'I fell over and banged my head,' Morton said dismissively.

Jeremy looked at the lump protruding from Morton's head and winced. 'And the smell of urine?' Jeremy asked.

Morton looked down at the large stain that splayed out from his jeans. Jeremy's jeans. 'Long story.'

'Is Dad seeing someone else?' Morton asked, as they began eating an unexpectedly tasty roast dinner cooked by Jeremy. He was warned by the paramedics of temporary memory loss but Morton searched through his store of memories and couldn't recall ever having seen Jeremy cook a meal. There was one time when he attempted to heat custard by spooning it into a china bowl then heating it on the hob, wondering why the bowl cracked into five pieces, sending yellow mess all over the oven.

'Someone *else?*' Jeremy said. 'As far as I'm aware he's just dating Madge.' Morton's brain didn't know which part of his answer to dissect first. *Dating?* His father had suddenly morphed into an American teenager.

'How long's *that* been going on then?' Morton demanded.

'God, two years or so now I would guess. She's lovely, you'd really like her. Oh, I should have introduced you; she was at my leaving party. You're not bothered about it are you, Morton? Surely not?'

'It might have been nice for someone to mention it,' he answered. He went to say, '*It might have been nice for someone to ask me,*' and was glad that he had not. Maybe he was over-reacting. It wasn't as if he ran home to report the latest news in *his* life. 'And who was the man in the photo?' Morton asked, realising as the words tumbled out that no mention had been made of the camera.

'What photo?'

Morton flushed. 'I found Father's digital camera and there were pictures on there at Coniston. Last summer I think they were taken.'

'Oh, that's Gary. He's Madge's son.'

'Right,' Morton said. How lovely, like the *Brady Bunch*.

'And my ex.'

'What?' Morton said, wondering if he really had suffered brain damage or if he'd somehow slipped into a parallel universe. He regretted how horrified he sounded. He didn't feel horrified, just surprised. His family simply didn't *do* candour.

'My ex. I dated him for a few months last year.'

'Does Father know?' Morton asked, instantly hating the fact that he sounded like a brainless homophobe, like he thought his father might sound if he knew. *Surely he couldn't know?* Jeremy would have told him before their father.

'Course he does,' Jeremy said matter-of-factly.

130

'Why didn't you tell me?' Morton said, wondering what the hell was going on with his family and dropping bombshells incongruously into conversations. Most people start with 'I think we need to talk,' or 'I've got something to tell you' but his family just *said* them while you're shoving a forkful of Yorkshire pudding into your mouth.

Jeremy shrugged. 'Why didn't you tell me you were straight?'

Juliette laughed. 'Good question. Why didn't you, Morton? Having said that, he actually *offered* to take me shopping to Brighton the other day. And he's bought himself a brand new Mini Cooper. How gay is that?'

'Got something to share, Brother dear?' Jeremy asked with a giggle.

'And is Father okay with it?' Morton asked, not quite able to reconcile his conservative father with a gay son.

'He went a bit quiet for a few days then when he realised nothing had changed he was fine. Back to his old self. A while later I introduced him to Gary then we met up for a meal and Gary's mum came along and they hit it off together. The rest is history.'

Morton shrank back and couldn't quite muster the courage to go and hug his brother and to say what he really wanted to say, which was 'Good for you, Jeremy. I'm pleased for you.'

131

Chapter Fourteen

Saturday

Morton had been lying awake for some time pondering last night. With every heartbeat his head thumped its anger for the lack of sleep and excessive quantity of his father's whiskey, right in the spot where Dunk had landed one on him. He should have had a dry, early night instead of getting drunk and staying up into the early hours, chatting. But he was glad he'd done it; he'd never felt as close to Jeremy in his life – a strange fraternal unity that had been lacking all these years. Jeremy's revelation seemed to have broken down an invisible wall that had slowly built up between them. In the new spirit of reciprocal candour, Morton told Jeremy about the *Coldrick Case* and all that had occurred. Jeremy had exclaimed, 'And you say *I* dropped a bombshell! Christ, Morton. I mean, Philip Windsor-Sackville is technically my boss. This is huge.' Taking Jeremy's tendency towards histrionics into account, hearing the whole charade in a linear fashion, one incident after another, seemed to be almost revelatory to Morton, as if it had all happened to someone else.

He climbed out of bed, careful not to wake Juliette, lying with her head scrunched uncomfortably between her pillow and his. Padding softly into the bathroom, he swallowed down two paracetamols and looked at himself in the mirror. The lump on the side of his head had grown to the size of a ping-pong ball. He gently touched the surface and it felt so firm that he thought there actually could have been a ping-pong ball under his skin. A fresh surge of pain bit into his head and he decided to leave the paracetamols to do their work. With a little help from a gallon of coffee, obviously. *It should help*, he thought, remembering something about caffeine dilating blood vessels. He went quietly downstairs, made a large mug of instant and opened up his brand-spanking-new Apple MacBook that Juliette had purchased for him in Tunbridge Wells. Not that he was going to get attached to this one, he was treating it as any other household electrical appliance, since it doubtless wouldn't be long before it was either stolen or blown up. There only seemed point in loading the basic programmes, rather than wasting time adding all his genealogy software.

Once the coffee was drunk, the paracetamols had kicked in and the Mac was up and running, Morton loaded up YouTube and typed the words 'Chief Constable Olivia Walker'. Four hits. *Chief Constable Olivia Walker swaps policing duties for a taster with Kent Fire and Rescue; Kent Chief Constable Olivia Walker gets tasered; Appointment of Chief Constable Olivia Walker; Chief Constable Olivia Walker welcomes Defence Secretary to Ashford.* Morton clicked the last hyperlink and watched a thirty-three second video clip of the Secretary of Defence shaking hands with a uniformed woman. The quality of the video (from a cheap mobile by the looks of things) was so terrible that the uniformed officer could just as easily have been Juliette as the woman he'd seen yesterday in the pinstripe suit. The first video clip showed Olivia Walker speaking directly to the camera about what she'd learnt by becoming a fire officer for the day. The clip had the *Meridian News* logo in the bottom left corner and, consequently, the video resolution was much higher and Morton could identify, beyond reasonable doubt, that she was the woman he'd seen yesterday at Charingsby. The same woman who'd been in charge of the investigation into Mary Coldrick's death was overseeing the investigation into Peter Coldrick's death. The same woman licensed on Daniel Dunk's car. With that in mind, Morton watched with gleeful *Schadenfreude* as Olivia Walker was willingly tasered by one of her minions. She seemed to be overacting, as if the video was actually for propaganda purposes. The last clip was filmed at a press conference where 'Cllr Paul Buzzard' announced that Olivia Walker was, by unanimous decision of the panel, to become the new Chief Constable of Kent Police. Morton watched as the camera panned to the right and Olivia read a short statement about how proud she was to be leading one of England's largest forces in crime prevention and detection. Morton wondered what part of crime prevention and detection her association with the Windsor-Sackvilles and Daniel Dunk had played?

Morton recalled what Juliette had said about it not being possible that he had seen Olivia canoodling with Philip Windsor-Sackville, as he was happily married to someone else. Just to be clear in his own mind, Morton returned to the family website and clicked the 'Family Tree' tab. Philip Windsor-Sackville had been married to Andrea Rhys-Jones since 1971. Judging by the unflattering photo of her on the website, where she seemed to have been snapped unawares, it seemed a classic case of her being traded in for a younger, more successful, more beautiful model. Arise Chief Constable Olivia Walker. Morton had to concede that Andrea did look a bit of a dowdy old frump. Still, she had borne him three children, all of whom were in the lower political ranks of government – one was the Junior Minister for the Environment - and that ought to count for something.

'Look. See, I told you,' Morton said, dumping the laptop down in the space he'd vacated in the bed. Juliette looked as though she hadn't moved a muscle since he'd got up more than an hour ago.

'What *now?*' Juliette moaned, struggling to open her eyes.

'Philip Windsor-Sackville is married to *her*, not Olivia Walker,' he said like a triumphant primary school child.

'Jesus, Morton, it's Saturday morning. Go away,' she said, turning her back sharply and almost heaving the new laptop off the bed. She pulled the duvet over her head and disappeared into a sleepy cocoon.

Taking the hint, he shut down the laptop and dressed in a new outfit from Jeremy's wardrobe. It was a big cliché, but his gay brother's wardrobe was infinitely more stylish than his own had ever been. He mentally went through his own wardrobe, considering all of his clothes that had gone up in smoke. Perhaps it wasn't a bad thing to start all over again, he thought, as he rooted through Jeremy's underwear drawer. Even Jeremy's boxer shorts were all Calvin Kleins. *How had he not suspected anything?* It certainly made him more interesting, especially since he was in the army - of all the careers that he could have chosen. In the process of telling Jeremy what had gone on in the past few days, Morton had confessed to borrowing various items of clothing. Jeremy had just grinned and said it was fine, that he could help himself.

Morton looked at his watch – ten twenty. Was ten twenty on a Saturday considered too early to disturb someone by phone? Maybe for some people but it was Soraya Benton that he wanted to call and she probably would have been woken by Finlay several hours ago. Ideally, he had wanted to visit her, but that involved too long a round trip with a banging head; not the best of ideas. Besides which, the paramedics had told him to rest for twenty-four hours and *definitely* not to drive. He felt bad for not having made contact with Soraya since Peter's funeral, but then what could he have said? *How did the cremation go?* It was hardly a question that needed asking, much less answering. He pulled out his phone, dialled her number and hoped for the best. She answered after several rings and sounded slightly breathless, as if she'd just run in from the garden. 'Sorry, it's just Morton,' he said, feeling the need to apologise.

'Oh, hi,' she said, sounding immediately brighter. 'I was just cleaning Fin's room. It's like a bomb's gone off in there. I'm trying to keep it tidy, what with it being my sister's study and all. Oh God, *bomb's gone off*, sorry, Morton. I wasn't thinking.'

'It's fine,' he said, having not actually made the connection between what she had said and his own demolished house. 'I had a couple of things I needed to ask you about. Is now a good time to talk?'

'Yeah, fire away. Fin's at his friend's all day and I'm just doing housework. I'd be glad of the distraction.'

'It's a bit delicate, really. I don't know how you feel and I really won't be offended…' Morton began, only to be interrupted.

'Oh, spit it out, for goodness' sake, Morton,' she said playfully.

'Sorry. I was wondering how you might feel about me taking some of Fin's DNA and comparing it to the Windsor-Sackvilles?' he asked, slightly nervously. Taking DNA was always a thorny subject to broach with clients. There seemed to be a general issue of mistrust of the technique among the older generation and a general issue of over-reliance on the technique among the younger generation.

'Of course you can,' Soraya said, without so much as a nanosecond's consideration. 'Go for it. What do you need? Blood?'

'Not quite - just a cheek swab will do. Are you sure you don't object? You'll have to sign a consent form.'

'No, not at all. I take it from all of this you're more sure that Fin's related to them, then?'

'At this stage it's no more than conjecture and coincidence,' Morton replied rather nebulously, contradicting his lack of belief in coincidence. 'Can I bring a test kit down tomorrow?'

'Yes, that's fine. One thing, though,' Soraya said. 'How do you plan on getting DNA from the Windsor-Sackvilles? I can't imagine any of them being compliant somehow.'

'Yeah, that might be an issue. I'm still thinking about that one. Which brings me to my next point: Sir David and Lady Maria Windsor-Sackville are opening the village fete in Sedlescombe today and I wondered if you wanted to come along?'

'Meet the enemy, you mean?'

'Something like that,' Morton said. 'What do you think?'

'I think I'll pass, I'm not sure I want to come face-to-face with them. Besides, I've got a lot to do here and there's still a lot of Peter's things to sort out. Let me know how you get on, though.'

'Okay, I'll see you tomorrow.'

'Good luck.'

Morton thanked her and ended the call.

It was a hot, airless afternoon when Juliette parked up in the makeshift parking area of an unsuitable, deeply rutted field being used for the Sedlescombe Village Fete. 'This had better not mess my car up,' she remarked to no-one in particular.

Morton, belted into the passenger seat beside her, was busy running his eyes across the agricultural fields in the distance to where he had cut through the Charingsby perimeter fence yesterday. 'Maybe we could go over and get my backpack?' Morton suggested, knowing the chances of it waiting patiently for him to return were somewhat less than slim. 'Safety in numbers and all that.'

'Good idea,' Jeremy said, casually sipping from a can of Coke in the back of the car. Having nothing better to do with his day, he decided to join them at the village fete. 'It's the last thing they'd expect. You've got to think tactically.'

'If you so much as step foot *near* that place, I swear to God that bump on the side of your head will become a football,' Juliette threatened. She wasn't joking either. 'Please, can we just have a normal day today, Morton; no explosions, muggings or stalkings?'

Morton plumped for Juliette's advice and quietly dropped the idea.

The three of them stepped from the car and followed the throng of crowds making their way across the field. It was already a good turnout by anyone's standards at such provincial gatherings.

A glum-looking pensioner in an over-sized, yellow hi-vis jacket that stretched down to his calves silently directed them into the 'Welcome Tent', where Morton handed over fifteen pounds for their entrance.

'Sir David and Lady Windsor-Sackville will be opening the fete in just under half-an-hour's time and there'll be a demonstration of Tractors Through the Ages at two o'clock and a falconry display at three,' a short, sun-wrinkled lady told them.

The three of them sauntered down the field, following a steady stream of people headed in the general direction of several large white marquees and a mass of assorted trestle tables.

'What *exactly* are we doing here?' Jeremy asked, taking a casual glance over a run of tatty paperbacks, as if he had only just realised where they were.

'That's what I'm wondering,' Juliette said, turning to face Morton.

'You two are so sceptical,' Morton said. 'I just wanted to actually *see* these people, that's all.'

Juliette gave him a doubtful look. 'That's what the internet's for.' She stopped to study the blurb of a well-worn Maeve Binchy novel. He knew that her mind was working overtime trying to establish an ulterior motive. She put the book down and the three of them walked on, passing motley tables of plants, ornaments, homemade jams and preserves, antique furniture and secondhand toys. A swarm of wasps besieged an open-sided gazebo where traditional apple-pressing was taking place. The hive of industry, of which the wasps seemed an integral part, resulted in a copious quantity of cloudy amber liquid oozing from a thick wooden press before being sold to a queuing public for one pound per plastic cup.

'Fancy some?' Morton asked.

'Maybe later,' Jeremy said, scrunching his nose up.

Morton led them past a long line of cakes and biscuits that might have looked remotely tempting if they weren't slowly wilting under the high heat of the day, much to the chagrin of their creators behind the tables. They moved further down the field, past a bouncy castle and face-painting tent towards a temporary stage on what was the only flat part of the field. An empty podium and microphone stood in the centre of the stage in anticipation of Sir David and Lady Windsor-Sackville. In front of the staging was a long thick red ribbon tied off between two wooden stakes at either side of the stage. Morton guessed that this was the symbolic ribbon that would be ceremonially cut in order to declare the fete open. It seemed to him like closing the gate after the horse had bolted, since the field was already heaving with visitors. In just a few minutes Morton would come face to face with his adversaries standing on that very stage. He wondered if they would know who he was. Probably not, the problem was much more likely being dealt with by the lower ranks of the family and staff.

Running his eyes over the crowds, Morton's attention was taken by something moving strangely in the distance. It was some kind of customised golfing buggy, speeding down the hill far too fast, scattering people left and right from its path. Heads, too many than can have fitted comfortably inside, bobbed about like Muppets, as the buggy jutted over ruts and fissures in the ground.

'If only I'd brought my speed trap radar,' Juliette commented, her attention having been drawn by the commotion of disgruntled families, heaving themselves out of the buggy's way.

It came to an abrupt halt in front of the stage, all the bobbing heads being flung sharply forwards then back. From Morton's perspective, it looked as though the front window had nudged into the ceremonial red ribbon. Morton immediately recognised the driver as Sir David James Peregrine Windsor-Sackville: still able to terrify the living daylights out of people with his bullish driving.

'Come on, you buggers,' Sir David said, referring to his legs, hoisting one and then the other out of the buggy, as if he had two lead weights attached to his pelvis.

One of his entourage jumped from the rear of the buggy and readied a pair of walking sticks in front of him. With the sticks firmly in his hands, he stood upright, a tall, formidable figure. He certainly seemed like a man used to getting his own way.

An equally wizened woman appeared from the passenger side, waving off the offer of assistance from a deferential aide. Lady Maria Charlotte Windsor-Sackville, née Spencer: a fearsome beast, if ever Morton saw one. She was dressed in an all-in-one lemon-coloured outfit with matching hat that wouldn't have looked out of place on the Queen. With one sweep of her hand, an aide came dashing over.

'Is that them?' Juliette whispered, an edge of disappointment in her voice. Morton wondered what she'd been expecting. Younger, more agile opponents maybe.

'Yeah, that's them,' he answered.

The redoubtable duo, armed with their walking sticks, ambled up the temporary steps onto the staging, closely followed by five attentive aides. Morton gazed at the scene in front of him; it was like some garish wedding rehearsal and he couldn't help but feel something akin to respect for their vigour. *Could that decrepit old pair really be responsible for murder? Was he now looking at James Coldrick's parents?* He wasn't sure, but the more that he observed them, the more obvious it became to him that the distinguished pair, despite their age, continued to wield and exert an incredible power over those around them.

Morton withdrew his phone and pulled up the scanned copy of James Coldrick's mother, holding it aloft beside Maria Charlotte Windsor-Sackville.

'What do you think?' Morton asked. 'One and the same?'

Jeremy and Juliette leaned in either side of him.

'No way, look at the nose,' Juliette said emphatically.

'It could be the same person,' Jeremy said. 'Look at the shape of her jawline. I think it could be the same woman.'

'I'm not sure,' Morton said, as his view of Lady Maria was supplanted by a humungous backside in black leggings.

138

A dishevelled mother, with far more children than can possibly have been healthy for her womb, parked herself and her family directly in front of them, marking their territory by pulling a picnic blanket from one of three large bags. Ordinarily, Morton would have taken exception to losing front row seats but the more he thought about it, the more he considered that being slightly camouflaged was no bad thing.

Morton craned his neck around a greasy-haired girl and watched as one of the Windsor-Sackville attendants, a young, slender woman sweltering in a tight pinstripe suit ushered them towards two gold-trimmed, red-velvet chairs in the centre of the stage. It was such a cliché as to be laughable. Morton, half expecting a pair of court jesters to leap out onto the stage, could see that the chairs were cheap fabrications. It was all about image, he realised as he studied them, bolt upright in their thrones, issuing orders to their minions. The image of the Windsor-Sackville family needed to be preserved at all costs. At any cost. Yes, Morton was starting to believe that they would consider murder an acceptable method to protect the family name.

A man, who screamed of self-importance, marched with his clipboard onto the stage and thrust his hand towards Sir David, who greeted him with a vague head gesture, large scowl and reluctant shake of the hand. A narrow, pathetic excuse of a smile passed across the scarlet-painted lips of Lady Maria, before her eyes surveyed the slowly gathering crowds with what looked to Morton like thinly-veiled contempt. The man continued to speak to the pair, gesticulating his clipboard in large circles as he spoke. The racket made by the growing number of people prevented Morton from catching what was being said on stage, but his interpretation was that his jokes and officiousness weren't going down too well with the knight and his good lady wife, who sat staring at the crowd indifferently.

A few minutes later, with a sufficiently large crowd assembled, the man with the clipboard stepped up to the podium and tapped the microphone. The volume of the crowd fell to a low murmur. 'Can everyone hear me okay?' he said with a large grin. A smattering of people in the crowd weakly replied that could hear him and so he carried on. 'Good, that's marvellous. I'm so glad to see the sun shining for us here today and I'm delighted that so many of you have turned out to enjoy all we've got on offer at the Sedlescombe Fete, including a marvellous falconry display with seven different species of owl, a Tai Kwan Do display and what I'm particularly looking forward to is

Tractors Through the Ages – I noticed a fine Massey-Ferguson similar to the one I used to plough this very field as a youth, but that's another story! Before I hand you over to our very special guests to open the fete, I would just like to use this opportunity of thanking Sir David and Lady Maria for their kind loan of this field to host the event.' He paused, anticipating some great reaction from the crowd, but what he actually got was a half-hearted, staggered clap, like a pitiable Mexican wave. He spoke over the last dregs of applause, 'Well, I'm sure none of you paid to hear me droning on, so, without further ado, would you please give a hearty welcome to Sir David and Lady Maria Windsor-Sackville.'

The crowd gave a unanimous round of applause as Sir David and Lady Maria rose from their thrones. Morton felt something akin to admiration for the pair as they approached the podium without the aid of their walking sticks. Sir David pulled the microphone closer and spoke with clean, crisp grandiloquence; a voice that seemed entirely ageless to Morton. He hoped that he would be so active at their age, but who knew what terrible hereditary illnesses and causes of premature deaths lurked in his unknown genes? For all that he knew, his mother and father could both have been dead by the time they were forty from some God awful disease.

Morton looked across at Jeremy, who was doing what could only be described as eye-flirting with one of the Windsor-Sackville aides, a slick Hollywood-handsome young man with perfect white teeth and bleached blond hair. At least Jeremy knew that there was a risk of cancer in his gene pool and could do something about it. And now heart disease needed to be added to the list. He wondered how his father was progressing today. Jeremy had called the ward this morning to be told the standard mantra that he'd had a 'comfortable night.' *Would they tell him if he'd had an uncomfortable night?*

Jeremy's relationship with the man on stage had progressed to the next level; they were now sharing in a silent, body-language-dependent conversation about Sir David's speech – eye rolling, smiling and frowning at each other like they were a pair of teenagers. Morton wondered if he would be more confident if he were gay. He couldn't imagine ever being so self-assured as a part of any gender combination to be doing what they were doing now.

Morton studied Sir David closely as he perorated. Was there an atavistic resemblance between him and Peter or Finlay? It was hard to picture Sir David's ancient, papery face as a young person to be able to make a comparison.

As Sir David finished, his wife, with considerable grace and elegance, made her way down to the red ribbon. Her trusty aides had a watchful eye over her, ready to lurch out should she take a tumble.

'It gives me enormous pleasure to be able to declare the Sedlescombe Fete...open!' the lady exclaimed loudly.

The gathering, now fully versed in crowd etiquette, clapped raucously.

Moments later everyone had dispersed in a hundred directions, many heading towards the burger and ice cream vans. Jeremy blithely bounced over to his new-found friend on the stage for the next phase in their relationship, whilst two of the entourage hurried walking sticks to the fragile Windsor-Sackvilles.

'Come on,' Morton said to Juliette, 'let's wait for Lothario's gay twin over here.'

'You've got to admit it, he's got a good taste in men,' Juliette remarked.

'Hmm,' Morton mumbled absent-mindedly. It was not something on which he felt in any way qualified to comment other than that the aide was handsome. Men were either handsome or ugly as far as Morton was concerned; there was no grey area in-between. They watched with veneration as a clear display of number-swapping took place, before the handsome aide was reabsorbed into the train of attendants following Sir David and Lady Maria back into the buggy where they were whisked off at high speed up the hill. Angry red brake lights flashed abruptly next to the apple-pressing tent and the party disembarked the vehicle once more.

'Come on,' Morton said, urging Juliette up the slope, just as Jeremy rejoined them.

'Guy,' Jeremy said, proudly wafting a piece of paper in the air. 'Australian.'

'Guy what?'

'Disney,' Jeremy answered. And he wasn't joking. Guy Disney.

'He looks fit,' Juliette said.

'I know!'

By the time they had reached the apple-pressing marquee, a number of people had gathered around Sir David and Lady Maria, as if they were some kind of celebrity couple. Juliette returned to rummaging through a stall of paperbacks. Jeremy made a beeline for

Guy and their relationship, which seemed to all intents and purposes to be on hyper-drive, progressed to the level of Guy placing his hand in the small of Jeremy's back while they spoke animatedly to each other.

He turned his attentions to the Windsor-Sackvilles, who were sipping apple juice from plastic beakers whilst speaking to the wasp-besieged proprietor about the need to maintain traditional agricultural practices. Sir David took a final swig of juice and tossed the cup into a large barrel then turned, his watery, aged eyes momentarily passing over Morton before flicking back in a brusque double-take.

Morton was in no doubt that the eyes that met his bore lucid and unmistakable recognition.

Sir David whispered something in his wife's ear then hurried towards one of his aides.

It was time to go.

Now.

Chapter Fifteen

Sunday

He had driven back to their former home in Rye, back to what felt to Morton like a different world, another lifetime. So much had happened in such a short time that it defied belief. Yet here he was, back where he used to call home. All alone. He looked at his watch – Juliette would right now be in the interview which decided the fate of her PCSO career. She had no idea which way it was going to go and if the last couple of weeks had taught Morton anything, then it was to expect the unexpected. 'Great, thanks for those wise words, Morton,' she'd replied before leaving home for the lion's den. Jeremy had thrown his arms around her and told her it would all work out fine. He would be at the hospital right now, visiting their father, contrary to his original plan of seeing Guy today. He'd rung the hospital first thing to check on their father's progress to be told that he'd 'had a very bad night'. He was still alive, though, which Morton thought was a minor miracle in itself. He wondered what would happen to his newfound relationship with Jeremy when their father did eventually leave this mortal coil. At the moment it was based in a surreal, parallel universe where they lived in the same house, shared clothing and went to village fetes together. It was like a dodgy American sitcom on the verge of being axed.

Morton stepped out of the Mini into the damnable heat of the day and stared at the gap occupying the space where his house had once stood. Apparently the two adjoining properties didn't feel able to support themselves without his house in the middle and had slumped into an unrecognisable pile of building materials, leaving in their wake a miniature Ground Zero. A spider's web of scaffolding encased the neighbouring properties, presumably to stop the whole of Church Square from dominoing into a pile of rubble. The spectacle had evidently become one of Rye's latest must-see attractions; a whole horde of people stood behind the hastily erected barricade, gazing at the half-a-dozen workmen who seemed to Morton to be doing very little to clear the wreckage.

A red Vauxhall Astra bearing the logo 'Fire Brigade' drew up to the cordon and a burly brick of a man climbed out carrying with him a Pampers Nappies box. Morton hadn't really expected to get anything back from the fire but seeing the sum total of thirty-nine years of life heading towards him in a nappy box actually choked him. That was everything: his whole life reduced to one box. Should he take heart that the box was relatively large? Had the Fire Brigade managed to retrieve many sentimental goods? Surely he wouldn't have bothered returning a packet of cornflakes or a sodden pair of socks, would he? Morton couldn't help but think about his school reports, greetings cards dating back to his first birthday, correspondence, an assortment of yellowing photo albums, family home videos – the list of his possessions ran like a tickertape through his mind and made the lump on the side of his head ache all the more.

'Morton Farrier?' the fire officer questioned.

Morton nodded and he thrust a meaty hand towards him. Morton's insides sagged when the fire officer managed to effortlessly balance the nappy box in his upturned left hand while the other rigorously shook Morton's hand. 'Assistant Divisional Officer Stephenson. I'm afraid that what the fire didn't destroy, the sheer quantity of water that we had to use probably did.' He passed over the Pampers box. 'Apart from this lot that my boys pulled out yesterday.'

'Thanks,' Morton said doubtfully. The box was virtually weightless.

Stephenson made a noise that sounded like a cross between an incredulous laugh and a scoff. 'Whoever did this used enough Semtex to bring down a large superstore. Amazing.'

'Yeah,' Morton agreed. He wasn't sure that amazing was the adjective he would have used, but it wasn't worth splitting hairs over.

'Is there anything else I can help you with?' Stephenson asked.

Rebuild my house? Catch the people who did this? Find me somewhere to live? Help me solve the Coldrick Case? What could the Assistant Divisional Officer help him with? Nothing, that was what. 'No, I don't think so.'

'Well, good luck with it,' he said, his job done. He turned on his heels and returned to his vehicle.

'Thanks,' Morton said vaguely, unsure of what he was thanking him for. It was a curious parting comment, he thought. He took one final glance at his house then he carried the Pampers box into town in search of a decent cup of coffee. It was a deliberate ploy to delay opening the box for as long as possible. Once he looked inside, he would know exactly what had survived and all the rest of his possessions would be forever consigned to oblivion. The longer away that moment was, the better.

He took a mini-statement from the hole-in-the-wall and stared at his bank balance, as if they were an assortment of random numbers.

From fifty to twenty-five thousand in seven days – that had to be some kind of record. Jesus. Where the hell had twenty-five grand disappeared to? He marched inside the bank, the ping-pong ball on the side of his head throbbing with each footfall, and demanded a full statement from a harassed-looking woman at the customer service desk.

The car had obviously taken a fair wodge and then there was his new Apple MacBook. The rest, in the spirit of egalitarianism, had been evenly distributed among Top Shop, Miss Selfridges, H&M, Mango, Laura Ashley, Debenhams, Karen Millen, John Lewis, French Connection, Jaeger, and Marks and Spencer. Juliette really had gone to town. Christ. *And* she'd complained because she'd had her shopping spree cut short because he'd had the audacity to ask her to collect him from Sedlescombe. Now he understood why rich businessmen had offshore accounts out of reach of their wives.

Jempsons always did a good cup of coffee. And they had air-conditioning. He tried to force his dwindling bank balance from his mind, as he sat down in a seat beside the window with a large latte. He stared at the passers-by and tried to avoid the inevitable: the time had come to open the Pampers box; a feeling of mild nausea prickled his stomach. He pulled open the box and took the items out one by one, setting them out on the table in front of him. A black granite squirrel. A darts trophy. A briefcase. A silver jewellery case. James Coldrick's copper box. It was like a sick joke – just five items had randomly survived the explosion. Well, four actually since the black granite squirrel didn't belong to him. It was the kind of thing Mrs McPherson next door might have owned though. Quite how it ended up in his box of last worldly goods was another matter. He realised then that he hadn't even asked the fire officer about his neighbours. Poor Mrs McPherson was in her eighties and had lived in that house since before the war; a shock like this could have killed her if the house crumbling around her hadn't already done the job. He'd have to find out where she was staying and return the squirrel to her: that might cheer her up. He looked at the other items. *How had the darts trophy that he won at the age of twelve survived the inferno?* It was made entirely of cheap, gold lacquered plastic.

He opened the small black briefcase and was relieved to find that actually the sales pitch about it being 'the black box for the home' was quite true. All their important documents, passports, certificates and insurances (including buildings and contents, thankfully up-to-date) were safe and untouched by the blaze. Last but not least there was

James Coldrick's copper box, blackened and scratched, but with the coat of arms still clearly visible on the top. He unhooked the clasp and fully expected to find the box empty, that someone had got to the contents first, but the letters and the photo had miraculously been preserved.

Morton swigged his latte and stared at the lamentable assortment of junk on the table in front of him. An elderly lady at the next table was staring, looking entirely flummoxed. 'The summary of my life,' Morton said helpfully.

'Oh,' the old lady replied.

Morton picked up the copper box. It was the only piece of tangible evidence still in his possession and he was stumped by it. Well and truly stumped. It was time to seek help from an old acquaintance.

He gulped down the remainder of his drink, left the coffee shop and made his way back to the car to visit Soraya.

As he walked, he dialled the headquarters of the Forensic Science Service in Birmingham.

'He's only been to school twice since it happened,' Soraya whispered to Morton. They had been sitting in her sister's lounge, a surprisingly large suburban townhouse, for some time whilst Morton brought her up to speed. She listened fixedly, yet to Morton her mind seemed elsewhere. Tired, dark circles curled under eyes and recent events seemed to be finally taking their toll on her.

Fin had yet to make an appearance, playing a Play Station game that sounded alarmingly destructive to Morton. He wondered if it was a sensible idea to allow an eight-year-old, whose dad's head had recently been blown apart, to play something so violent. *What was wrong with Connect Four or Kerplunk?* It had been good enough for him as a child, a revelation which made him suddenly feel old.

'They're sending round the educational psychologist to talk to him and try and get him back to school properly. Honestly, Morton, the sooner this whole business is over the better,' she said, rubbing her eyes.

'I couldn't agree more,' Morton replied, which was a bit of an understatement, all things considered. The way that Soraya spoke was as if all of Fin's problems would be miraculously solved if a DNA connection could be established with the Windsor-Sackvilles. As far as Morton was concerned, that would be when the trouble started.

146

'It doesn't help living out of a suitcase either, neither of us feels settled. My sister's been great, but we just want to be back home again.'

'Well, let's get this test done then,' he said.

Soraya nodded and called for Fin. Four polite requests and a final threat to have his Play Station unplugged later and Fin finally, and very sullenly, appeared in the lounge. He seemed surprised to see Morton, and not in a good way.

'Fin, you remember my nice friend, Morton, don't you?' Soraya said, over-cxaggerating the words, like an animated primary school teacher. *Nice friend*, Morton, that was one way of describing him. Much better than *that-horrible-man-who-made-you-cry-last-time*, Morton. This wasn't going to be pleasant, he could tell already. *How was he even going to take the swab?* There was no sensible reason (beyond telling the truth, and he wasn't about to open *that* can of worms) that Morton could pluck from his brain to justify shoving a stick into Fin's mouth and wiping the inside of his cheek eight times.

'What game are you playing?' Morton asked. It was a lame question, but it was the only one he could think of.

'War Storm Four,' Fin murmured, unable to look Morton in the eyes.

'War Storm Four?' he said, attempting to mock incredulity. 'What was wrong with the other three?'

Finlay shrugged. 'They were rubbish.' Morton wanted to give a hearty, supportive laugh, but what came out of his mouth was more of a mocking snigger. He *really* shouldn't have kids.

'Fin, Morton's got an extra special test to do for your diabetes.'

Fin looked uncertain. 'Will it hurt?'

'No, not a bit,' Morton said. 'Look.' He pulled out a swab stick slightly larger than a nail file and held it aloft. If he'd used his brain he would have brought two along and demonstrated it on himself first. 'All I have to do is rub this on your cheek.'

'My cheek?' he said, raising a finger to the side of his face.

Morton nodded. 'Inside.' The boy clamped his mouth shut and looked horrified. 'Don't worry, it won't go down your throat or anything,' he quickly added, but the horror remained in Fin's eyes.

'It's okay, it really won't hurt at all,' Soraya said, hamming up her reassurance. 'Okay?'

Fin nodded and Morton approached him, trying to hold the swab stick in such a way as to not make it look like he was brandishing a weapon of torture. Fin opened his mouth and allowed Morton to take to the swab without a fuss.

'There, all done,' Morton said, delighted with the small triumph of not making an eight-year-old boy cry again. 'You can go back to War Storm Four if you want.'

Seconds later the sounds of explosions and gunfire came from Fin's bedroom.

'Well done,' Soraya said with a smile, 'you're good with kids.'

He wondered if she was being sarcastic. Not making a child cry was hardly a cause for procreation in his book.

'I didn't know he had diabetes,' Morton ventured, unsure as to why the fact had struck him as being important. If Fin was anything like Morton was at the age of eight, then he would have a substantial back-catalogue of medical history. Bumps, breaks, stitches, allergies and all the contagious diseases available had blighted his first decade on the planet, much to the vexation of his parents, whose own biological progeny had been beset by far fewer problems (and most of those had been inadvertently passed on from Morton).

'Yeah, he's had it since birth. Peter had it, too. It's okay, we control it,' she said, not quite sounding as if she believed herself. 'What should we do if the result is positive?' she asked.

Now there was a question. Positive as in a match with the Windsor-Sackvilles, or positive as in a good, optimistic outcome? 'Cross that bridge when we come to it,' Morton parried. *If we come to it.*

'But it's looking like the most likely scenario, isn't it?'

'It's certainly a possibility,' Morton answered, unsure whether or not her question was rhetorical.

Soraya ran her fingers through her hair and sighed heavily.

'I'll be in touch,' Morton said, glancing down at his watch. 'I've got somewhere I need to be.' Morton stood and made his way to the door.

Soraya followed. 'Another lead?' she asked.

'No, just help with existing ones,' Morton answered cryptically.

He said goodbye and sped off to the railway station.

It really had been a case of desperate times calling for desperate measures when Morton telephoned Dr Baumgartner at the Forensic Science Service. His call to his former university lecturer was redirected to a mobile as, rather fortuitously for Morton, he was in London for a few days and was 'absolutely delighted' to meet him for a beer. It was always a beer, preferably a local variety, that he would opt for, irrespective of the time of day or the task in hand. He'd once paid for a round of drinks for the whole class of forty students after trooping them down to a nearby pub to study vernacular architecture. Vernacular architecture over a vernacular beer. Morton supposed that it had done the trick; he'd certainly never forgotten that lecture. The call hadn't come entirely out of the blue; he'd been in touch with Dr Baumgartner several times since leaving university, what with various reference requests and attending the odd public seminar that he'd delivered. There had apparently been a sharp rise in the number of people interested in the Forensic Science Service after the glut of CSI programmes that had filled the television schedules in recent years, though Dr Baumgartner was always quick to point out that real life forensic study bore little resemblance to the slick, exacting procedures found onscreen.

They'd agreed to meet in the *Sherlock Holmes* pub off Charing Cross, which Morton considered to be a bit of an irony. He wondered what Holmes and Watson would have made of all the advances in crime detection technology. 'Deoxyribo Nucleic Acid, my dear Watson' didn't quite have the same ring to it.

The only difference that the elapsed time had made to Dr Baumgartner's appearance was that his thick black beard had turned to concrete grey, but for the revealing yellow stain around his mouth. Ten roll-ups a day since he was fourteen, something that he inexplicably sought to tell the class on a regular basis. Apart from that minor change, he looked just the same as the last time that Morton had seen him, which, if he remembered correctly was at a photo analysis conference in Eastbourne three years ago.

They sat at a table mercifully distanced from the rest of the pub's clientele. Morton explained the whole *Coldrick Case*, point by point, without exaggeration or embellishment. The more he summarised the *Coldrick Case*, the more far-fetched it sounded, like some awful Sunday night drama on ITV that he would avoid like the plague. Dr Baumgartner didn't seem in the slightest bit fazed and actually praised Morton for his thoroughness. 'You always were a fastidious bugger at university. I think most genealogists would have thrown in the towel long ago, so you should be congratulated for sticking at it. This is *exactly* your kind of work, make the most of it.' Morton hadn't thought about it like that before. He supposed that, despite the obvious drawbacks to stalking, mugging, explosions, espionage and a throbbing

149

lump on the side of his head, it certainly livened up what could otherwise be a rather dull job.

'And what is that you'd like my help with?' Dr Baumgartner asked.

Morton delved inside his bag and pulled an apologetic face. 'I'm hoping that you'll be able to compare Finlay Coldrick's DNA,' he said, raising the swab stick, 'with Sir David James Peregrine Windsor-Sackville's.' Morton raised the plastic beaker he had procured from the apple-pressing marquee yesterday – entirely illegal of course, but Morton hoped that it was the kind of 'thinking outside the box' of which Dr Baumgartner might approve.

'Fine, no problems at all,' he said, without as much as a flash of hesitation. 'If I were in my lab in Birmingham I could have given you the result in under an hour but it'll be a bit longer than that, I'm afraid. Give me a day or two and we'll see what I can come up with.'

'No worries. I've another request, too, if you don't mind. Could you see what you think about this?' he said, passing over James Coldrick's copper box. It felt a bit presumptuous to be asking his former lecturer to do him such large favours but Morton was desperate. Dr Baumgartner might just be able to offer a new perspective, spot an anomaly that years in the Forensic Science Service had taught him. The main thing was, Morton trusted Dr Baumgartner implicitly.

Dr Baumgartner opened the box and took a cursory glance at the photograph. 'Yes, I'll gladly give you my advice, for what it's worth, but you seem to be doing a pretty exhaustive job by yourself,' he said, setting his thick-rimmed glasses down on the table and giving his beard a contemplative stroke. 'Listen, Morton. You have a doubtless natural genealogical instinct that you need to trust a bit more. You've come all this way by yourself, which is frankly admirable. It's more than I would expect of some of my top people at the FSS. Have faith in your abilities.' He gave his beard another gentle tug, reset his glasses and read the letter. Once he had finished reading, he set the letter down and stared up at the ceiling, his eyes drifting thoughtfully. 'It certainly does come across like she knows the end is nigh,' he finally said. 'Can I take it away and see if I can come up with something?'

'By all means – thank you,' Morton said. 'I'd appreciate some fresh eyes.'

'Great,' he said with a smile, carefully placing the two items back in the box. 'Now, I think it's time for another beer. My shout.'

Morton watched as Dr Baumgartner toddled off to the bar, an eccentric but redoubtable figure. It felt good to Morton to be back in his company and to receive his approval.

Morton was more than happy to have his Pampers box of treats quietly side lined by the news of Juliette's interview. It wasn't like he was relishing telling her that his darts trophy had survived the blast when everything she valued and cherished as sentimental had perished. On the way home he had even considered dumping the damned box and all of its contents and telling her that nothing had survived. That way they were on an equal 'let's start again' footing. He stowed the box at the bottom of the stairs and joined Juliette in the kitchen.

'You'll never guess who conducted the interview?' she said, pouring herself a cold beer and perching herself on the edge of the table. She didn't give him much time to guess but if she had, then Jones and Hawk would have been his first answer. 'Only Olivia Walker!' Nope, it was safe to say that she definitely had not been anywhere near his top-ten-guess list.

'I did say 'Expect the unexpected',' Morton said sagely.

'Yeah, but you didn't tell me to expect *her* to be acting like my best friend. Christ, I was waiting for the camera crew to leap out, she was so sickeningly friendly. She said she was so grateful that I'd spotted her error in not changing the ownership of her car and that she was sorry that I'd been suspended – administrative error - and that I could start back to work there and then if I wanted to. She's been hearing great things about me around the station! I mean, can you believe it?'

Morton couldn't believe it. But then again, with a moment's thought, he actually could believe it. What was that old saying about keeping your friends close and your enemies closer? PCSO Juliette Meade was much more easily monitored within the warm bosom of Kent Police than conducting her own undercover operations whilst being suspended on full pay. They were effectively tagging her.

'Honest to God, Morton,' she continued, 'it was all so relaxed and informal, like we're old friends catching up in Starbucks. 'Do you want a tea or coffee, Juliette? I can't even *think* about functioning until I've got at least a gallon of caffeine running through my veins!" Juliette did an exaggerated impression of a stereotypical toff in a fit of laughter. 'She even had the nerve to say 'I hear you've had a bit of a to-do with your house; you have had a spell of bad luck." Another bout of toff laughter followed by a swig of the beer.

151

A 'to-do' with the house: that was one way of describing it. Morton wondered if now was a good time to say, 'Talking of the house, take a look in the Pampers box and see what treats I've got for you!' No, it wasn't the time. But then again, there never would be a good time.

'So, I'm back to work seven tomorrow morning, speed-trapping as if nothing had ever happened.'

'I thought you wanted to go back?'

'I do, I love my job, but not like this. They're playing me, Morton, surely you can see that?' He could see it, as clear as day.

'Did she talk about me or the *Coldrick Case* at all?' Morton asked.

'Not a single word. Bizarre.'

Morton had other questions to ask but at that moment Jeremy appeared in the kitchen doorway, his face puffed and red as though he'd been crying. Morton stared at him. Was this it? Was it their father? Had he finally succumbed?

'What's the matter?' Juliette asked.

'It's Dad, he's got worse,' Jeremy said, on the verge of tears. Morton could spot the signs a mile off, having made his younger brother cry more times than he could remember. 'He had another heart attack and they've scheduled him for a triple heart bypass tomorrow evening. He's in a terrible state.' Morton could tell that Jeremy wanted to say more but he would burst into tears if he did.

Juliette went over to the doorway and hugged him. After several seconds she pulled back and looked him in the eyes. 'The operation's a good thing, Jeremy. At least it will help him.'

'I know. Even Dad thinks this is the end for him now,' Jeremy said. 'He wants to see you, Morton, before he goes down. He's got something to tell you.'

Morton nodded, his stomach immediately turning itself in knots over whatever chastisement his father wanted to issue.

Jeremy took a beer from the fridge and sat at the table with Morton, his face etched with grief.

Nobody spoke because nobody had anything more to say.

An hour later Juliette called to Morton. 'Morton? Why's one of Mrs McPherson's ornaments in a Pampers box at the bottom of the stairs?'

A few seconds ticked by whilst Morton braced himself for the penny to drop.

And it did.

'Is this it? Is this all that's left? Oh my god.'

152

Chapter Sixteen

Monday

The lump on the side of his head had throbbed for the entire night, maintaining a regular musical beat. When sleep had finally arrived for him, he was plagued by dreams of his father's deathbed confession, a revelation that a somnolent Morton knew was monumental; an utterance which would change everything. The dream started with him getting out of the Mini in the car park of the Conquest Hospital and running through the building at top speed, as concerned nurses wordlessly directed him through the labyrinth of identical wards until he eventually reached his father, just in time for his last moment on earth. But as Morton drew his ear close to his father's mouth to catch those momentous words, the dream restarted and he was back in the car park.

The only answer was to get up and, at precisely four twenty-two, Morton abandoned both sleep and any attempt at catching his father's nocturnal message. If he were remotely superstitious or religious then he would have made a mad dash to the hospital, believing the dream to have been some kind of prophecy, urging him to see his father before it was all too late. But, since he was neither religious nor superstitious he headed down to the kitchen to make a coffee.

He switched on his laptop and sat in the nascent dawn light that filtered in through the patio door and kitchen windows. He had switched on the lights at first, but they gave the room a strange street-lamp hue that was a stark reminder of the unearthly hour at which he had risen. He hoped to goodness that he wasn't turning into his father. For as long as Morton had been aware, his father had got up at five o'clock in the morning. Weekends, days off, holidays, they were all the same: five o'clock prompt. The strangest thing was that he had never needed an alarm, which Morton had always found particularly baffling when the clocks changed. Morton would willingly be placed in front of a firing squad rather than get up at five o'clock in the morning voluntarily. Today was different, of course.

Morton opened the online folder pertaining to the case and clicked on the photograph of James's mother holding him as a baby. He looked into the dark eyes that stared out from the grounds of wartime Charingsby. Whoever she was, she looked genuinely happy. Seeing

Lady Maria Charlotte Windsor-Sackville in the flesh at the Sedlescombe village fete two days ago had done nothing to help Morton ascertain whether or not she could have been James Coldrick's elusive mother. Even his trusted friend Google couldn't help. Evidently she wasn't high profile enough or a close enough relation to Princess Diana to warrant an archive of online images. He had found, though, that her ancestral home of Mote Ridge, buried deep in the Kentish countryside, had been in the care of the National Trust since her father's death in 1969 and was, five days per week, open to the general public. Monday was one such day.

'Morning,' an unfamiliar antipodean voice chirped cheerfully, startling Morton. He turned to see Guy parading into the room wearing nothing more than a pair of white boxer shorts. Two things sprang into Morton's mind simultaneously. One, where did he come from? As far as Morton knew Jeremy went to bed at the same time as him. There were definitely no Australians in the house at that time; surely he would have noticed when he went round checking that the windows were shut and the doors were locked? The second thought that Morton had was how impossibly handsome Guy looked, despite the ungodly hour of the day. 'Jeez, you're chatty in the mornings,' Guy said, filling an empty pint glass with water.

'Sorry,' Morton said, 'you made me jump. I'm still half asleep.'

'What you up to?' he said, leaning in and looking at the laptop screen. 'Ah, Lady Maria. You interested in her?'

'Kind of,' Morton answered dismissively, unsure of how much Jeremy had revealed in pillow talk. Hopefully nothing.

'She's a real feisty bird but she's got a soft spot for me so I tend to get the better jobs around the house. Not that I can complain, decent wages, free apartment in Charingsby; it's alright really,' he said.

Morton wondered if it was potentially a stroke of luck having an employee of the Windsor-Sackvilles standing half-naked in his kitchen. Someone to question about the inner workings of the estate. *But what if he's on their side?* he thought. Morton decided it was a risk worth taking. After all, he was there when Jeremy and Guy met. That would have been impossible for the Windsor-Sackvilles to orchestrate in advance. 'I expect they have a lot of security and police protection, what with their son being Defence Secretary and all,' Morton finally said, dropping a giant unsubtle fishing hook into their conversation.

'I guess so,' Guy answered cryptically. 'All sorts of people come and go; it's hard to keep track of who's who really. I've only been over here for a year so I'm not really familiar with all your politicians.'

'Is there a man called Daniel Dunk that works for them?' Morton asked, sounding as casual as he could.

'Yeah, he's a kind of security bloke, handyman. Bit shady if you ask me, but they rate him. His wife used to work at Charingsby before I started there and I think his dad might have even worked for them way back in the past. I guess his family are part of the furniture. Why's that, you know him?'

'Know of him,' Morton said, touching the memento Dunk had left on the side of his head.

'Well, I'm going back to bed. Night.'

'Night,' Morton replied, wondering if his life could get any stranger. He returned his attention to the laptop and clicked on the 'opening hours' tab for Mote Ridge. Their doors would open in four hours' time and Morton would be there.

A while later, Morton headed into the bedroom and began to dress by the muted light straining through the curtains.

'Just say it, Morton,' Juliette suddenly snapped from the bed, still with her eyes shut, curled into the foetal position.

'Say what?' Morton said innocently, as he pulled on a clean shirt and pair of jeans.

'You're banging and clattering around the room, which usually means you want me to wake up. Just say it. What's happened now?'

'Nothing,' Morton said indignantly, hating the way that Juliette could see through him as though he were a sheet of glass. He hadn't consciously been trying to wake her up. Well, maybe he had. 'I just brought you up a cup of tea. But since you're awake, you'll never guess who just strode into the kitchen half naked at four this morning?'

'Guy,' she said. Not so much a guess as a statement. She still hadn't so much as twitched a muscle.

'How do you know?'

'I let him in last night.'

'Why didn't you tell me?'

'Why would I?'

'Because.'

'We're not sniggering fifteen-year-old girls, Morton. Jeremy's an adult and this is his house, he doesn't need our permission to have people to stay over. Now let me get some sleep.'

'I didn't say he needed our permission, but his usual place of residence is Charingsby after all. Talk about Trojan Horse.'

Juliette made a grunting sound that spelled the end of the conversation.

When Morton arrived at Mote Ridge it seemed to be under siege from every W.I. platoon in the country. At least, that was Morton's impression as he queued behind a neat single-file line of pensioners that snaked towards the ticket office, a plain wooden box manned by two overworked staff. Typical, Morton thought. Of all the days he could choose, he picked today. But then again, he wasn't here for a day out, he was here for research, to find out once and for all if 'M', the woman who gave birth to James Coldrick, was Lady Maria Charlotte.

The trail of old ladies collected their tickets then bee-lined for the tearoom and Morton finally made it to the small window in the side of the ticket office.

In exchange for the ten pounds entrance fee, Morton received a brief guide to Mote Ridge, a map of the extensive grounds and a long hard stare at his ping-pong-ball lump from the beleaguered young girl behind the window.

Morton pocketed the map and crossed a dry moat into the heart of a large, rectangular courtyard with high, flint walls that made the place feel more like a fortress than a home. It had most probably been both at some time in its chequered history. He couldn't imagine growing up somewhere so detached and formal. He wondered at the implications of having more servants living with you than family. What was it that Guy had called Lady Maria? *A feisty old bird*. Translation into English: surly old dragon. Was it really any wonder, though, looking at this place? What kind of an upbringing had she had?

The house itself was an eclectic mixture of architectural styles. The main part comprised of a large stone tower with small lead-framed windows, which reminded Morton of a classic fourteenth-century church. Fused to the tower was a stunning example of a typical medieval hall house – iconic black beams and white wattle and daub plaster with tall mullioned windows. Rising up from the rear were four ornate herringbone brickwork chimneys. Morton stared at the building

156

with a feeling akin to admiration. Such a fine house would usually take him a whole day to explore but today he was here for work.

A sign with 'Entrance' and a large red arrow directed visitors through the one-way labyrinth of the Mote Ridge mansion. Morton sped through manicured guest bedrooms, servants' quarters, kitchens, sculleries and formal dining areas, all replete with original furniture and belongings from the house's heyday, searching for something which would confirm or disprove the idea that Lady Maria was James Coldrick's mother.

Overtaking hordes of ambling visitors, Morton finally reached Lady Maria Charlotte's childhood bedroom. The word that sprang into his mind when he took in the room, was *clinical*. He realised that, of course, it might not have been that way when she was growing up here, that this mocked-up version of her bedroom might be nothing more than a National Trust volunteer second-guessing history. All the furniture, the walnut wardrobe, bedstead, chest of drawers and writing bureau were kept several feet away from the public by a thick sausage of red rope and a multi-lingual sign stating, 'Do Not Cross'.

Morton took another cursory glance around the room and, for the first time, noticed a large sepia photograph hanging beside the door. A label below the photograph read 'Maria Charlotte Spencer, 1921'. He studied the photo carefully and put his training from Dr Baumgartner to work. She was diminutive, shyly looking out at the hundreds of visitors who trooped through her bedroom every week. Her dress was a high-quality pristine-white pearl-lined yoke with a matching ribbon tied neatly atop her dark wavy hair. Behind her was the painted backdrop of a grand staircase, which told Morton that it was a studio portrait. His assessment of the photograph type and clothing agreed with the stated date of the early 1920s. He withdrew his phone, selected the close-up photo of James Coldrick's mother and held it beside the photograph of Lady Maria; he was certain that they were *not* the same person. James Coldrick's mother had much softer, rounder features with a natural beauty that came without the aid of the careful make-up and lighting used in the photograph of Lady Maria. Their eye shapes were, almost imperceptibly, different; Lady Maria's were more pinched and severe than the almond, smiling eyes of James's mother. Although their hair colour and thickness were initially similar, when Morton studied their hairlines, he noticed they were entirely different.

A National Trust volunteer entered the room and he quickly lowered his mobile. Not quite quickly enough. 'What's that you've got

157

there then?' the volunteer asked curiously. She was a fragile-looking woman in her mid to late eighties. Her name badge identified her as Jean.

'Just a picture,' Morton said vaguely. He had hoped to slip quickly and quietly in and out of Mote Ridge but reasoned that it wouldn't do any harm to speak to a volunteer. From past experience, Morton found that these people were usually pretty clued up on the property in which they volunteered. They were often privy to snippets and anecdotes which were absent from the laminated information sheets or guide books. 'Do you think that the woman in this photo could be Lady Maria?' Morton asked, raising the phone level with the portrait photograph.

Jean raised her glasses from the string around her neck but quickly shook her head emphatically. 'No, I wouldn't say so. Do you know when it was taken?'

Morton considered giving the very precise answer of the seventh of May 1944, but settled for, '1944.'

'Definitely not, then. She was in America at that point. If you go over to the Old Stables at the far side of the courtyard, we have a photo exhibition and among them are pictures of her during the war.'

'America? What was she doing there?'

'Her father sent her out there for safety as soon as the Germans started bombing, sometime early in 1940,' Jean said.

'When did she come back to Britain?'

'1945, only a few months prior to her marriage to Sir David.'

'Oh, I see,' Morton said. It was looking highly unlikely that she was James Coldrick's mother. There was only one further possibility, and that was that she gave birth in America, which would explain why there was no birth entry in the English registers. Morton posed the question of a possible child to Jean, who burst into laughter.

She seemed almost offended at the very idea. 'Heavens above! What on earth made you ask me that? Goodness me, no, absolutely not. No,' she said. 'Her first child was Philip, whom she gave birth to in 1946. Heavens!'

Morton shrugged. 'Just an idea.' He left Jean in a fit of giggles and made his way back towards the courtyard. He wouldn't be fulfilling the *forensic* part of his job title if he didn't take a look at the photo exhibition. On his way across the courtyard Morton spotted the gift shop. He ducked inside and picked up a brand new pair of binoculars to replace his father's pair that had inadvertently become another casualty of the *Coldrick Case*.

He pulled out the map of Mote Ridge and made his way to the Old Stables, a converted stable block containing a potted history of the Spencer family and their ties with Mote Ridge. Morton moved among a gaggle of pensioners, closely reading the frankly over-the-top quantity of material relating to Princess Diana, despite her only connection to Mote Ridge being that her great great great grandfather had been born there. It was hardly her ancestral seat, but the pensioners seemed to be lapping up the displays, cooing over pictures of the infant princes. Photographs of the infant Prince George seemed to be particularly popular with the visitors.

Morton passed by the information pertaining to centuries-old members of the Spencer family until he came to Lady Maria. Just as Jean had said, there were four photographs of her in America during the war. The sceptic in him said that the photos had nothing in them identifiably American, but that wasn't the point. The point was that the woman in photos was the same as the girl in the portrait he had just seen, the same as the old, doddery lady at the Sedlescombe Fete on Saturday; *not* James Coldrick's mother. There was no doubt now in Morton's mind: M did not stand for Maria Charlotte Windsor-Sackville née Spencer.

Feeling dejectedly back at square one with the question of James Coldrick's parentage, he left Mote Ridge.

Morton was relieved to find that it wasn't a case of *déjà vu* he'd experienced the previous night. He arrived at the Conquest Hospital and nothing he had dreamt about had actually occurred. He parked a long way from the main entrance, paid the parking fee and made his way to the Atkinson Ward. What he hadn't expected, however, was to find a tattooed skinhead ('Matt Hargreaves,' the dry-wipe board above his head announced) in place of his father. Morton stared at him and received a snarl that, if Matt Hargreaves hadn't been wired up to so many machines, including an oxygen mask, would have undoubtedly turned into a '*What are you staring at?*'

It was like he'd stumbled onto the wrong ward. Maybe he had, they were all replicas of each other, after all. But no, it was the correct ward. The men in the neighbouring beds were the same men as before, watching their televisions, oblivious to Morton's growing panic. *Was that it?* Had his father died and nobody had contacted him? Maybe his phone had run out of battery. He checked it and it still had three bars of power and a full signal. No missed calls. No text messages. *Surely Jeremy would have called? Maybe he'd phoned Juliette first?* He stared at his father's replacement.

'What?' Matt Hargreaves managed to rasp angrily.

'Where's my father gone? He was here.'

Matt Hargreaves growled something and turned his head toward the window, as if he couldn't quite cope with life if he were unable to shout or head-butt anyone who irritated him.

Morton was rooted to the spot, staring disbelievingly at him.

'Hello? You look for Mr Farrier?' a deep, heavy Eastern-European accent said to him. He turned to see a tall shaven-haired nurse with a kindly smile on her face. He nodded and waited for the worst. 'He go down for heart operation.'

'Oh,' was all Morton could manage to say. He left the ward and dialled Jeremy, who was three floors above eating a cold Cornish pasty and drinking a hot cup of tea.

'They had a cancellation, so they brought Dad's op forward,' Jeremy said, thrusting the last of the ketchup-drenched pasty into his mouth. Morton wondered if cancellation was a euphemism for death.

'How long's he been down?' Morton asked, sitting opposite Jeremy in the deserted cafeteria.

'About two hours now,' he answered with his mouth full. 'It'll probably take another hour.'

'How was he before he went down?' Morton asked, suddenly feeling nauseous.

'Terrified, but then so would I be if I had to have my ribcage cranked open and my heart stopped.' Morton imagined his father right now on the operating table, neither dead nor alive, occupying some half-way space in the universe while fate or God or whatever, decided which way he was going to go. 'He was actually more gutted that he hadn't had a chance to speak to you yet,' Jeremy added.

'Did he say what it was about?' Morton asked.

'No, no idea. I wouldn't worry about it, though.'

'No,' Morton answered. But he was worried. He needed to hear whatever his father had had to say to him.

'Do you want a drink?' Jeremy asked, standing and downing the last of his tea. 'I think we could be here a while.'

'Coffee please. Strong.'

As Jeremy stood at the counter and filled two polystyrene cups, Morton's mobile rang. It was Dr Baumgartner. He told Morton that the results of the DNA test would be back by the morning and he wanted to arrange a meeting to talk about the contents of the copper box before his return to Birmingham on Wednesday. They agreed to meet tomorrow afternoon, back in the *Sherlock Holmes*, which seemed as good a place as any to learn the truth about whether or not Sir David Windsor-Sackville was James Coldrick's father. With Morton's certainty over Lady Maria not being James Coldrick's mother, he still could not rule out Sir David being his father. *Something* tied the Coldricks to the Windsor-Sackvilles, why else would they have spent the best part of seventy years hiding the past?

Morton ended the call wondering at the subtle undercurrent of intrigue he'd detected in Dr Baumgartner's voice. But Morton knew better than to push for a premature assessment. 'Never, ever, ever, ever, ever, hurry your work,' Dr Baumgartner would say on a regular basis to slapdash students presenting half-baked case files to him.

Jeremy returned with the two drinks. 'Everything okay? You look like you're not really with it.'

Morton snapped back from his daydream. 'Yeah, just thinking about Father.'

Jeremy offered a comforting smile. 'He does love you, you know, Morton.'

'I know.'

And so they waited.

They had finished their drinks and moved down to the ICU waiting room, which was the mirror image of every other waiting room in the hospital. Their conversation had naturally run dry and the two men sat in comfortable silence, each engrossed in their own thoughts. Morton wondered what was going through his adoptive brother's head. His own mind leapt like a manic frog between disparate problems. He wondered how Juliette had got on with her first day back at work. He imagined that the senior officers in the station would be keeping a close watch, monitoring her every move. He would ring her once he'd heard news of his father but who knew when that would be? Nobody was in any hurry to talk to them, it seemed. He felt like going over to the nurses' station and asking how soon his father would be able to talk; but that seemed a rather crass and frivolous question to be asking of a man with a ten-inch hole in his chest and no heartbeat.

Morton wondered if he'd dozed off and was in a bizarre dream when he heard the faint opening bars of *Dancing Queen*, steadily increasing in volume. He glanced around the room and realised that he was fully awake and that there could be no doubt over his brother's sexuality when Jeremy fumbled in his pocket and pulled out his mobile. He answered the phone and Abba stopped singing. It only took a few sentences of half conversation for Morton to realise that he was talking to Guy. Jeremy was evidently rebutting a suggestion of going out tonight.

'Go, Jeremy, it's fine. I can wait here,' Morton interrupted.

Jeremy covered the handset. 'No, I'd rather wait here.'

'Jeremy, he's not going anywhere and I've got your mobile number. Go out. Have fun.'

'Sure?'

'Sure.'

It felt as though he had been alone in the waiting room for several hours before a young, female nurse appeared in the doorway with a smile on her face. Morton hoped she wasn't one of those people with that condition where they smiled after bad news. His best friend at university, Jon, had burst into hysterical laughter when he was told that his parents had been killed in a coach crash in Switzerland. He literally couldn't stop smiling all day long and Morton wondered if he was secretly pleased that his parents were dead. Morton only realised that wasn't the case when Jon was incarcerated in a mental hospital the following day.

'Okay, so the operation went very well. It took a bit longer than we would have liked,' the nurse said and Morton glanced at the clock. Jeremy had been told it would take around three hours. His father had been operated on for four and a half hours. 'We've moved him to ICU, which is standard procedure after major surgery like this. You can see him but he won't come round from the anaesthetic for some time.'

Morton followed the nurse into ICU. He found his father, mouth agape and milky eyes half-opened so that he resembled the living dead. He was hooked up to an even greater quantity of beeping and flashing machines than before.

He stood watching his father's chest rise and fall mechanically beneath the off-white crust of bandages strapped to his torso. Wherever his father was right now in the universe, his body looked peaceful. There was still a large part of Morton that believed his father

162

would never recover, but he realised for the first time standing there that he wanted him to pull through; he wanted his father to live.

'You can go in and see him,' the nurse said.

Morton sat down beside his father and tentatively said hello. He spoke quietly because it felt odd talking to someone who you knew wouldn't respond. They always said on television medical dramas that the person could hear you and that familiar voices might help them to recover. That was all well and good on television, but the reality of sitting within earshot of the nurse whilst he spoke to an inanimate object left him feeling rather stupid.

He gently picked up his father's gelid, bloodless hand. A large black bruise splayed out from the entry point of the IV drip in his left hand. His skin had turned into thin tea-stained paper, sagging into the hollows of his cheeks and eye sockets. Morton looked pitifully at the frail man who had raised him. Despite everything, he still couldn't quite tally the word *father* with his emotions; it was like there was a link missing somewhere in the chain. *Could that link be nothing more than a separate DNA structure? Or was there more to it than that?* His father's Victorian style of child-rearing couldn't have helped matters, but then it had done nothing to damage the relationship between him and Jeremy. If anything was going to damage their father-son bond, then it would be Jeremy's sexuality. Morton just couldn't see his father, a man who frowned upon sex before marriage, sitting at the breakfast table eating his daily fry-up whilst a half-naked Australian man draped himself over Jeremy.

'What did you have to tell me?' Morton asked softly. He glanced over at the nurse, who was either oblivious to him, or she was acting as though she was. She must see this kind of thing all the time, Morton reasoned. *Just talk*, he told himself, but the words wouldn't come. If he was going to talk to an inert object, then there was no point in asking questions and waiting for a reply; he just had to speak.

He chose to talk to his lifeless father about when his mother died, which he thought, from a psychological point of view, was very revealing. Of all the subjects, in all the world that he could have chosen to talk about, he chose what he considered to be the defining moment of his life. The point where it all changed. When everything he had known was turned upside down. A moment in history that had never been discussed.

After his father had told him that he was adopted, Morton shrank inside a cocooned version of himself, perfunctorily carrying on with life

163

as if nothing had ever happened. Over the years he had wondered at the timing of the revelation. Had his father deliberately dropped the hit-and-run statement into the emotional turmoil of his mother's death, knowing that it would provide a convenient smokescreen? He thought he could remember his father muttering something about wanting to tell him before, but the hours that followed boiled down to a handful of crystal-clear words; the rest a blur. There followed brief empty conversations with his father, where the topic was skirted around like a decaying animal in the road. That slowly-rotting carcass was his relationship with his father and his mother's tarnished memory. It took him two years to summon the courage to ask his father *the* question. It was on his return home from the first term at university and Morton had found that his father had, for the first time since his wife's death, lavished the house in Christmas decorations and was bounding around it with renewed zeal. Morton had barely set down his bags when he decided to snatch the presented opportunity of festive cheer and pose the question as to who his real parents were. He should have anticipated his father's reaction. A long agonising silence, in which Morton hoped that his father's clenching jaw was simply concentration, was followed by the single longest diatribe Morton had ever heard from his father's lips. Morton's scheduled two-week break came to a sharp end after a record hour and a quarter before he caught the train to Jon's house and spent a peaceful happy Christmas with his family. When he had returned home the following summer, Morton found that his bedroom had been stripped of *everything* and turned into a guest-room. 'Well, after you absconded at Christmas, we didn't think you were coming home again,' his father said. And so he resided in the guest-room for the duration of the summer, spending as little time as possible there. His father ended the summer holidays by informing him that, in his opinion, university had turned him into a sulky introvert and maybe it hadn't been a good idea to go there after all. Morton's response, which he knew retrospectively to have been spiteful, was to ask who his real father was. Jeremy then waded into the argument and informed Morton that he'd broken his father's heart and the subject was never to be raised again. And it wasn't.

But now his father had had his heart repaired.

Maybe it was time to ask the question again.

Chapter Seventeen

Tuesday

For the first time since he had been attacked, Morton wasn't woken by the pain from the lump on his head. This morning he was woken by the welcome aroma of coffee. Good quality strong filter coffee, wafting up to his bedroom. Juliette was already up. He heard her laughing at something downstairs and he sat up in bed to listen. *Was she on the phone?* No, she was talking to Jeremy and Guy, who'd evidently stayed the night again. Christ, Morton thought, he really was turning into his father, casting judgements on his brother's relationship.

A round of goodbyes downstairs was followed by the closing of the front door. Morton looked at the alarm clock: nine fifty-five. There was just enough time to grab a bite to eat, take a shower and catch up with Juliette before she went off to work. He was curious to know how her first day had gone yesterday. He suspected either brilliantly or terribly. There was rarely a grey middle-ground where Juliette was concerned. She'd been sound asleep by the time he'd returned from the hospital last night; once he'd begun pouring out thirty-nine years of angst at his father, it was hard to stop. It flowed out of him like an unstoppable reservoir of anguish, whose dam had been unceremoniously ruptured. He'd quickly become oblivious to the nursing staff, the outpouring continuing until he was entirely emotionally drained. His reservoir was empty and he felt utter relief at having said everything he'd ever wanted to say to his unconscious father. Then he left the hospital.

Morton climbed out of bed, unable to ignore the coffee aroma any longer. Juliette was in the kitchen in her work uniform, sipping a drink. 'Morning,' she said cheerfully. 'You were late at the hospital last night.'

'I decided to make use of the fact the old man couldn't answer me back, so I told him everything I've ever felt. *Ever*,' he replied, pouring himself a coffee. 'He obviously agreed with me because he didn't argue back.'

Juliette smiled. 'How is he? How did the operation go?'

'Fine, as well as can be expected. He'll be in ICU for a while then he'll move to a regular ward,' Morton said. He couldn't quite bring himself to say the next part, 'and then home', because that would mean he and Juliette would have to face up to the reality of being homeless. It was funny, they'd not once talked about getting a new place, they'd just replaced some clothes and moved in to his father's house, as if that was the most natural thing to do in the world. It was like they were flying the nest but in reverse. He changed the subject. 'How was your first day back at work?'

Juliette raised her eyebrows in a 'there's a story' kind of way. 'Suspiciously fantastic,' she said. 'Usually the Chief doesn't have much time for the PCSOs, but he was totally OTT with me, asking me how I was and actually listening to my answer, rather than nodding and wandering off in his own little world. Oh, and they split me and Dan, my usual partner up, and paired me with straight-laced Roger who does *everything* exactly by the book. The bosses hate him, but they know he wouldn't dare put a foot wrong.'

'Unless you corrupt him,' Morton said.

'Believe me, straight-laced Roger is incorruptible.'

'So nothing new with the *Coldrick Case* then?'

'Not that I've been told, no, but I'll keep my ear to the ground. I could hardly log on and start fishing on my first day back. Hopefully I'll see someone involved in the investigation later on. What have you got planned for today, then? Anymore illegal activities?'

'Hopefully not. I'm meeting Dr Baumgartner for *the* results.'

Juliette nodded but Morton could tell she didn't have the foggiest which results he was talking about.

The train from Hastings station took an hour and thirty-two minutes to reach Charing Cross. Morton had spent the journey on his phone, re-examining photos and documents from the *Coldrick Case,* seeing if there was anything he had missed or overlooked. If Dr Baumgartner had nothing with the DNA or copper box, he was well and truly stumped. No further leads to pursue. The outcome of the case depended on this meeting. Morton marched purposefully along Northumberland Street, the gold lettering of the pub name coming into view. As he approached the pub, he began to worry. *What if Dr Baumgartner had been mugged? Or had his hotel room ransacked? Or worse?* The people working for the Windsor-Sackvilles had proven that they would stop at nothing to prevent him from discovering the truth. He opened the door and glanced around. There was no sign of him. Morton looked at his watch: they were due to have met five minutes ago. *Should he be worried?* It was only five minutes, after all.

The barman looked across at him. 'Can I help you, mate?'

166

'There haven't been any messages left for Morton Farrier, have there?'

The barman shook his head. 'No, mate, sorry.' Morton's mind went into overdrive, recreating all manner of possible fates that could have consumed his former university lecturer. *How could he have been so stupid as to drag him into all this mess?* It was bad enough that Jeremy and Juliette were involved. He looked at his watch again – another two minutes had passed. A month ago Morton wouldn't have thought twice about ordering the drinks, grabbing a table and waiting patiently. Now his heart was racing faster than if he'd just sprinted to the pub. It was ridiculous, but this was what the *Coldrick Case* had done to him; reduced him to a nervous wreck. He thought back over his previous jobs, scanning for a single hint of danger among them. He came up with nothing more than a heated row with a parking attendant after over-running at Eastbourne Library by three minutes. Perilous indeed.

'Morton!' It was Dr Baumgartner, standing in the doorway looking completely unfazed, unmugged, and undead. 'Not late am I?' his chirpy voice boomed across the room as he extended his hand to Morton.

'No, you're not late,' Morton said with a wry smile, shaking the extended hand. 'Beer?'

'Oh yes, that would be smashing. Same as last time.'

Morton carried two pints over to the table that Dr Baumgartner had chosen. They exchanged pleasantries about Dr Baumgartner's hotel and Morton's now marble-sized lump before Dr Baumgartner cut straight down to business. 'Right, the DNA test,' he said, with a gentle tug of his grey beard. 'It came back this morning and the chances of your boy Finlay and old Windsor-Sackville sharing a common ancestor within the last forty-thousand years are somewhere in the region of a billion to one.'

Morton nodded. The firm, concrete news that the Windsor-Sackvilles and the Coldricks were completely unrelated hit him hard, knocking him back to square one. Yet deep down, he had known it all along; his gut reaction, his 'natural genealogical instinct' had told him so.

'In layman's terms,' Dr Baumgartner simplified, 'not that a forensic genealogist is in *any way* a layman, but they are quite frankly genetic chalk and cheese. All forty-three markers we tested came back negative.' He must have seen something like disappointment on Morton's face as he felt the need to add, 'sorry.'

'No, it's fine,' Morton said, trying his damndest to stop his mind going into free-fall. All of that work for nothing. It was too late; his thoughts exploded in a hundred directions as he considered all that he'd done and had done to him was in vain. 'Well, that's it then. I've nowhere else to take it.'

'Morton, that's not what I expect from a first-class student like you,' Dr Baumgartner said, his scraggy eyebrows pulled tight into a grimace. He was being deadly serious.

'But that's it, there's nowhere else to go.'

'Don't you want to know about these before you throw in the towel so hastily?' Dr Baumgartner said, placing the copper box on the table. 'Very interesting indeed.'

Morton sat up, ready to listen.

Dr Baumgartner placed the headshot photograph of James Coldrick's mother on the table between them and pulled out a large, heavyweight magnifying glass. The exact same one he'd used during his time lecturing at university. He placed the magnifying glass on the photo and raised his eyebrows suggestively to Morton, just like he used to at university. Dr Baumgartner had never been a fan of spoon-feeding his students. If they didn't have the skills to find the answers for themselves then they were in the wrong field. Simple as that. Morton leant forwards and studied the image. He'd looked at it over and over again – the last time just twenty minutes ago on the train here. There was nothing new to see, no reflection in her eyes, nothing at all in the background. It simply was a photograph of her head and shoulders. She wore small gold studs in her ears and some kind of necklace. What had he missed? Maybe nothing, maybe this was a bizarre lesson in learning when to admit defeat. No, that really wasn't Dr Baumgartner's style at all. There was no such thing as defeat in his book. Plus, his smug face made it clear that he knew something. Morton looked up for further guidance, another clue.

'Why do you think the photo is cut like that?' Dr Baumgartner asked. 'The sides and top are neatly trimmed equidistanced around the woman's head, yet the bottom slopes sharply from left to right. What has the person who cut this photo tried to remove?'

God, it really was like being back in his classroom. 'Her clothes?'

'Exactly! She was wearing something that would identify her immediately, but whoever cut this picture left us one very large clue around her neck.'

168

Morton studied the photograph. What was he not getting? A simple gold chain culminated in a pendant of some kind, ninety per cent of which was not in the photo. Only three narrow bars with rounded edges stacked one above the other, slightly offset remained. 'A bird's wingtip?' Morton ventured uncertainly.

'Yes!' Dr Baumgartner screeched loudly. 'Any particular bird?'

'Eagle?' Morton guessed, still not getting Dr Baumgartner's excitement.

It all became clear when Dr Baumgartner slid a piece of paper across the table. Morton unfolded it and was stunned.

'Christ.'

'Still want to give in?'

'No.'

It felt as if he had undergone a transformation, as though he was a fully re-subscribed born-again genealogist. Make that a born-again *forensic* genealogist. The distinction was important. '*Deidre*, how are you today?' Morton had greeted brashly as he burst whirlwind-like into East Sussex Archives. 'These are literally *flying* from your shelves,' he said emphatically, shoving a great stack of his business cards into the holder made vacant since his previous visit. Evidently Morton's greeting was like a tranquilliser to her cold black heart because she stared, dumbstruck at him, unable to lance him with an icy jab. He scribbled a high-speed entry in the admissions book and bounced up the stairs into the search room. He had wondered what he would say if he were confronted by Max Fairbrother. He still held a great mistrust for the man and was sure that he hadn't told him everything he knew. As it turned out, it didn't matter; Max was, according to Quiet Brian, currently enjoying two weeks' leave in Florence. A fortnight in southern Italy sounded like the most perfect post-*Coldrick Case* antidote Morton could think of. He'd reclassified the Coldrick job back up to the *Coldrick Case* in light of the evidence found dangling around James Coldrick's mother's neck. 'The *Reichsadler*,' Dr Baumgartner had told him, having handed him an A4 printout of the full pendant. The bird's wingtip, the only part visible in the photograph, belonged to an eagle clutching a wreath of oak leaves, inside of which was a large, unequivocal swastika. James Coldrick's mother was wearing the Nazi party emblem around her neck. In Britain. During the peak of World War Two. The *Coldrick Case* had suddenly taken a giant step forward into the unknown. Dr Baumgartner had passed Morton the phone number of one Professor Geoffrey Daniels, who worked at the National Archives of Berlin and whose field of expertise was Germany and the Second World War, just in case he needed it.

Quiet Brian told Morton where to find the files containing information on enemy aliens, as Germans and Austrians had been called during the war, as if they had all arrived via a UFO from Mars rather than on a boat from mainland Europe.

Morton withdrew a chunky folder from the shelf and took a seat in the crowded search room. He read, with a sudden and unexpected twinge of sympathy, through the countless and increasingly aggressive directives and instructions from the Home Office to the local County Council regarding what to do with anyone of German or Austrian descent. Was James Coldrick's mother one of the thousands of aliens rounded up within forty-eight hours of Churchill coming to power in 1940? It seemed so unlikely, somehow. He flicked past various letters and pieces of correspondence marked 'confidential' or 'secret' until he reached the files that he had come to see: 'Home Office: Aliens Department: Aliens Personal Files HO 382.' He quickly scribbled down the reference number, located the relevant (and alarmingly bulky) film and hurried over to the bank of microfilm readers, only one of which was vacant – the rest having been commandeered by family historians.

Morton threaded up the reel and wound on to the first page, which contained a brief synopsis of the microfilm's contents. He was sure that he could feel the cool surge of adrenalin rush into his heart. Could it *really* be that the answer to the Coldrick's ancestral history was contained within the fat celluloid roll in front of him? *Really?* A small part of him didn't want to read on, didn't want to risk another dead end. He'd given everything to the *Coldrick Case* and if the answer wasn't here then he didn't think that he had the stamina to continue. There was a lot to be said for the predictability of mundane family history research jobs.

He took a deep breath and read the first page on the film. *The Vice Chief of the Imperial General Staff said that, in the light of the possibility of invasion, it was very desirable that all enemy aliens in counties in the south-east should be interned. No doubt ninety per cent of such aliens were well disposed to this country, but it was impossible to pick out the small proportion of aliens who probably constituted a dangerous element. In the circumstances, the only course seemed to be that all aliens in this area should be interned for the present. The number is probably four to five thousand. These aliens should be categorised thus:*

170

'A' are known Nazis who are interned immediately, 'B' are the doubtful ones who will have restrictions placed on them and 'C' were all the rest, mostly Jewish refugees.

Morton desperately hoped that James Coldrick's mother would appear in the 'C' category, constituting one of the ninety percent of aliens 'well-disposed to this country', yet he doubted that a Jewish refugee would have been willingly photographed with a swastika around her neck.

He wound the film on and discovered that the files were arranged haphazardly and in no particular order. At first he read each and every word on the record cards. After all, he had no idea of James Coldrick's mother's name and he hoped that it would be the detail that would finally reveal the truth.

It was going to be a long search, which might well stretch into days huddled at a microfilm reader.

After several hours of fruitless searching, Morton began to skim-read the entries, his eyelids gravitating towards earth, like shop blinds at closing time. He looked at the clock: in little over two hours' time Deidre Latimer would take great pleasure in shooing him away.

He ploughed on, but it had become an effort to stay focussed and the names that he read received diminished process-time in his brain. *Fritz Karthauser, Rozsa Balogh, Charlottenne Hellman, Eva Loewenheim, Walter Tauchert, Hans Hacault, Magda Mueller, Leni Raubal, Geli Reitsh…* the names skewed and twisted in his addled mind. He wasn't even sure if Leni and Geli were men or women. He ached all over and the idea of making a note of where he'd reached in the reel, packing up for the day and returning home and snuggling up with Juliette took hold. There was no guarantee that he'd find James Coldrick's mother anyway. She could easily have been one of the names he had read, having blithely skipped over her. Then he thought of Dr Baumgartner and the way that he held Morton in such high esteem. What would he think about him struggling to stay awake and casually casting his eyes over the records, as if he were reading the Sunday papers, wanting to give up halfway through? He'd be mortified, that's what. Morton wasn't that person. He needed to do this properly.

He switched off the machine, stood, and contracted his tight leg and arm muscles. A brisk walk and a shot of caffeine would see him through the last quarter of the reel. He strode boldly past Deidre Latimer, across the car park and down to Nero's. He had a plentiful choice of vacant seats, but Morton chose to sit in the same comfy leather armchair where he had sat the last time he was here, where Max had finally confessed the snippet of information about William Dunk that had led him back here again. There was something oddly comforting in sitting in the same place, in remembering Max pulling apart his double-chocolate muffin, casually revealing his corruption. Morton drank his coffee, feeling like an echo of himself that day, a third-party observer watching the discussion taking place again.

A loud crash and sound of smashing crockery as a tray of drinks hit the floor snapped Morton from his reveries. He was back in the room, back to the present time. He finished his drink and hurried back to the archives.

He returned to the microfilm reader with a renewed zeal and desire to find the answer. He'd been scanning the reel for several minutes when his mobile rang. Damn, in his haste to minimise contact with Deidre Latimer in the lobby he'd forgotten to switch off his phone, and now the amplified iPhone ringtone was attracting the attention of the dozen or so disgruntled researchers, who were currently glaring at him as though he'd just committed a terrible atrocity. Leaving your mobile switched on *was* a kind of atrocity here, he supposed. He elongated their pain as he deliberated whether or not to answer: it was Jeremy, he had to answer. Just in case.

'Hi,' Morton whispered.

'Morton, just thought I'd tell you that Dad's been moved back to the Atkinson Ward. He seems to be doing well.'

'Oh, thank God,' Morton said, genuinely relieved that his father seemed to be pulling through.

'The only trouble is that he keeps asking when you're going to come in.'

'Okay, tell him I'll be there this evening,' Morton answered. Whatever it was that his father wanted to say had better be worth it, especially now that Quiet Brian was making a beeline towards him with a condemning look on his face. At that moment Morton's eyes did an involuntary double-take at the microfilm reader and both Jeremy's tinny voice and Quiet Brian's admonishing whisper sharply faded away, the aural equivalent of them blurring into the background.

He'd found her.

Surname: Koldrich
Forename: Marlene
Date and place of birth: 18 November 1913, Berlin
Nationality: German
Police Regn. Cert. No: 470188
Address: Sedlescombe, Sussex

The committee have decided that the alien should be placed in Category 'A' – sent to Lingfield Internment Camp immediately.
Date: 20 May 1940

M stood for Marlene. Marlene Koldrich, the un-anglicised name of James Coldrick's mother, Peter Coldrick's grandmother and Finlay Coldrick's great grandmother. He wasn't surprised to see that she was classified as a category A alien; it kind of went with the territory of wearing a swastika in World War Two. He hit the print button and watched excitedly as a black and white copy spewed from the machine. He snatched the photocopy and considered his next move. He supposed it would be to find out what records still existed for Lingfield Internment Camp and take it from there. He'd ask Quiet Brian, he always seemed to be a mine of military history information. For no reason other than to be completely satisfied that the entry was complete, Morton wound the film reel on one page and was startled by the short entry.

The committee have decided to declassify Marlene Koldrich
Date: 27 May 1940

Morton reread the entry. From category A to declassified in one week. How did *that* happen? The more he thought of it, the more likely it seemed to him that *someone* in high authority had pulled the right strings. Someone in government, perhaps. He doubted that Marlene had ever even made it to Lingfield Internment Camp in the intervening week.

Morton left the archives, carefully clutching his two printouts, his head in a tailspin. What on earth could have possessed the Regional Advisory Committee to take such action? After a grovelling apology to Quiet Brian for using his mobile, Morton asked if there were any other records that might help him, but Quiet Brian seemed quite certain that there were none that had survived. Morton had briefly considered calling up street directories or electoral registers for Sedlescombe in 1940, but remembered that they weren't produced during wartime. There was also no 1941 census taken. National security and all that.

As he crossed the car park towards the Mini, Morton pulled out the torn corner of a newspaper from his back pocket on which Dr Baumgartner had scribbled the phone number of Professor Geoffrey Daniels. The phone rang for several seconds before a gruff, disgruntled voice answered. When Morton explained that he was a very good friend of Gerald Baumgartner the voice swiftly softened.

Someone had evidently noticed that the waiting room at the Conquest Hospital wasn't a particularly great advert for the place. The blue plastic chairs had been wiped, the payphone mended and a colourful set of three posters now adorned the walls. Morton gazed across the glossy attempts to educate and inform the ill and injured public. The first one showed four Russian Matryoshka nesting dolls standing beside one another, painted as a father, mother, son and daughter. Above the family a tagline read 'Diabetes often runs in families.' The next featured a middle-aged distorted face with accompanying stroke advice. The last poster gave frank information on the symptoms of bowel cancer.

He carried the cup of tea, requested by his father, to the Atkinson Ward and placed it on the cabinet beside him, receiving an appreciative nod from him.

'How's work?' his father asked in a raspy, weak voice. Jeremy had said on the phone that their father was doing well but Morton had seen no evidence of it so far. He looked pasty and sallow, a haunted version of his pre-operative state. Morton still couldn't quite believe that he wasn't at death's door.

'Very busy,' Morton said.

His father nodded. 'I suppose that's why you haven't been here much.' It was a rhetorical question; Morton didn't need to answer it. Actually, it was bait and Morton did answer it.

'I was here last night, actually.'

'I know,' he answered airily.

How could he know? Morton wondered. Had Jeremy or one of the nurses told him that Morton had kept a stoic bedside vigil? Or had his father heard every word of his extensive tirade? He didn't want to ask.

He just wanted to know whatever it was that his father's cracked and sore lips were struggling to say.

With what seemed the greatest effort in the world, his father lifted his hand and placed it on Morton's. He gripped Morton's four fingers tightly. 'I've got something to tell you,' his sandpapery voice said, his eyes meeting Morton's earnestly for the first time. Morton knew that he was about to be told something big, something life-changing. 'It's about your past. It's time you knew.'

Chapter Eighteen

Wednesday

Well, the kitchen table of the Farrier residence sure was an uncomfortable place to be. Morton, Juliette, Jeremy and Guy sat half-heartedly eating their way through the pile of toast in the centre of the table, an awkward silence lingering over the cafetière that sat between them. Morton felt sorry for Jeremy and Juliette; he knew that their brains were being eaten alive with questions that they wanted answering but that neither of them could quite articulate. Questions that he himself had asked his father last night. He felt most sorry, though, for the bewildered-looking Guy, trying - and failing - to make the three stunned, voiceless people at the table engage in small talk. The poor chap had even resorted to commenting on the weather. He'd only arrived moments before breakfast and hadn't been privy to the long and emotionally intense night that had followed Morton's arrival back from the Conquest Hospital. He'd left there in a state of shock: every fragment of his childhood had been pulverised and mashed up beyond all recognition by that one, short conversation with his father; as far as he was concerned, he had no past. That small box in his brain where he stored painful memories or parts of his life that he'd rather forget had exploded with more force than had his own house. Only this time, there were no salvageable trinkets or trophies.

Morton had left his father's bedside with the intention of driving straight home to clear his head but when he saw that *The Harrow* pub was open, he parked up and went inside. He felt like a walking cliché as he downed two double whiskeys. But what he really sought from the pub was to be a faceless blur in the corner, giving the news and the alcohol time to sink in. It had been many years since he'd last drunk in there and so he sat, incognito, stewing over what he had just been told. 'Your biological mother was raped at the age of sixteen,' his father had said, matter-of-factly. 'And in those days you didn't just pop a pill and the baby was gone, you put it up for adoption, which is exactly what she did. And *that's* how your mother and I came to have you.' The way that his father emphasised the word *that's* had made it sound as though it were the end of a long, self-explanatory speech that required no further questioning. And, as if to underline the point, his father closed his eyes and emitted a deep satisfying sigh, a crushing weight evidently having been lifted from his reconditioned heart. Over the years, Morton had convinced himself that nature was indeed stronger than nurture and that no part of his character attributes, or what had made him the person he was today, stemmed from his adoptive parents, which now left him with the stark and numbing realisation that fifty percent of his biological make-up came from a rapist. And to think that he was embarrassed at school to say that his father worked in a hardware store. He imagined the reaction of standing up and telling his class that his father was a man who liked to force schoolgirls to have sex with him.

'So, you knew my mother then?' Morton ventured.

'Of course I knew her, I married her, didn't I?'

'My *biological* mother,' Morton clarified.

For a brief moment it appeared as though someone had pressed a pause button on his father, for he lay frozen without so much as a flicker of movement. Even his glassy eyes were devoid of animation. As Morton was assimilating the possibility that his father had just pegged out in front of him, right at the critical revelatory moment, which would have been just the kind of thing likely to happen to him, he turned and met Morton's anxious eyes. 'Yes, we knew her.' Another lengthy pause. *God, this was like pulling teeth*, Morton thought. 'Who was she?' he asked, his whole body physically aching to know the answer that he'd waited almost twenty years to hear.

'She was just a girl, a *sixteen*-year-old girl.'

Morton suffered another pause. 'But what was her name?'

'Her name's irrelevant,' he said, now barely audible. His eyes closed again and turned his head. 'All long ago in the past.'

'Please,' Morton pleaded gently.

'I need to rest.'

'Please,' he repeated, alarmed to discover that he was on the verge of tears. He couldn't say anything else; he was emotionally parched.

His father was unresponsive and Morton stood to leave. And then the answer came. Without fanfare and even without his father opening his eyes or moving a muscle – just five simple words.

'Her name was Margaret Farrier.'

Morton ordered a pint of beer and tried to imagine his Aunty Margaret aged sixteen. He was sure that he'd seen photographs of her beaming brightly in her school uniform, a moment captured on camera before her innocence was barbarically stolen by Morton's natural father. It was odd but he felt a strange level of responsibility for his biological father's actions. The flip side to that, however, was the simple truth that if his father hadn't raped Aunty Margaret then he wouldn't be here now. It was a sickening and horrifying feeling to know that he owed his entire existence to a rapist.

It took a second pint for Morton to go home and muster the courage to go back to break the news to Juliette and Jeremy. The irony of finally discovering a latent fraternal bond with Jeremy, to now discover that he was actually his cousin, was not lost on Morton as he neared the house.

He tried his hardest to put on something resembling a brave face. Even just an ordinary face would have done. He wanted to stride into the kitchen confidently and say, 'Hi, everything okay? You'll *never* guess what I've just found out!' *Wasn't that how his family did things?* Dropped emotional bombshells and then ran away? He was sure that his father would have walked away if it were at all possible as soon as he'd uttered the words, 'And *that's* how your mother and I came to have you.' Job done. Cheerio. But Morton couldn't appear any other way than totally shell-shocked and mildly drunk. Of course, they had both spotted it as soon as he walked through the front door. 'What's happened?' Juliette had asked. 'It's Dad, isn't it?' Jeremy had said, the pair of them haranguing him before he'd even drawn breath. He'd just managed to keep his composure while he relayed what his father had told him and had just finished telling them everything, when Guy arrived. Suddenly, the world fell silent and a raft of questions from Juliette and Jeremy were left unspoken.

'Right,' Jeremy said assertively. 'We're going to get ready, then go and visit Dad.' Guy set down the piece of toast he was in the middle of eating and obediently followed Jeremy from the room.

Morton nodded and slumped down onto his arms, unable to talk anymore. He was tired, more tired than he'd ever been before and he just wanted to rest and not to think.

'Did they ever find the bloke who raped her?' Juliette asked, her voice loaded with sympathy. That must be her PCSO voice, Morton thought. He expected that she was itching to get into work and see what she could dig up. Morton shrugged. He had no idea if *the bloke* - his father - had escaped scot-free and gone on to rape other schoolgirls or if he was behind bars. He might even be dead by now.

'I'm going to bed,' Morton mumbled.

'I'll come too.'

When he woke up he was drenched in sweat, yet, according to the clock, he'd only been asleep for forty minutes. He sat up and stripped off his sodden t-shirt. A flicker of his dream flashed in his mind, like a snippet from a grainy film. A fat Russian Matryoshka nesting doll had spoken to him. He couldn't remember what he'd said; just that it was an old man who didn't look in the slightest bit Russian. He resembled someone haggard from years of working on the land and after he had spoken, the top half of his body tilted open sideways and out popped another man whom Morton identified as James Coldrick. He said something incoherent - at least, the memory of the dream was now incoherent - then he too opened up and out sprang Peter Coldrick. Then, just like the two men before him, his body severed across the waist to reveal Finlay Coldrick, who promptly burst into tears. Morton wondered why his exhausted brain had picked Russian nesting dolls to feature in what must surely be the oddest dream he'd ever had. Then he remembered the posters he'd seen yesterday in the waiting room of the Conquest Hospital.

Then a thought struck him, which fully woke him up.

Diabetes often runs in families the poster had said.

Finlay Coldrick had diabetes. Peter Coldrick had diabetes. *Didn't William Dunk's death certificate cite diabetes as a cause of death?* Morton reached for his phone and accessed his cloud space, where he quickly located a photo of William Dunk's death certificate, since the original had perished with everything else on the *Coldrick Case Incident Wall.* Yes, there it was: diabetes mellitus.

Coincidence?

There was only one way to be sure. Another DNA test.

Morton climbed out of bed as quietly as possible, doing his utmost not to disturb Juliette. There was no way on God's green earth she would allow him to do what he was about to do. He quickly dressed and left the house.

As Morton made the fifty-minute journey from Hastings to Dungeness, he mulled over the implications of his bizarre dream. If the diabetes was not a coincidence, then he had finally found James Coldrick's father: William Dunk. It was certainly possible in terms of the timeframe and location; William would have been thirty-one at the time of James's birth and he would likely have been living in Sedlescombe by then. According to a quick search on Ancestry,

179

William Dunk had never married, Daniel having been born in 1969 out of wedlock to one Sharon Higgins. *Could Daniel Dunk and James Coldrick have the same father in William Dunk? Were James Coldrick's parents really a Nazi woman and a handyman for the local gentry? If so, then what part did the Windsor-Sackvilles play?* He needed yet more evidence.

Mercifully there were no top-spec cars registered to the Chief Constable of Kent Police parked on Daniel Dunk's property; there were no cars at all in fact. Morton parked a safe distance away and pulled out the new pair of National Trust binoculars to spy on the house. He really must put the binoculars back in his father's wardrobe since it appeared that, contrary to Morton's initial belief, his father was making a decent recovery. Jeremy had texted to say that the doctors expected him to be allowed home within days. Another miracle; his family was full of them. His *real* family. He hadn't yet digested the news that his Aunty Margaret was his real, bona-fide biological mother. But then, how could you digest something like that? It was about as digestible as a stack of bricks. He doubted that he would ever even be able to *begin* to comprehend such life-changing information, although it did make some kind of sense on some kind of level. If you'd asked him at any point in his life to honestly state with whom in his family he felt the closest affinity, he would unquestioningly have chosen Aunty Margaret. He never could fathom where this syrupy high-esteem in which he held her had come from. After all, he could count the number of visits she had made to the family home and his reciprocal visits to her in Cornwall on one hand. Was *he* the reason that she had upped sticks as an eighteen-year-old and moved so far away? Was there significance to be found in the fact that her home was minutes away from Lands End, as if she couldn't live any further away without needing a submarine to get home? He raked through his back catalogue of memories of Aunty Margaret and he realised that it was a mawkish romanticised *idea* of her that he most loved; the kind of mother he'd wished that his own had been. Safe, constant, fun, Aunty Margaret's visits always cast a heavy and palpable shadow over his own restrained, conservative mother. He realised that he had always viewed Aunty Margaret's interactions and close relationship with her two daughters with an envious eye. And now, at the age of thirty-nine, he finally understood the affinity he had with Aunty Margaret. His mother.

Morton raised the binoculars to Dunk's house once more and was convinced that it was deserted. No doubt Dunk was off doing whatever hitmen do when not engaged in the business of killing

180

innocents. *Line-dancing, perhaps? Or lace-making, maybe?* Morton placed the binoculars in a rucksack he'd found in Jeremy's wardrobe, which he'd hastily packed the moment that the realisation of his dream had sunk in. He'd managed to sneak out of the house leaving Juliette sleeping in blissful ignorance of the plan that he'd impulsively hatched. He was going to enter Dunk's house to gather DNA material: that was about as organised and detailed as his plan got. He switched his phone to silent, knowing that the first thing that Juliette would do when she woke was to phone or text him, and the last time she did that, he was within hitting range of Daniel Dunk, and that didn't end too well.

He locked the car and walked towards Smuggler's Keep with the air of someone who had a God-given right to be there. Like a Jehovah's Witness or an Avon lady. *Not that either of those categories have a God-given right to do anything, least of all knock on strangers' doors,* thought Morton. He marched haughtily past Dunk's gummy neighbour's property and brazenly rapped the knocker on the wooden door, layers of peeling paint revealing its entire colourful history. He knew that he should have a back-up plan, at least *something* to say if Dunk should answer the door, but then what do you say to someone who knocked you unconscious the last time you saw them? *Hi, me again!* But he didn't need to worry; there was nobody home. Morton walked the length of the house, or glorified shed as it might better be designated, stopping at each window to try to catch a glimpse inside, but each was covered by old, sun-bleached curtains. He reached the back door and glanced around him, not quite able to believe that the *Coldrick Case* had reduced him to breaking and entering. He wondered if his sudden moral degradation was an atavistic trait that he could attribute to his father. He still couldn't comprehend that he was the by-product of a rape and he felt nauseous when the thought caught him unawares. He couldn't stop himself from imagining what his father did to her and what that made him, the carrier of his Y-chromosome. Not that a faulty gene pool made his actions defensible. If he were caught by the police he wouldn't have a defence; his bag was filled with a whole bunch of equipment to help him enter Dunk's property. *Tooled up* – wasn't that the parlance of those involved in such iniquitous activities?

He set down the bag and pulled out a large rusting crowbar. After a deep breath and a final check to make sure that he was truly alone, he placed the crowbar in the crevice beside the lock. Before he had even applied the slightest pressure the door creaked open, slowly but noisily.

181

Morton stared incredulously through the small gap that had opened up. It was never a good sign in films when a door creaked open to reveal a dark unwelcoming room. On the plus side, he seemed to recall that it wasn't illegal to enter a house where the door had been left open. And it wasn't as if he was going to steal anything. Well, maybe a little of Dunk's flaky skin but that was hardly the crime of the century.

He gently pushed the door open with his foot. With a bit of daylight streaming in, it wasn't quite the uninviting killer's workshop that he had feared it might be. It was just a normal, if slightly run-down, lounge. It actually reminded him of Peter Coldrick's house with its assortment of dilapidated furniture and rubbish strewn everywhere. The only addition were the multiple copies of *The Sun* and *Nutz* magazine, scattered liberally around the room. *It shouldn't be hard to pick up a DNA trace of Dunk among all this crap*, Morton thought.

He reluctantly closed the door and stood for a few moments, waiting for his eyes to adjust to the subdued lighting. Within a couple of minutes he was able to see that tucked at the end of the lounge was a tiny kitchen. To even describe it as a kitchenette would be an over-exaggeration. A stand-alone cooker was piled high with a variety of crockery and saucepans, their contents in various stages of decomposition. It was book-ended by a fridge-freezer and a sink with another pile of dirty plates and pots. It didn't surprise him that Dunk was a bit of a slob; it kind of went with the territory of a murdering thug.

Morton approached the sink and immediately recoiled at the disgusting stench. A plague of fat blue bottles that had been contentedly feasting on a putrefied plate of mess were disturbed by his presence and began pinging around his head.

With a pained grimace, Morton delved his hand into the abyss and pulled a wine glass from the sink. His disbelief that Dunk would even know what wine tasted like was confirmed by a perfect pair of rouge lip prints around the glass rim. He looked around the room but couldn't see anything else remotely female. He suspected that whoever the lips belonged to didn't actually reside here. *What had Guy said? That Dunk's wife or girlfriend had once worked at Charingsby?* Something along those lines. Then a thought occurred to him. What if the lipstick marks belonged to Olivia Walker? He considered the implications of this as he rooted in the sink, retrieving a pint glass containing the last dregs of beer with the words 'Stella Artois' emblazoned on the side. It had to be Dunk's. Morton carefully placed the glass in his bag and moved into a short

182

dark hallway that fed into two rooms: a bathroom with predictably blackened, grimy grout and broken tiles on the wall and a small simple bedroom containing a double bed, a chest of drawers and small volcanoes of clothes dotted around the floor.

Then he noticed a large mahogany and glass gun cabinet mounted to the wall. Morton took a closer inspection. The velvet-lined case had capacity to hold four guns: only three were present. Which either meant, as he suspected all along, that Dunk had murdered Coldrick or that Dunk was currently roaming the Kentish countryside with a – what was it Juliette had called it? – 'regular shotgun'.

As he gazed around the room, Morton suddenly realised that he was taking an inordinate amount of time over the simplest of tasks; he just needed to get Dunk's DNA and get out. He didn't need to be dawdling around like he was considering buying the place. He hurried over to the bed and, from the tell-tale concave impression in the pillow scraped a few hairs and pieces of dandruff into a plastic bag. That had to be enough of Dunk's scalp to get a result.

Morton took one final look around the room, then cautiously opened the front door. No sign of any murderous yobs. Or bent police chiefs. Or gummy neighbours. All was still and silent in Dungeness.

Safely inside the Mini with the doors centrally locked, Morton took a moment to breathe deeply. He'd done it. Now he needed to get to Euston in record speed. Dr Baumgartner's train would be leaving for Birmingham in two hours' time.

Morton predictably had to park a million miles away from Euston. He might as well have parked in Croydon. He ran through the heaving station, pushing past crowds of people, desperately hoping that he wasn't too late. He glanced up at the huge yellow and black digital display which presided over the gates that led to the waiting trains. The train for Birmingham was due to leave in three minutes. They'd arranged to meet outside *WH Smith's* but Dr Baumgartner was nowhere to be seen.

Morton desperately flicked his head left and right, craning his neck around the hordes of people trooping through the station.

He was fast running out of time.

Looking back at the time table display, he noted the platform number for the Birmingham train and made a run for it. As he neared the ticket barriers he wondered if he should get all *Hollywood cop* about it and leap over the barrier yelling something about him being a forensic genealogist and 'would somebody stop the damn train'. Not really his style. Fortunately for him, a petite Asian lady had wedged open the disabled ticket barrier and was fixated by a youth in absurdly tight jeans and spiked purple hair staggering towards the train.

Morton ran past her, easily breaching the ticket barrier, where he caught sight of Dr Baumgartner, hanging his upper torso from the nearest train door and waving wildly.

'Dr Baumgartner!' Morton greeted.

'Thought you weren't going to make it,' he replied.

'Here,' Morton said, thrusting his holdall into Dr Baumgartner's waiting hand.

At that moment the train conductor blew his whistle and the train doors emitted their high-pitched warning to announce that they were about to close.

'I should have the results by tomorrow,' Dr Baumgartner just managed to say, before the doors abruptly smacked together in front of his face. And then he was gone. Back to Birmingham. Back to the headquarters of the Forensic Science Service.

With the rear end of the train almost faded from sight, Morton pulled out his mobile. Sixteen missed calls and two text messages. Not bad for a few hours in silent mode. Four were from Dr Baumgartner in unsurprising regular three-minute intervals preceding their scheduled meeting. One was from Jeremy and the rest were from Juliette. He dialled her mobile as he began his epic journey back towards the Mini.

'Where the hell have you been?' she greeted congenially.

'Sorry, phone battery died,' Morton lied, though why he didn't just tell the truth, he wasn't too sure. He vaguely thought that the truth was too complicated and he didn't know who might be listening. Anyhow, it was a stupid mistake trying to pull the wool over Juliette's eyes.

'Liar. Your phone wouldn't have even rung if your battery was dead.' *Oh yeah*, Morton thought, forgetting whom he was talking to. She sounded like she was speaking from a dungeon.

'Where are you?' he asked.

'Don't change the subject. Where have you been?'

'I'll tell you when you get home. Where are you?'

'I should be in a primary school with Roger giving a 'Stranger Danger' talk, but I told him I didn't feel well and I had paperwork to catch up on so now I'm in the basement searching through a stack of bloody microfiches for anything on your aunty or mum or whoever she

184

is to you now. PNC came back with nothing but then it wouldn't because of how long ago the crime was committed.'

'How likely is it that you'll come up with something?'

'Not. I don't have the criminal's name, date of birth, et cetera which would make the task a bit easier. Besides which, these records are regularly weeded for Data Protection.'

'Well, thanks for trying.'

'See you later.'

Morton hit the red button on his phone with a cynical intuition that Juliette wasn't going to locate any records pertaining to his Aunty Margaret's rape. He just had a hunch that his biological father had escaped justice and was freely roaming the streets. He remembered that Jeremy had tried to call him so he phoned his mobile.

'Bad news, I'm afraid,' Jeremy began and Morton immediately feared the worst for his father. 'I'm going back to Cyprus tomorrow.'

'So soon?' Morton said, feeling suddenly bereft of his newly-acquired relationship.

'Now that Dad's on the mend there's no justification for the compassionate leave. Looks like his care is over to you and Juliette now.'

'Hmm,' Morton answered pensively. He doubted that it would be the last he'd hear of him, though. He'd overheard some of the blokes at the party talking about videos they'd uploaded to Facebook whilst in Afghanistan, so he doubted communication could be any more stunted in Cyprus.

Two hours later, a near-empty bottle of red wine had helped to distil Morton's erratic thoughts. The house was silent but for the muted ticking from the grandfather clock in the hallway. He was sitting in his father's lounge, staring at a family portrait that had hung over the fireplace since it had been taken. He couldn't recall if the photo had been taken for any particular birthday or anniversary but he remembered that he and Jeremy were told of their mother's cancer days later. Possibly even the next day. He'd never really connected the two ideas before but now, looking up at himself as a fourteen-year-old boy with a grinning Jeremy - minus his top front teeth – sat beside him and their parents standing stoically behind them, he wondered if the picture had been taken as a desperate final snapshot of their dissolving nuclear family unit. Proof that they'd existed. Proof that could never be tarnished by insidious underlying family secrets. *Say cheese!* It was an

185

image that should, under normal circumstances, be found amidst the yellowing pages of a photo album, not hanging proudly on the wall: Morton on a day trip to Hastings with his aunt, uncle and cousin. He felt sure that he could cope with their bizarre family foibles if it'd been like that.

Morton's mobile suddenly sounded loudly from his pocket. 'Hello,' he answered, hoping that the voice on the other end was calling with good news.

'Morton?' Professor Geoffrey Daniels asked in a gruff, baritone voice.

'Yup, speaking.'

'Have you checked your emails yet?'

'No, not today, why's that then?'

'I've found Marlene Koldrich's birth certificate and have emailed you a translation.'

'Oh, brilliant, that's fantastic,' Morton answered, wondering what the email could contain that required a follow-up phone call. He moved into the kitchen and switched on his laptop.

'It's fairly run-of-the-mill stuff,' he qualified, instantly deflating Morton's expectations of a grand discovery. 'The usual name of parents and address.'

'Okay,' Morton said, hearing in the Professor's intonation that there was a caveat looming. 'I'm just looking at my emails now.'

There was a pregnant pause as he clicked on his emails and, at the top of the email inbox, found the tantalising gold unopened envelope beside the name Geoffrey Daniels. He opened the message and read the brief contents: *Morton, still on trail, but found this which you might be interested in. Regards, Geoffrey.* Below his email was a translation of Marlene's birth certificate.

Marlene, the daughter of Eberhard and Gaelle Koldrich, born 18 November 1913, Markgrafenstrasse 5, Berlin

'Eberhard and Gaelle Koldrich,' Morton said, more for his own benefit than the Professor's.

'Yes, which is why I'm calling. Eberhard Koldrich – ever heard of him?'

Morton said the name repeatedly in his mind: definitely no entries in his brain under that name. 'No, should I have heard of him then?'

'Depends on your knowledge of World War Two; I understood from Gerald Baumgartner that you were a first-class student.'

'Apparently not.'

The Professor dropped his oblique indictment and continued. 'Eberhard Koldrich was a high-ranking member of the *Nationalsozialistische Deutsche Arbeiterpartei*. One of his main wartime tasks was the conversion of influential British aristocrats who might be sympathetic to a peace treaty with Germany, effectively allowing the Nazis free rein in occupied Europe.'

'Kind of like the Duke of Hamilton meeting Rudolf Hess in 1941?' Morton said, if only to prove that he did actually have some depth of historical knowledge.

'Something like that, yes, only more discreet and more organised. I've done a lot of research into him and his group over the years. Eberhard Koldrich was responsible for sending over a surprising number of young men and women to make political unions with important British families.'

Finlay's great, great grandfather was a top Nazi. Morton wondered when the best time would be to break that particular piece of news to Soraya. 'And Marlene was one of those women? Sent to link up with the Windsor-Sackvilles?'

'I've always presumed Eberhard's daughter was involved but she disappeared without trace. Looks like you might have found her. The fact that the Regional Advisory Committee released her a week after being deemed internable suggests that some higher authority pulled some strings.'

'Frederick Windsor-Sackville?'

'*That* would need evidence, my dear boy.'

'Hmm,' Morton concurred. He thought about the copper box being created for a marriage between David Windsor-Sackville and an unknown person. 'Do you know if the Koldrichs had a family crest?'

'Yes, they did.'

'Any chance you could email me a copy of it?'

'Of course.'

'Thank you. Do you know what happened to Eberhard and Gaelle?'

'He was executed at Nuremberg in 1945, Gaelle died in 1962. Marlene was their only child, so the family line has ended.'

Morton was about to explain that the family name lived on in a new, anglicised form but at that moment the front door banged shut

187

and Juliette casually strolled into the kitchen. She had that characteristic look in her eyes that spoke of having something to say. Everyone had something to say to Morton at the moment, yet nothing that seemed to make any sense. He tried to recall a single moment in his life that was as confusing, personally and professionally, as the last two weeks. Nothing even came close. Morton thanked the Professor and hung up. He would send a follow-up email to him once the case was closed.

'Good day?' he asked Juliette.

She leant on the worktop and stared out into the garden. 'Curious,' she answered cryptically. He hoped that her curious day had something to do with his parentage. Perhaps she had the name of his father. 'Just after I spoke to you on the phone, the door opened in the basement and in walked Olivia Walker.'

'Oh.'

'Yeah, that's what I thought. According to the schedule, I was telling eight-year-olds not to wander off with strangers and there I was actually rooting around in semi-darkness among closed case files. But Miss Walker didn't say a word about it. She said she'd looked at my application for the police force last year and couldn't fathom why I'd been turned down.'

'What did you say?'

Juliette shrugged. 'Not a lot I could say really. She implied that if I were to apply again it'd pretty well be guaranteed. The whole time she was eyeballing the files I was looking at.'

'Could she have known what you were looking at?'

'No, no way. I didn't find anything. I'm sorry, Morton, but we're going to need more to go on to find out who your dad is.'

'I'm still not sure that I *need* to know anything beyond that he was a rapist.'

Juliette filled the kettle and turned to face him. 'So, are you going to tell me where you disappeared off to in the early hours this morning?'

So he told her. Everything.

'That was quite possibly the most stupid thing you've done since – oh, let me see, you broke into Charingsby,' she said. 'What's got into you lately? You've broken the law more times in the last two weeks than in the entire time I've known you.'

She had a point. But his crimes were fairly pathetic and piffling, all things considered. It barely even registered as a felony to walk into an open house and scrape some dandruff into a bag. In Juliette's eyes, though, a crime was a crime.

He suddenly remembered the memory of the lipstick mark on the wineglass in Dunk's house and what Guy had said about Daniel Dunk having a wife or girlfriend who had once worked at Charingsby. He turned back to his laptop, ignoring Juliette's admonishing glare.

He opened up the Ancestry website and ran an online marriage search for Daniel Dunk. There was only one possibility:

Daniel Dunk. May 2005. Hastings and Rother. Vol. 456. Page 100. Ent. C22.

Morton clicked the 'Find Spouse' button.
    'Shit.'

Chapter Nineteen

Thursday

It was the endgame. Morton couldn't help but lie in bed, conjuring up grandiose descriptions for how the day would pan out. He had had so little sleep and when his eyes had finally succumbed to the acute tiredness weighing down his body, he had dreamed of today. This time tomorrow it would all be over, he hoped, as he stared fixedly at the stain on the ceiling, as if it might generate further inspiration for the conclusion to the *Coldrick Case*. Not that he needed inspiration; he had a plan and it was almost time to put it into effect. He glanced over at the red digital clock display: 2.04 a.m. There seemed hardly any point trying to go back to sleep for fifty-six minutes.

There was a noise. A repetitive sound that Morton couldn't place in his dream. *What was it? A plague of killer bees?* No. He sat up in bed and opened his eyes. It was the heart-stopping shriek of the alarm. He stumbled out of bed like a new-born giraffe and whacked the stop button.

'You're really going through with this...' Juliette's croaky voice mumbled from under the duvet.

'Absolutely,' Morton answered, surprising himself at just how agile he felt on so little sleep. It had to be the adrenalin which had begun circulating his veins the moment the alarm sounded.

'Go and wake the boys, then,' Juliette said, barely managing to lift her head from the pillow.

Morton went to wake *the boys*, as they were now regularly being called. It was an appellation that rendered them permanently youthful, which he supposed they still were. Unlike him. Old and crotchety.

He gently knocked, then pushed open the door. 'Morning!' he said brightly, as though he was waking a pair of six-year-olds. Jeremy and Guy were spooned tightly together, sleeping soundly. His topless brother and his topless brother's topless boyfriend. It almost seemed a shame to wake them. The sight of them evoked a strange, envy-tinged parental pride in him. It was good to see Jeremy so comfortable with himself. Morton would be mortified if his father walked in to see him and Juliette *spooning. Was he uptight?* He was fairly sure that he was. He needed to relax. 'It's time to get up, *boys*,' he said a little louder.

Finally Jeremy stirred. 'Oh crap,' he muttered, as the reality of the day dawned on him. His return to Cyprus was looming. He leaned over and planted a tender kiss on Guy's forehead. 'Time to get up.'

'I'll see you downstairs,' Morton said, making a hasty retreat on the basis that if they were topless they were probably also bottomless, and that wasn't a sight he wanted to see at three in the morning.

It wasn't too long before Morton was joined in the kitchen by his three weary accomplices. He wondered how he managed to look so damn rough in the mornings when Guy and Jeremy managed to effortlessly appear like they'd just stepped out of the Next catalogue; ripped jeans, fashionable cardigans and ruffled, out-of-bed hair. But their attire didn't manage to disguise their deep-seated reservations about the plan that he'd cooked up last night. They were quite right: of course there were far too many *ifs*, *buts* and *maybes* attached to his plan but he had to give it a go. He was wearing suitably dark clothing and had repacked the breaking-and-entering rucksack that he'd almost used to get into Dunk's house yesterday.

Juliette, Jeremy and Guy stared blankly in various directions around the kitchen while Morton rehearsed, with military precision, exactly how things were going to happen.

'Since I'll be thirty thousand feet in the air when this ridiculous thing unfolds, can I skip this part and make a drink, please?' Jeremy asked.

Morton acceded with a nod of his head and continued explaining the plan. He asked if they had any questions but there were none. For Morton and Guy, it was time to say goodbye to Jeremy until he was next granted leave to come home.

'Right,' Morton said, breaking a silence that was close to becoming uncomfortable. It was weird, in the last few days Morton had learned so much about so many things, yet what he most cherished was discovering that he actually liked, no *loved* his brother/cousin, and now here he was about to disappear off with the possibility of not returning for at least six months and an even greater possibility of being posted to Afghanistan. How could Morton put everything he felt into something that even attempted to summarise his feelings? He couldn't.

The silence in the pre-dawn kitchen tipped over into the realm of discomfort as Juliette and Guy began to shift awkwardly. Juliette even resorted to a close inspection of her fingernails, which was something in itself. Morton had never known her to care about her nails a single day that he'd known her. It was just too fussy, too girly. He knew that he needed to be the one to break the stalemate but the words wouldn't come, they were stuck somewhere in his larynx, refusing to accept the fact that all was well between the two brothers. Instead of speaking, Morton opened his arms and drew Jeremy into a long embrace that he hoped would impart everything he needed to say. As he held Jeremy, a tear escaped down his cheek.

'Take care,' the pair of them said simultaneously.

The car radio blasted out a dull documentary about women in Uganda when Morton switched on the ignition, producing enough decibels to wake the whole street. Just what was needed at four in the morning. He switched it off and drove in silence, his car mimicking the movements of Juliette's black Ford Ka in front. Juliette had once suggested that he buy a Ka, a proposal at which he took great offence. It was times like that that he wondered if he was the marrying kind. One person forever, even when they suggest things like buying a Ka. He knew that now the final bastion to their nuptials had been unceremoniously crushed he had no reason not to marry her. But then, was that a good reason *to* marry someone? Just because you've run out of reasons not to? It seemed a little thin. At least upon marriage Juliette would be taking a name that kind of belonged to him, it was his mother's maiden name after all. Née Farrier. He recalled the – what would it be now, thousands? – of marriage certificates that he'd seen in his career. Would he do as many illegitimates had done before him on marriage certificates and leave his father's name and occupation blank, or should he write 'rapist' under occupation? He was fairly sure that hadn't been done before and might raise the registrar's eyebrows.

The village streets that he passed through were unsurprisingly silent; just the Mini and the Ka playing pre-dawn cat and mouse.

The Ka slowed as it entered Sedlescombe village then pulled in beside the Clockhouse Tearoom, close to where Morton had woken with urine-soaked boxers and a large pair of pendulous breasts staring him in the face. Such a fond memory. Morton tucked the Mini neatly behind the Ka and climbed out. The village was, as he expected, completely dead. Not a single light but for the sporadic sodium street lamps dotted along the road and not a single noise but for Guy, climbing out of the driver's side and unlocking the Ka boot.

'Ready?' Guy whispered.

Morton nodded. Ready as he ever would be, he thought, acknowledging for the first time the prickling in his intestines.

'It's not too late to go back, you know,' Guy said. 'Call this whole thing off?'

'Nope. Let's do it,' Morton said, bundling himself into the tiny confines of the Ka boot. He wasn't someone who had suffered claustrophobia before but the split-second that the lid came down and the lock crunched darkness into place, he felt as though he'd been mummified. It was a good job this was going to be a short journey. He was grateful not to be in pitch darkness; a muted red glow penetrated in from the rear lights. Not that there was anything to see squashed in the foetal position in a car boot at four in the morning anyway.

As the Ka began to move off, Morton suddenly had the thought that he could just have walked into the biggest trap of his life. What if Guy was double-crossing him? *He might be an undercover operative working for the Windsor-Sackvilles.* No, that would just be ridiculous, he'd seen the way that Jeremy and Guy got together at the Sedlescombe Village Fete; that was *so* not pre-planned. *Unless Jeremy was involved, too.* No, this was just hysteria talking. Either way, it would be just a few seconds until he found out.

The Ka sped along for a few seconds then drew to an abrupt halt. They were at the front gates of Charingsby.

He heard talking and strained his ears but couldn't catch what was being said. Guy had mentioned that despite his being well-known on the gate, there would still be questions when he arrived at such an hour. Whomever he was talking to was evidently satisfied with his explanation and the car moved off again. They crawled along slowly, the sound of crunched gravel filling the boot space.

The car stopped and the engine was cut. Morton took a deep breath as the lights were switched off and his prison was plunged into total darkness.

His heart began to race when he heard Guy's heavy footfall on the stones.

Getting closer and closer.

A key turned in the boot lock and the lid was tugged open, sending in a waft of clean cold air but no extra light.

Good old-fashioned fear and paranoia pinned Morton inside the boot. He closed his eyes and regressed back to the childlike mentality that if he kept perfectly still and didn't look out, then he couldn't be seen.

A torch beam fell on his face. 'What're you doing, you weirdo?' Guy asked. 'Crap, are you dead?'

Morton opened his eyes and almost blinded himself. He raised a hand to shield himself from the brain-frazzling glare.

'Sorry, mate,' Guy said, switching the torch off. 'Come on, we need to get a move on.'

Guy extended a hand to Morton and helped him out of the boot, his eyes gradually adjusting. The car was parked on a rectangle of shingle surrounded on three sides by an overabundance of dense foliage - cherry laurel, if his memory of the lectures on fauna and flora with Dr Baumgartner was correct. On the fourth side, the direction in which they were now facing, was the unmistakable grey stone façade of Charingsby, resembling a sinister country house from a Bronte novel. It might have been the cold night air seeping through his clothing, chilling his core but he had deep misgivings about the place and what had occurred here all those years ago.

'Ready?' Guy asked.

'Let's do it,' Morton answered and he followed Guy across the car park area to a Gothic archway in which was set a heavy black-studded, oak door protected by keypad entry. Guy tapped in a six-digit code which Morton did his best to memorise. Then Morton watched as he pressed his thumb onto a scanning pad. *Christ, they really didn't want intruders getting inside*, Morton thought.

A small green LED illuminated and a heavy clunk sounded from the door's internal mechanisms. Guy pushed it open and they stepped into a dim narrow passageway that smacked of a servants' rat-run. Upstairs Downstairs and all that.

Morton's heart began to pound even faster, which he hadn't thought possible without rigorous exercise. They had rehearsed the plan over and again into the early hours; Guy had even drawn a map of the internal layout of Charingsby and, in true *Mission Impossible* style, fed the paper into Morton's father's shredding machine. He suspected that Guy was disappointed not to have a hearty fire to dramatically toss it onto. They hadn't managed to resolve the question of what would actually happen if they were discovered. Better not to dwell on that.

They moved silently down the passageway until it terminated at a perpendicular, slightly wider corridor. From his memory of Guy's improvised map, Morton knew that left would lead them to the servants' quarters – the direction in which Guy should be heading if he were going to his room. Silently, the pair turned right and followed the

194

corridor until it reached a tightly-closed chunky oak door. Guy stopped and placed his ear at the keyhole. This was the moment when things could go dangerously wrong. Beyond the door was the main downstairs lobby, the heart of the house and the place at which they would most likely be caught. Several armed security guards patrolled the house day and night, and numerous CCTV cameras kept a twenty-four-seven vigil on unpatrolled areas.

Guy was evidently satisfied that the coast was clear. It was the kind of setting where the door should creak loudly, announcing to all and sundry their arrival. But it didn't, it just opened gently to reveal what Morton could only think of as a magnificent entrance hall that put Mote Ridge to shame. An ornate multi-branched chandelier cast a diffused yellow glow over the room. There was just enough light to see the massive gold-framed portraits of long-deceased Windsor-Sackvilles, glaring down at him, as if they were aware of his potential to destroy everything that they stood for. A grand staircase wound its way up before splitting into two and curving out of sight. An intricate woven rug formed the centre-piece of the immaculately polished mahogany flooring.

'Impressive, huh?' Guy whispered, breaking a self-imposed rule that there should be no talking unless absolutely necessary. It hardly seemed necessary to Morton to ask if he found it impressive. A nodded response sufficed.

Guy closed the door behind them and they began the long journey to the door beside the foot of the staircase. If it was going to go wrong anywhere, then it was here. To avoid the CCTV cameras, they had to creep around the room's extremities, which would take them a whole lot longer than simply walking directly across the floor.

Guy strangely acted like he'd done this before, ducking carefully this way and that, circumventing protruding furniture like a professional dancer. Maybe he *had* done this before. Morton's paranoia resurfaced; could this all be a trap? Guy did seem to have a very in-depth knowledge of the internal workings and security of a house in which he was simply a – what *was* his job? Footman? Butler? Did this sort of a place still have those roles? Whatever, now wasn't the time to start asking questions; they'd finally reached *the* door – the door behind which all of the darkest Windsor-Sackville secrets were kept. *This* was the door into the walled garden to which Peter Coldrick wanted access. Where other genealogists had failed to conquer, Morton was here, on the verge of discovery.

All things considered, the door to the archives of Charingsby offered little in the way of resistance. It was protected by nothing more than an outlandishly large lock, for which Guy had the outlandishly large key.

Five seconds later, they were inside. Guy tapped in another six digit code to prevent the alarm from sounding.

Morton quietly closed the door and took stock of the room. It was huge, effortlessly dwarfing East Sussex Archives. There were no windows and no other exit points other than that through which they had just entered. The walls were lined with floor-to-ceiling bookshelves containing books, box files and folders. A long line of tall, metal cabinets filled the centre of the room. All of this to search in under an hour.

Both men instinctively made their way to the bulky cabinets in the centre of the room and began to search indiscriminately among the files.

'Where do I start?' Guy whispered.

Morton exhaled and looked in awe at the room; he had no idea where he should start. 'I don't know, just look for anything we can hold against them. Or anything to do with the Coldricks or the war.'

East Sussex Archives had a great number of obvious downsides but at least they had a decent system of cataloguing that made some semblance of sense to the public. Here the system only had to make sense to one person – the archivist.

'Do you know the archivist at all?' Morton asked.

'There isn't one; it's just another job for the secretary,' Guy answered, pushing closed another drawer. 'That's that cabinet done. What now?'

'We've just got to keep searching,' Morton instructed, as a pang of despair crept into his head.

Pushing shut a heavy drawer containing land purchases in the eighteenth century, Morton took a deep breath and looked around the room. *Time was running out. There had to be some kind of logic to the material gathered here.* His eyes moved slowly and systematically around the shelves, trying to piece together some kind of order from the haphazard assortment of documents. In his peripheral vision, Morton spotted something of interest. Turning to a stack of nondescript folders at the bottom of a nearby shelving unit, he had just selected a red box file when he heard a low unnatural thud behind him. He turned. Any doubts that Morton had about Guy's allegiances were dispelled; he was lying crumpled in a heap on the floor, possibly unconscious, possibly dead. Morton's nemesis, Daniel Dunk stood like a demented Bond villain over the body.

For someone who felt so inadequate in so many ways, it surprised Morton greatly to discover that his fight-or-flight reaction was actually to fight. Without thinking about it – because if he had thought about it he would very likely have reconsidered – Morton picked up a bronze bust statue of Sir Winston Churchill that stood proudly on a lectern nearby and threw it at Daniel Dunk. Sir Winston seemed to cut through the air in slow motion – at least it was slow in comparison with the raft of thoughts firing through his brain. *What if Sir Winston struck Dunk on the head and killed him?* There was certainly no pleading self-defence. Then again, there were always stories that incited outrage where the burglar got knocked out by a defiant home-owner and the home-owner was the one locked up while the burglar walked off scot-free with compensation. *He* was that burglar.

Morton was actually slightly relieved, and not at all surprised, that Sir Winston fell short of his target, crashing down at Dunk's feet. Not even close enough to bruise his big toe but at least it showed Dunk that he was a force to be reckoned with. Well, sort of. The only damage he managed to inflict was on poor Sir Winston, whose nose had been severed from his face.

Dunk emitted a primeval grunt as he lunged across the cabinet that separated them, his hands aimed at Morton's throat.

Morton again surprised himself by instinctively punching Daniel Dunk in the face. Not only had he punched him but he had punched him hard, sending Dunk to the floor. He had, quite literally, floored someone. Amazing. The last fight that he'd had was with Jonathan Stainer in the third year at primary school. And he'd lost.

Without missing a beat, Morton sent his right foot into Dunk's ribcage, wincing when he heard what sounded like the cracking of bones. It was enough; Dunk was down and out of action, so Morton grabbed the rucksack and the box file and ran from the room. He didn't know what to do about Guy but, whether dead or unconscious, he was still left with the problem of a large immoveable Australian. He dialled Juliette; it was time for phase two of the plan.

As Morton ran back in the direction that they had entered the house he could hear some kind of commotion going on nearby, the sound of men running towards him. He hurried down the narrow

197

passageways and reached the large oak door that led to the outside world. He yanked on the handle but it was locked.

The angry shouts of several men were drawing closer; they had entered the passageway and would appear within seconds.

Morton's fight or flight reaction was now severely leaning towards the latter.

He tried the door again but it was locked fast. Then he spotted the small green button beside the door. He pressed it and the heavy clunking mechanism released the door.

He ran out into the cold darkness of the shingle car park. As he turned to run behind the house, he caught a glimpse of blue flashing lights. Then the sirens started, echoing violently around him, hurtling towards the house. A police car and a police riot van – both heading this way. Good old Juliette. It was hopefully enough to clot the flow of enraged security guards who would now stop at nothing to hunt him down.

Morton didn't hang around to find out if the plan had worked or not, he kept on running until he reached the woods that he hoped led past the shooting box. From there he could make his way back to the village and the sanctity of his car.

By the time he reached the shooting box, Morton was sweating and suffering tachycardia. He needed to stop just for a moment to catch his breath. He leant up against the abandoned building and tried to regulate his breathing. He looked out into the dense woodland but could see nothing - it was like staring down a bottomless well with squinted eyes. He hoped that if he were being chased, his assailants would make enough noise for him to know that they were following.

It was time to move on, to get out of Sedlescombe once and for all. Morton ran over to the point in the fence that he had entered by previously but found it had been repaired. He was fully prepared for this eventuality and pulled out the wire-cutters from the rucksack. He hoped that this would be the last time he would have to sabotage the Charingsby perimeter as he snipped a hole large enough to crawl through.

He took one final glance behind him then squeezed himself through the gap into safety.

And just like that, he'd escaped the clutches of the Windsor-Sackvilles. It actually wasn't as hard as he'd thought it would be.

Having regained his energy, he ran across the field towards the village, which was now bathed in a washed-out orange from the

198

nascent sunrise. The Mini appeared in view and he heaved a sigh of relief. This thing, this monster project that he'd daubed the *Coldrick Case* was almost over. All he needed to do now was get to the police station. Climbing into the safety of the Mini, he locked the doors and pulled out his mobile. Fourteen missed calls from Juliette in the last ten minutes. He started the car and dialled her back. The phone dialled endlessly, as he sped the car along the deserted street. He began to panic. *What if the plan had failed? What if Dunk's henchmen had realised that the large intimidating riot van only contained Juliette and the accompanying police only contained her partner, Dan?*

Finally, the call connected and he heard Juliette's reassuring voice.

'Did you find Guy? He was knocked out by Dunk,' Morton blurted out.

'Yeah, we found him. He'll be okay, bit of a bump to the head. Listen, we stopped most of them but a couple managed to escape in a BMW.'

Morton glanced in his rear-view mirror and saw a pair of headlights in the distance. Headlights that were quickly gaining speed.

'I think I found the BMW,' Morton said, watching the car zoom closer. 'Or at least, it's found me.'

'Where are you?'

'Er, just leaving Sedlescombe,' was all Morton managed, before he dropped his phone from the force of a rear shunt. The Mini lost control and swerved dangerously towards the edge of the road. Morton knew the occupants of the BMW had one aim: to force him down the steep embankment they were currently speeding past. He yanked the steering wheel hard and managed to level the Mini as it bumped the hard curb.

When Morton realised that the BMW was trying to get alongside him for a final swipe, it was too late to stop it. The BMW was driving neck and neck with him.

He knew this was it.

He looked across at his assailants: Daniel Dunk and Philip Windsor-Sackville. He watched, as if detached from the scene, as Dunk wrenched his steering wheel and smashed into the side of the Mini. They had achieved their objective.

His head was spinning faster than the worst of the worst drinking sessions put together. A wave of nausea came and went. His hands felt like they were on fire. He swallowed down against another wave of nausea and tasted blood. A lot of blood. It was too dark to know where he was. He was on his side, pinned in.

That smell, he knew it. Clear, fetid, like ammonia. But what was it? Petrol. Something in his brain, something intense was able to push through the soupy confusion and tell him that he needed to get out of the car. But there was another, separate reason why he must escape. Something to do with the rucksack that he found his face buried in. Grab the rucksack and get out; that was all he knew.

The door was welded shut. The window? He ran his hand around the door, knowing that there should be a handle or a button, something to make the glass move. Then he realised that there was no window; it was just an open space that led out into darkness. Trees. What was he doing in a wood? He caught a flashback of the shooting box at Charingsby. Was that where he was? Something to do with Sir Winston Churchill. And Daniel Dunk.

The pungent stench of petrol sent a fresh wave of sickness surging around his stomach. He grabbed the rucksack and pulled himself towards the vacant space beside him.

There was talking nearby. Men. That was it; the reason why he needed to get out. The men mustn't get their hands on the rucksack.

He tugged furiously at it but it wouldn't budge. Besides which, he couldn't actually move. Was it his injuries? Was he really so badly hurt? He tentatively felt around his torso, tapping his fingers over his jacket. No, he wasn't so damaged to prevent escape. Then his turbid brain realised: it was the seatbelt; that was what was pinning him in. He fumbled for the release button and slumped forward as the belt pinged back over his shoulder. He spat out a mouthful of blood and held his stomach to prevent him from being sick.

The men were talking more loudly, moving towards him.

He pulled at the rucksack but it was stuck fast. He couldn't remember quite why but he knew that he couldn't let them get their hands on it. Then he caught sight of something glinting at his feet – it was the rucksack buckle.

Another flash of clarity and he realised that he'd been pulling on the flaccid airbag.

Morton lunged at the rucksack, wincing at the pain in his hands, and wriggled out of the open window, flopping heavily down onto something prickly.

The merry-go-rounding inside his head and the surging waves of nausea were too much – he vomited beside the car.

His frangible, addled brain was able to decipher some of the men's voices. 'He has to be dead,' one of them said. He recognised the voice, then recalled the last two faces he had seen. It belonged to one of them but he couldn't remember which.

'About bloody time, you kept him alive too long,' the other said. 'I told you to get rid of him days ago. You didn't have this much trouble with Peter.'

As Morton lay on the prickly plant beside a pool of his own vomit, he knew, with certain lucidity, what he had to do. He dipped his painful right hand inside the rucksack and rummaged until he found the box of matches.

The men had fallen silent but for their heavy breathing. They had almost reached him; Morton was out of time. He struck a match and threw it towards the car's underbelly. For a moment the match lay on the ground, the flame flickering, as if deciding whether or not it was up to the task. A second later a growing lozenge of flame flowed like a river towards his car. His brand new car.

Morton knew that he had to move. He began to drag himself and the rucksack along the woodland floor, just as a massive explosion ripped open the carcass of the Mini.

From the torn fabric of his mind, Morton thought that it sounded like some of his attackers had been caught in the blast. One thing he knew, they were making a hasty retreat back up the bank. Morton dragged himself further and further into the enveloping woods.

Then he vomited again.

Then everything went dark.

Morton Farrier left the Conquest Hospital shortly after one o'clock in the afternoon with the assistance of Juliette, who was dressed in full superhero PCSO uniform. He climbed into the police van holding his bandaged hands awkwardly out in front of him, partly to elicit sympathy from Juliette and partly because they were hurting like hell. That dastardly Paul from the Mini showroom had failed to warn him during his spiel about the car's many features that, by clinging onto the steering wheel at the moment of any possible collision, he would end up in a hospital with first-degree burns to his hands and wrists from the firing of the airbag. Aside from the burns, he had also suffered concussion and a three-inch gash to the left side of his head, which required five stitches to seal the gap. As the nurse meticulously wove the black thread through his gaping skin, Morton hoped that the cut

201

would scar nice and visibly, giving him something of the hard edge of Daniel Dunk. The doctor wanted to make sure that Morton was fully *compos mentis* and asked him the day of the week, which he was unable to give and he was unable to satisfy the doctor that this had nothing to do with the head injury. He was finally released after correctly answering the ironic question as to who the Secretary of Defence was. It would have taken a full lobotomy for him to forget the name of Philip Windsor-Sackville.

'Right, to the station, then,' Juliette said rather fatalistically as she brought the throaty police van to life, the same van that she had used to storm Charingsby a few hours previously. Morton noticed that she had parked in a disabled bay *and* not paid for parking. Oh the joys of being above the law.

'We just need to do a quick detour first,' Morton said.

'Oh, for Christ's sake, what now?'

Morton went to explain when his mobile rang.

Dr Baumgartner's name flashed up onscreen.

The results.

Morton carefully carried the chunky red box file towards the house. He had told Juliette to keep the van running – what he had to do would only take a moment. He banged loudly on the front door of the imposing townhouse.

A rattling of bolts then Soraya Benton appeared before him. She was dressed just the same as the first day he'd met her in an oversized cream jumper and baggy jeans. Lacking now, however, was the sparkle in her eyes and the welcoming smile. 'Hi,' Soraya said, 'come in.'

Morton followed her into the lounge and sat himself down.

'So what have you been up to, then?' she asked, taking a seat opposite him. He could see her eyeing up the box file on his lap. 'You look a bit worse for wear.' She even managed a stinted, cracked attempt at laughter.

Morton smiled. 'It's over, Soraya,' he said quietly.

'What do you mean? Did you find what you needed?'

He paused to consider the question. 'Yes, I did. I also found a lot more than I bargained for. Like your marriage to Daniel Dunk.'

'What?' she gasped, a look of terror flicking across her face. 'I don't know what you're talking—'

'It's over. Stop pretending,' he interjected.

Soraya's eyes fell as she waited for Morton to continue.

He tapped the red file with his knuckles and revealed the handwritten title, 'Misc. Charingsby' emblazoned on the spine. It sent shockwaves of pain through him but it was worth every moment to see the look of sheer horror on her face.

'It's funny really,' he said, 'there I was, flailing around in the archives of Charingsby, not a hope in hell of pulling all the records I needed out before being caught, then I discover this little red box which someone had painstakingly already put together.'

Soraya bit her lip and stared at him, the epitome of the rabbit trapped in the headlights. Morton, with a good deal of concentration and pain, managed to prise open the box file. 'Everything I needed, everything I've been searching for these last two weeks is in here.' He withdrew a pile of paper and provided a running commentary for each item. 'The 1944 admission register for St George's Children's Home, bank statements confirming payments to James Coldrick totalling hundreds of thousands of pounds, documents unequivocally confirming Frederick and David Windsor-Sackville's involvement with the Nazis in the first half of World War Two, including vast, multi-million pound payments made to the family from Berlin ...' Morton put the papers down. 'I don't really need to tell you about the rest of the folder, do I, Soraya?'

She shook her head.

'I'd suspected something was amiss for a while now. I became suspicious that day at Peter's house when we went there together to search for his will and you miraculously found the *All About Sedlescombe* book, which I knew hadn't been there at the time of his death. You put it there, didn't you?'

Soraya nodded.

'Having first filtered the contents to suit your own needs?'

Another nod.

'The day that I met Peter he warned me not to trust anyone. He meant you. He knew you were up to something.' Morton held up the box file and pointed to the word on the spine. 'Do you know what gave you away?' Morton asked rhetorically. 'It was the letter *a*. As soon as I spotted this on the shelf I knew.' He paused, allowing her the opportunity to say something in defence, but nothing was forthcoming. '*You* compiled this file.' Another pause. 'Which didn't make sense to me. Why, I thought, would she need me to research everything that she already knew? Then it clicked – the stuff in here might well bring down the Windsor-Sackvilles, but to what end? What would you gain from that? Then it came to me - you don't want to bring them down at all - you want to be part of them, but you needed me to find something concrete to prove that your son is heir to the vast Windsor-Sackville empire. You needed the genealogical link that's missing from this file. Well, I found you the link to Finlay's family. A will arrived in the post this morning; I guess you could call it Finlay's inheritance. Here,' Morton said, handing over a single sheet of paper.

Soraya cast her eyes down the paper then looked up, perplexed.

'It's a search for the estate of William Dunk,' Morton said cryptically.

'I don't understand,' Soraya mumbled.

'William Dunk, your father-in-law - he left nothing behind other than the delightful house in which your *husband* now resides,' Morton said with a large grin.

'What's Daniel's dad got to do with anything?' Soraya asked.

'Oh yes, sorry, I forgot that bit. William Dunk was James Coldrick's father.'

'No,' Soraya exclaimed incredulously. 'Absolutely impossible.'

'I'm afraid not, William Dunk is undoubtedly the biological father of James Coldrick.'

'How could that be?'

'William was the estate handyman – Marlene obviously fell in love with him, unbeknownst to the Windsor-Sackvilles. The result was James Coldrick. Marlene wasn't silly enough to declare the truth. In short, your son has no relationship whatever with the Windsor-Sackvilles.'

'You're making all this up,' Soraya protested.

'Why would I do that?'

'To stop Fin from getting what he's entitled to.'

'He's entitled to nothing, Soraya. Absolutely nothing.'

'Then why have they been buying James Coldrick's silence all these years, then? Why go to such lengths to protect the truth?' she demanded, anger rising in her voice. 'If James was William's son then why have the Windsor-Sackvilles spent all these years covering up the truth?'

'They didn't know. They believed James was the son of David Windsor-Sackville. Simple as that.'

Morton briefly summarised what he had learnt from Professor Geoffrey Daniels about the plans to unite the Koldrichs and the Windsor-Sackvilles. 'Ultimately, they believed that James had been created as part of that union, but D-Day marked a change of direction in the war. The last thing a prominent English family wanted in mid-1944 was a link to Nazi Germany. As you know from these documents in my lap, a wedding was even planned. They went as far as to draw up a new coat of arms for the pair, which they had emblazoned on a copper box,' he said. Professor Daniels had emailed Morton a copy of the Koldrich family crest, which was a confirmed match for the other half on the copper box.

'How are you so damn sure that William Dunk was James' father?' she demanded.

'DNA. I borrowed a sample from your husband. It's ironic really that he's done so much damage to James Coldrick's family. I wonder if he would have done the Windsor-Sackville's bidding if he'd known that James Coldrick was his half-brother.'

Soraya stared in disbelief, taking in the news.

'One thing I'm still not sure of, though. You married Dunk in 2005, yet had Finlay with Peter in 2008. Was your relationship with Peter purely because you'd discovered in the archives that the Windsor-Sackvilles were paying off an illegitimate son? Did you go out looking for Peter in order to procure a child with him?'

Soraya sat dumbstruck, her silence speaking for her.

Morton let Soraya's guilt hang quietly between them before saying, 'I'm on my way to the police station right now. Your husband, your deceased father-in-law, the Windsor-Sackvilles, Olivia Walker, will all be implicated. I'm giving you a chance.'

'What do you mean?'

'I mean, I'll do what I can to save your back but you need to disappear. Now.'

'Why would you do that?'

'Finlay. I was always working for him remember – not you – and as my client, he doesn't deserve the fallout from all this. Take him and leave.'

Right on cue, Finlay Coldrick strolled into the room. Rather bizarrely, Morton thought, the boy actually grinned from ear to ear when he spotted him. 'Hi, Morton!' he greeted. Even more bizarrely, he bent down and gave Morton a hug. 'What happened to your arms?'

'Long story,' Morton said, genuinely taken aback by the child's reaction. Maybe children weren't such an alien species after all.

'Fin,' Soraya said sharply, 'go to your room and pack some clothes into your holdall, like you used to when you went to stay at...' Her sentence faded and their eyes locked momentarily before Fin hurried from the room.

'Would it really have been worth it, Soraya? I take it all this comes down to money?' Morton asked, not pausing for an answer. 'You realise that your husband is responsible for Peter's and his mum's deaths, don't you?'

Soraya suddenly burst into tears - uncontrollable, angry tears.

'Goodbye, Soraya,' Morton said. He took one last pitying glance at her then left the house, knowing that he would see neither Soraya nor Finlay ever again.

'Done?' Juliette asked him as he climbed back inside the hot police van.

'Done. To the station,' Morton replied emptily. None of the previous genealogy jobs he had completed had ever had even one percent of the drama of the *Coldrick Case* but they had all ended with a satisfying conclusion; this left him feeling hollow inside. So many lives had been destroyed and were about to be destroyed because of the *Coldrick Case*.

It took six hours. Six long gruelling hours in the void that was Interview Room Three of Ashford Police Station and Morton had told Barnaby McHale, the middle-aged, yet spry Deputy Commissioner for the Metropolitan Police the entirety of the *Coldrick Case*, inside and out. He even confessed to the innumerable illegalities which he had committed along the way. McHale passively scribed several pages of notes, only occasionally interjecting to clarify a point which sounded quite ludicrous. 'Your house blew up?' he had asked, to which Morton nodded. 'What, all of it?' which seemed a slightly obtuse question. Morton nodded again and then continued with the interview. The only careful and discreet economies with the truth surrounded Soraya Benton and Max Fairbrother's involvement. In the case of the bald-pated stalwart of East Sussex Archives, Morton felt his involvement to have been so insignificant and so long ago as to be ignorable but he couldn't quite see how Soraya would escape investigation, seeing as she was married to the murderer that was Daniel Dunk. He wondered if killing more than one person made Dunk a serial killer or mass murderer. Neither was a great character trait in a husband, he reasoned, as he handed over all the documentation in his possession. McHale mentioned Olivia Walker's astonishing rise to the top, muttering something about questionable nepotism by the Secretary of Defence.

206

He told Morton that he would be personally overseeing an investigation into Mary and Peter Coldrick's deaths. Then McHale shook his hand, acknowledged the possibility of Morton's facing his own charges but concluded nonetheless, 'Very brave thing you've done, Mr Farrier.' But Morton didn't feel brave; he felt like the clichéd fish out of water, albeit a very stubborn one, like a belligerent salmon, hacking its way against the prevailing current. Maybe a dog with a bone was more apt if he was going for animal analogies.

Once the interview was over, McHale led Morton down the labyrinth of indistinguishable internal corridors until they reached the front doors where he was released back into the wild to find that the day had grown grey and chilly as a fine, almost imperceptible coating of drizzle fell from the sky.

Juliette was waiting in civvies in her car and together they left the compound.

She leant over and kissed him. 'How did it go?'

'Fine, I think,' he answered. After all that had gone on, he didn't feel he was in much of a position to fully appreciate the implications of what he had just done. Before Morton was even half-way through his revelations to McHale it had become obvious that the ramifications for the Windsor-Sackvilles' political careers would be huge. Not to mention Olivia Walker's high-flying career in the police and Dunk's career in serial-killing. What the police didn't tear apart, the newspapers surely would. It was all out of his hands now. *Que sera sera* and all that.

'Could we make a quick detour on our way home, please?' Morton asked.

Juliette groaned.

Morton nudged open the lych gate to Sedlescombe church with the tips of his bandaged hand. Among the documentation that he'd handed over to McHale was the burial certificate for Marlene Koldrich in this very churchyard. With the drizzle increasing to a constant saturating rain, he headed straight for the vestibule where, on his last visit, he had noticed a map of the churchyard pinned to the notice board. It told him that Marlene was buried in section R, grave number 22, which, according to the map was in the back right area of the churchyard.

Oh the irony! On his previous visit here, he had been so absorbed with the task in hand as not to see the blindingly obvious. In front of him, sheltered by the overhang of an oversized yew, was the clean black granite grave of James and Mary Coldrick, the tell-tale signs of fresh earth and fresh flowers pronouncing Peter's recent interment and behind it, *directly* behind it, was a subtle jaded wooden cross with a simple brass plaque at the centre.

Marlene, died 6th June 1944.

Here they all were.

Together.

If he had been a religious man, he might have uttered a prayer, or quoted some appropriate lines from the Bible about eternal unity, but he simply stood in the dusky wet churchyard as sporadic droplets fell from the yew above him. His head slightly bowed, he felt a profound sorrow for the remains of the tragic family before him; all of them innocent pawns in someone else's game. He saw it all clearly now - the whole jigsaw completed, all making sense. Marlene, daughter of Eberhard Koldrich, sent to England as a young woman to ingratiate herself into English aristocracy in anticipation of a Nazi victory, finds willing hosts in the Windsor-Sackvilles, a family so self-important that their only care regarding the war was to be on the victors' side, regardless of consequence, ends up not falling in love with the son of an important government minister, but with the loutish estate handyman. She falls pregnant, manages to convince the Windsor-Sackvilles that they have a male heir on the way, then bang! D-Day happens and the course of the war changes direction and Nazi-sympathisers beat a hasty retreat. Among the documents in the box file was a small newspaper cutting that spoke of the death of 'an unknown visitor', only known by the name of Marlene, having committed suicide on the village green on 6th June 1944. Goodbye, Marlene. Lo and behold, the Windsor-Sackvilles are there celebrating at Chartwell with Churchill soon after VE Day and David James Peregrine Windsor-Sackville's company, WS Construction, lands one of the biggest reconstruction contracts in Europe. Then follows the knighthood and nothing else is mentioned again until Mary Coldrick starts researching her husband's family tree in 1987. Cue fire, cue death, cue huge payments landing in James Coldrick's bank. Problem solved, until Peter Coldrick becomes curious. Cue gunshot wound to the head. Cue death.

But what these people hadn't reckoned on was the services of Morton Farrier, Forensic Genealogist.

Morton stared at Marlene's austere grave.

'Goodbye,' Morton said. He turned and left the family at peace.

Chapter Twenty

6th June 1944

Emily held the baby tightly and ran from the house. She navigated the orchard easily - nobody knew it better than she - and made it to the periphery of the woods. As the baby began to scream and pain spiked her bare feet as she ran, she knew she could never escape, yet she kept running – pushing further and further into the darkness, her nightie catching and snagging on branches. Behind her, the crunching of heavy boots was gaining ground, easily homing in on the sound of the screaming child. She pulled him tightly into her bosom, hoping to stifle his cries. From the blackness behind her, an unseen hand reached out and grabbed Emily's shoulder. It was over.

'It's finished, Emily,' her assailant shouted.

Emily turned to face him. 'My name's not Emily!' she shouted back.

'Fine. It's finished, *Marlene.*'

Emily visibly sagged. All the lies, all the pretense, all the hopes for the future were gone, another casualty of the global conflict. A political union between two prominent families, as orchestrated by her father, Eberhard, and Frederick Windsor-Sackville, was crushed and buried. She cared nothing at all of it, her initial aspirations shattered the moment her baby son arrived. James. *What would become of him?*

'Hand the boy over, Marlene,' he ordered.

'What will you do with him?'

'That all depends on what happens next. If you do as I ask, then he'll live. If you don't, then neither of you will see this war out.'

Marlene nodded. There was nothing she wouldn't do for James. She set the suitcase down, gently kissed him on the forehead and handed him over.

'Well done. Now, listen – '

Marlene didn't wait to hear the end of the sentence; she abandoned the suitcase and bolted into a thicket of coppiced horse-chestnut trees. She knew that she was only a few hundred yards from the Charingsby perimeter fence. *If she could just run faster!*

A sudden loud crack echoed through the dusky woods, a bullet was fired into the back of Marlene Koldrich's skull. She dropped to the floor like a pile of old rags.

David Windsor-Sackville pulled the safety-catch over the shotgun and returned to the crying baby. He knew what his father wanted him to do to the baby but, as he held him in his arms and watched as the tears abated, he knew he couldn't do it. He would take him to St George's where he could start a new life. The baby looked up at him and smiled.

Chapter Twenty-One

Friday

The house felt different without Jeremy there. Aside from his physical presence, there was something clearly missing. Quite what that something was, Morton wasn't sure. He'd taken the plane as planned, back to Cyprus, back to his maddening vocation in the military. Morton was still having trouble reconciling that particular career choice with his gay brother.

'God, look at the time,' Juliette said, thrusting her finger towards the clock above the fireplace.

'Damn it,' Morton said. They were supposed to collect his father from hospital fifteen minutes ago. The house needed to be perfect for him. Everything in its place. It also needed not to look like they'd been squatting there for the last couple of weeks, news of which he'd yet to break to his father. Morton had to give Jeremy his due, he'd certainly gone to town in cleaning and tidying the house in preparation for his arrival. He'd make someone a lovely husband one day. And vice versa hopefully. There was just one last thing to do. 'I'll be two minutes.' Morton hurried up the stairs, grabbed the new pair of National Trust binoculars that he'd purchased from Mote Ridge and pulled open his father's wardrobe. In his clumsy haste, and having only minimal movement in his fingers, Morton upset the box of junk in which he was trying to insert the binoculars.

'Bloody hell,' he muttered. *Why now, of all times?* His father was going to be in a foul mood as it was. 'Can you give me a hand, please?' he called.

When Juliette entered the room, he stood back and allowed her to scoop up all of the rubbish and put it back inside the box, including the National Trust binoculars.

'Stop!' Morton yelled, with unnecessary drama.

Juliette looked perplexed. 'What?' She looked down at the scrap of torn newspaper; yellowed, crinkled, dated January 1974, and knew instantly.

It was an archetypal e-fit criminal: swept over dark hair, menacing, deathly eyes, thick black moustache and long sideburns.

His real, bone fide biological father.

Say hello to Daddy.

They scrutinised the photo. The face that peered out bore no atavistic resemblance to Morton, of that he was sure. Definitely not the kind of photo he'd be putting in his wallet anytime soon.

Juliette read the story beneath accompanying the e-fit. 'This is the suspect whom police want to talk to after a teenage girl was raped last weekend. The casually-dressed man lured his victim to a secluded spot in the town centre after befriending her during the evening of last Saturday. The attack occurred around 10 p.m. close to the Bell and Whistle pub. Detectives are appealing to the public to help catch the sex predator.' She finished reading and looked at Morton. He knew that she was staring at him but he couldn't take his eyes off the e-fit.

His father.

No! Not his father; his father was in hospital waiting for him to collect him, moaning and groaning to the nurse and doctors no doubt about how incapable he was.

'What do you want me to do?' Juliette asked uncertainly, the piece of paper hanging limply in her hand.

'Put it all back,' he said. 'Let's go and bring Dad home.'

Further Information

Website & Newsletter: www.nathandylangoodwin.com
Twitter: @NathanDGoodwin
Facebook: www.facebook.com/NathanDylanGoodwin
Pinterest: www.pinterest.com/NathanDylanGoodwin
Instagram: www.instagram.com/NathanDylanGoodwin
Blog: theforensicgenealogist.blogspot.co.uk
LinkedIn: www.linkedin.com/in/NathanDylanGoodwin

Hiding the Past
(The Forensic Genealogist #1)

Peter Coldrick had no past; that was the conclusion drawn by years of personal and professional research. Then he employed the services of one Morton Farrier, Forensic Genealogist – a stubborn, determined man who uses whatever means necessary to uncover the past. With the Coldrick Case, Morton faces his toughest and most dangerous assignment yet, where all of his investigative and genealogical skills are put to the test. However, others are also interested in the Coldrick family, people who will stop at nothing, including murder, to hide the past. As Morton begins to unearth his client's mysterious past, he is forced to confront his own family's dark history, a history which he knows little about.

'Flicking between the present and stories and extracts from the past, the pace never lets up in an excellent addition to this unique genre of literature'
Your Family Tree

'At times amusing and shocking, this is a fast-moving modern crime mystery with genealogical twists. The blend of well fleshed-out characters, complete with flaws and foibles, will keep you guessing until the end'
Family Tree

'Once I started reading *Hiding the Past* I had great difficulty putting it down - not only did I want to know what happened next, I actually cared'
Lost Cousins

The Lost Ancestor
(The Forensic Genealogist #2)

From acclaimed author, Nathan Dylan Goodwin comes this exciting new genealogical crime mystery, featuring the redoubtable forensic genealogist, Morton Farrier. When Morton is called upon by Ray Mercer to investigate the 1911 disappearance of his great aunt, a housemaid working in a large Edwardian country house, he has no idea of the perilous journey into the past that he is about to make. Morton must use his not inconsiderable genealogical skills to solve the mystery of Mary Mercer's disappearance, in the face of the dangers posed by those others who are determined to end his investigation at any cost.

'If you enjoy a novel with a keen eye for historical detail, solid writing, believable settings and a sturdy protagonist, *The Lost Ancestor* is a safe bet. Here British author Nathan Dylan Goodwin spins a riveting genealogical crime mystery with a pulsing, realistic storyline'
Your Family Tree

'Finely paced and full of realistic genealogical terms and tricks, this is an enjoyable whodunit with engaging research twists that keep you guessing until the end. If you enjoy genealogical fiction and Ruth Rendell mysteries, you'll find this a pleasing page-turner'
Family Tree

The Orange Lilies
(The Forensic Genealogist #3)

Morton Farrier has spent his entire career as a forensic genealogist solving other people's family history secrets, all the while knowing so little of his very own family's mysterious past. However, this poignant Christmastime novella sees Morton's skills put to use much closer to home, as he must confront his own past, present and future through events both present-day and one hundred years ago. It seems that not every soldier saw a truce on the Western Front that 1914 Christmas...

'The Orange Lilies sees Morton for once investigating his own tree (and about time too!). Moving smoothly between Christmas 1914 and Christmas 2014, the author weaves an intriguing tale with more than a few twists - several times I thought I'd figured it all out, but each time there was a surprise waiting in the next chapter... Thoroughly recommended - and I can't wait for the next novel'
Lost Cousins

'Morton confronts a long-standing mystery in his own family—one that leads him just a little closer to the truth about his personal origins. This Christmas-time tale flashes back to Christmas 1914, to a turning point in his relatives' lives. Don't miss it!'
Lisa Louise Cooke

The America Ground
(The Forensic Genealogist #4)

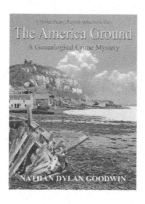

Morton Farrier, the esteemed English forensic genealogist, had cleared a space in his busy schedule to track down his own elusive father finally. But he is then presented with a case that challenges his research skills in his quest to find the killer of a woman murdered more than one hundred and eighty years ago. Thoughts of his own family history are quickly and violently pushed to one side as Morton rushes to complete his investigation before other sinister elements succeed in derailing the case.

'As in the earlier novels, each chapter slips smoothly from past to present, revealing murderous events as the likeable Morton uncovers evidence in the present, while trying to solve the mystery of his own paternity. Packed once more with glorious detail of records familiar to family historians, *The America Ground* is a delightfully pacey read'
Family Tree

'Like most genealogical mysteries this book has several threads, cleverly woven together by the author - and there are plenty of surprises for the reader as the story approaches its conclusion. A jolly good read!'
Lost Cousins

The Spyglass File
(The Forensic Genealogist #5)

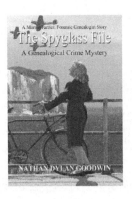

Morton Farrier was no longer at the top of his game. His forensic genealogy career was faltering and he was refusing to accept any new cases, preferring instead to concentrate on locating his own elusive biological father. Yet, when a particular case presents itself, that of finding the family of a woman abandoned in the midst of the Battle of Britain, Morton is compelled to help her to unravel her past. Using all of his genealogical skills, he soon discovers that the case is connected to The Spyglass File—a secretive document which throws up links which threaten to disturb the wrongdoings of others, who would rather its contents, as well as their actions, remain hidden forever.

'If you like a good mystery, and the detective work of genealogy, this is another mystery novel from Nathan which will have you whizzing through the pages with time slipping by unnoticed'
Your Family History

'The first page was so overwhelming that I had to stop for breath...Well, the rest of the book certainly lived up to that impressive start, with twists and turns that kept me guessing right to the end... As the story neared its conclusion I found myself conflicted, for much as I wanted to know how Morton's assignment panned out, I was enjoying it so much that I really didn't want this book to end!'
Lost Cousins

The Missing Man
(The Forensic Genealogist #6)

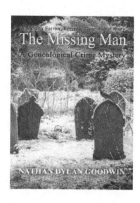

It was to be the most important case of Morton Farrier's career in forensic genealogy so far. A case that had eluded him for many years: finding his own father. Harley 'Jack' Jacklin disappeared just six days after a fatal fire at his Cape Cod home on Christmas Eve in 1976, leaving no trace behind. Now his son, Morton must travel to the East Coast of America to unravel the family's dark secrets in order to discover what really happened to him.

'One of the hallmarks of genealogical mystery novels is the way that they weave together multiple threads and this book is no exception, cleverly skipping across the generations - and there's also a pleasing symmetry that helps to endear us to one of the key characters...If you've read the other books in this series you won't need me to tell you to rush out and buy this one'
Lost Cousins

'Nathan Dylan Goodwin has delivered another page-turning mystery laden with forensic genealogical clues that will keep any family historian glued to the book until the mystery is solved'
Eastman's Online Genealogy Newsletter

The Wicked Trade
(The Forensic Genealogist #7)

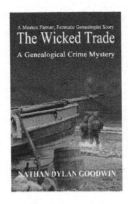

When Morton Farrier is presented with a case revolving around a mysterious letter written by disreputable criminal, Ann Fothergill in 1827, he quickly finds himself delving into a shadowy Georgian underworld of smuggling and murder on the Kent and Sussex border. Morton must use his skills as a forensic genealogist to untangle Ann's association with the notorious Aldington Gang and also with the brutal killing of Quartermaster Richard Morgan. As his research continues, Morton suspects that his client's family might have more troubling and dangerous expectations of his findings.

'Once again the author has carefully built the story around real places, real people, and historical facts - and whilst the tale itself is fictional, it's so well written that you'd be forgiven for thinking it was true'
Lost Cousins

'I can thoroughly recommend this book, which is a superior example of its genre. It is an ideal purchase for anyone with an interest in reading thrillers and in family history studies. I look forward to the next instalment of Morton Farrier's quest!'
Waltham Forest FHS

Made in the USA
Monee, IL
28 October 2020